Supernatural Consultant, Volume Two

Dragon Detective

Nickel might be a water elemental dragon, but even he has limits—and the sudden rain storms, hail, and snow in midsummer are way over the line. Luckily, he works for Dane's Supernatural Consulting firm and can use those resources to figure out who keeps mucking with the weather and get them to stop.

Soon Nickel realizes he isn't the only one searching for the weather worker: the enemy he has been hunting for ten years has finally reappeared, and it's a race to see who will reach the weather worker first. Nickel isn't certain he'll win, or even survive, the attempt, but he'll do whatever it takes to save the dragons.

Dragon Soldier

The aftermath of the last battle has left Nickel weak in bed and grounded for the next decade. Despite being in trouble, Nickel wants to return to the battle against the enemy as soon as he can, but thoughts of Platinum, the dragon helping to nurse him back to health, keep distracting him.

Platinum can't believe how much his life has changed. He went from being a lonely fugitive on the run to part of a family in only hours. The last few days have been his happiest, especially now that he's met Nickel. He knows it's only temporary, though. The enemy that kept him captive for most of his life isn't finished with him yet, but even Platinum and Nickel's combined powers might not be enough to save them all.

Dragon Adventures

Aqua and Rios are bored, which is always a recipe for disaster. Going on a trip might not solve the cause of the boredom, but they know it will distract them for a while. Except, Rios runs into a nix trying to save his river from drug smugglers and Aqua is kidnapped by a bunch of angry fire salamanders. Their fun adventure quickly turns into a desperate fight for survival, and they're not certain they'll be able get back home ever again.

SUPERNATURAL CONSULTANT

Volume Two

Mell Eight

A NineStar Press Publication

www.ninestarpress.com

Supernatural Consultant, Volume Two

© 2021 Mell Eight

Cover Art © 2021 Natasha Snow

Printed in the USA

ISBN: 978-1-64890-231-4

First Edition, March, 2021

DRAGON

DETECTIVE

Chapter One

Nickel walked into the office and shut his umbrella with a snap that spattered water droplets all over his pant legs. He grimaced and tossed the umbrella onto the stand by the door with a sigh of disgust.

"It's not that bad, dear," Becky said cheerfully from her oversized secretary's desk in the middle of the room. He scowled at her in return, which she ignored with the ease of knowing him for over ten years. Becky looked warm and dry while wearing a nice summer-weight cardigan. The rain hadn't started until an hour ago, so she had already been safely ensconced on her throne. Nickel, on the other hand, had been out and about getting lunch. He had been lucky to be near a shop selling umbrellas when it had suddenly started pouring, but that hadn't saved his shoes.

Admittedly, Nickel liked rain. He was usually the first one to run outside to play when the skies darkened and thunder rumbled overhead, just not when he was wearing a nice suit. He might be able to save his shoes, but only if the scamp napping on his desk chair moved.

"Lumie, scram," Nickel snapped.

Lumie popped one red eye open, saw that Nickel was the one speaking to him, and went right back to sleep. His long red hair flopped over his face as he took ignoring Nickel to another level. Nickel growled and ran a hand through his much shorter blue hair in exasperation. There was no talking to Lumie when he was in one of his moods. Instead of fighting for his chair, Nickel dropped to the floor.

His shoes popped off with wet squelching sounds, and his socks left a puddle on the floor. Nickel's magic fizzled between his fingers for a moment before he directed it to pull on the water, calling it out of his shoes and socks. It was a gradual process. Water moved slowly. It was sticky, according to the science teacher Dane had hired to teach all the kits, and was therefore happier to remain attached to something than not. It was why water always hesitated on the edge of a counter before the push from behind and gravity below finally sent it falling. Of course, once the first drop fell, all the water built up behind it fell too because it was all stuck together. It took some doing before the water obeyed his magic, but once one drop and then another began to coalesce in Nickel's hand, it wasn't long before he had a small river flowing from his shoes and socks into his cupped palms.

The water was cool and welcoming, just the way Nickel liked it. He continued to call out the water slowly. Easy, routine magic, it was also good practice for when he worked larger spells. Except the water was starting to heat in his hands. First it was only just warm, which happened sometimes when he was being a touch careless, but when bubbles started to form between his hands, Nickel turned to glare at Lumie.

"Knock it off!" Nickel snapped. Lumie continued to breathe evenly, as if he really were asleep. Experience told

Nickel that Lumie was a dammed good actor, though. The heat continued to rise until the water stopped protecting Nickel's hands and they began to get uncomfortably hot. His shoes also began to smell. 'Ron had stuck a hairdryer into a pair of sneakers once to try to dry them. The bathroom had reeked of sweaty feet for days when she was done, and the office was quickly taking on the smell of that awful aroma.

Nickel tossed the water before it could start burning his hands. It arced beautifully in the air, steaming as it continued to boil, and landed directly on Lumie's head.

Lumie shrieked and jumped out of Nickel's chair. His red hair was plastered to his face and dripping onto his shirt. He looked like a soaked puppy, especially as he scowled. Nickel couldn't help grinning at the sight.

"What was that for?" Lumie shook his head back and forth, deliberately spraying Nickel with more water. The water steamed off Lumie quickly, leaving his hair dry and slightly fluffy.

"You know why!" Nickel snapped back, his good mood forgotten with the reminder that Lumie had just tried to boil Nickel's hands off and destroy the office with a pervasive stench.

"Sleeping in your chair is no reason for you to throw water all over me!" Lumie yelled. His eyes flashed with magic, so Nickel prepared himself to block anything Lumie was about to throw at him. "And ugh, what's that smell anyway?" Lumie asked. He turned his head away from Nickel, the water incident already forgotten as he sniffed the air.

"I was just trying to help!" Alloy whined. He poked his head out from underneath the desk. His mixed red-and-blue hair was disheveled, and his eyes—one bright red and the other blue—were wide as he tried to hold back tears. Nickel jumped in surprise and then growled at himself. How had he missed the fact that Alloy was curled underneath the desk? He shouldn't have. Apparently, the distraction of Lumie taking his chair combined with his wet shoes had been enough for Nickel to miss Alloy. That wasn't acceptable; Nickel snarled to himself. He had to be better than that. Alloy wasn't an enemy, but next time Nickel might not be so lucky.

Still, yelling at Alloy wouldn't have any effect. Either Alloy would pretend to be Lumie and conveniently forget the scolding a few minutes later, or he would run to Copper and Copper would smooth over any hard lessons Nickel had tried to impart.

"You remember the time 'Ron tried to dry her shoes in the bathroom?" Nickel asked Alloy as calmly as he could. Alloy's nose wrinkled in disgust so Nickel took that as a yes. "She used the hot air from the hairdryer, and the heat made her shoes stink. That's why heating up the water in my shoes started to smell bad."

"Oh," Alloy said slowly as he began to understand the mistake he had made. "I should have helped your water magic, then?" he asked curiously. For any other dragon, what Alloy had said would have been an impossibility. Elemental dragons like them used one element of magic. That was it. Nickel used water, and Lumie used fire. Alloy was the result of a cruel experiment gone wrong and had somehow been born with power over both water and fire.

"That would have been better," Nickel agreed. "But you should always ask first before you interrupt someone's spell. You could have burned me if I hadn't gotten Lumie wet instead." Alloy giggled and Nickel couldn't help cracking a smile at the memory of Lumie jumping up in surprise.

"Shut up," Lumie grumped. At some point, he had left Nickel's desk and had wandered over to Becky's instead. He was busy plundering her candy jar, but he still shot them a disgruntled glare that only faded when he finally found a Cinnamon Bomb. He bounced off into Dane's empty office with his prize in hand, Nickel and Alloy promptly forgotten.

Nickel could only shake his head. Lumie had to grow up eventually, Nickel hoped. Alloy was certainly more mature.

"Oh, don't worry, dears," Becky said in her best old-lady voice. She looked like one at the moment, although in another minute she might look like someone Nickel's age or even someone in their thirties. Her outward appearance wasn't confined by age. "I have enough candy for everyone."

She reached into her plundered candy jar and pulled out a package of red Laffy Taffy. It was cinnamon flavored, but Alloy liked the high sugar content too. For Nickel, she waved a stick of blue rock candy. She had apparently been shopping overnight, because Nickel was certain there hadn't been any of his favorite candy left yesterday. He had checked.

Was it demeaning to allow himself to be bribed by candy? Nickel couldn't help wondering even as he padded barefoot across the office to take the proffered candy. Alloy looked at his candy and then down at Nickel's shoes. He whined to himself and plopped down on the ground. Nickel felt the swirl of water magic in the air a moment later. He took Alloy's candy too and brought it over. Nickel called on his own water magic and sat next to Alloy to help.

By the time Nickel couldn't feel any more water in his shoes and socks, Alloy's mouth was pink, and Nickel knew his own was blue. The air smelled a lot better too; Becky must have turned on the air-conditioning or something. Her powers of premonition only worked to predict when someone was going to get brutally murdered—and her banshee scream allowed her to deal with threats accordingly. She couldn't have predicted Alloy's mistake, but she knew how to deal with it when it happened.

The front door opened, letting in a blast of freezing air, and Dane stepped inside. He was preternaturally beautiful even when his glamour was in place. His hair was long and very blond, almost like bottled sunshine, his eyes were bluer than Nickel's own, and his bladed nose only served to complement the rest of him. Dane was owner of the Supernatural Consulting Firm and was mated to Mercury, Nickel's adoptive father. Nickel and all his siblings had tried calling him 'Dad,' but it hadn't stuck. Dane was simply Dane to him. At the moment a very disgruntled look marred his face.

"It's snowing," Dane grumped.

There was a pause as everyone in the room processed that statement.

"It's July?" Becky asked. "Right?" It was midsummer. She was correct.

Nickel moved to the window and saw big snowflakes drifting down from a cloudy sky that only moments before had been pouring rain. As Nickel watched, the snow stopped falling and the sky began to clear. After only a minute of watching, the sun shined, the snow melted, and it was suddenly a regular July day outside again.

"Okay, that's weird," Dane said from over Nickel's shoulder. Sudden afternoon rainstorms were common enough during the heat of the summer in the area. They had been getting far more of those than anyone expected lately, which Nickel knew from firsthand, damp experience, but no one could have predicted snow in July. "You want to look into it?" he asked.

Nickel shrugged. He was technically in between cases at the moment, so he might as well try to figure out what was screwing with the weather.

"How did the Mitchell case work out?" Dane stepped away from the window and moved to Becky's desk to pick up any messages he had missed while he was out at lunch.

Nickel wandered back to his own desk to pick up the file Lumie and Alloy had thankfully left untouched. He flipped it open even though he didn't need to double-check any of the information he had carefully penned before leaving for his own lunch.

"Turns out Mrs. Mitchell was right. Her husband was cheating on her with a man," Nickel began delicately. Dane nodded, unsurprised. "Turns out it was the same man Mrs. Mitchell was cheating on her husband with."

Dane looked up suddenly from reading his messages and pinned Nickel with his stare. "Repeat that?" he asked, a grin slowly growing across his face.

"Mr. Mitchell and Mrs. Mitchell were both cheating on each other, but it was with the same man."

Becky tittered and Dane let out a loud laugh. "Please tell me you're going to set them up as a threesome?" Dane asked.

Nickel grumbled under his breath at Dane. "I was just going to provide Mrs. Mitchell with the picture of the man Mr. Mitchell was sleeping with and let her do the math on her own."

"Ugh, math," Alloy groaned.

Dane looked startled again; he was apparently just noticing that Alloy was sitting on the floor by Nickel's desk. "When did you get here? Or how?"

Alloy shrugged. "Lumie said he wanted to visit, so we walked here." Dane quirked one eyebrow at Alloy, looking utterly perplexed. Home for everyone in the office—except Becky—was quite far away; it was much more than the distance a quick morning's walk would cover. Then again, it had been Lumie's idea, and Lumie's magic was as odd as Lumie himself.

"Which means Lumie must be in my office," Dane concluded.

Alloy nodded eagerly. "That's where he went after Nickel dropped a lot of water on his head."

"I won't ask," Dane said with a wide grin before walking into his private office. He didn't close the door behind him, and Nickel saw him pause at his desk chair, shake his head, and then move to take a chair on the visitor's side of the desk. Lumie must have resumed his interrupted nap in Dane's chair.

Nickel sat down in his own chair and pulled himself closer to the desk. He banged his knees on the low surface and hissed in pain. The desk had appeared ten years ago when he had first started seriously working with Dane. Unfortunately, it hadn't grown with him now that he was eighteen, and he was almost constantly banging his knees and elbows on it. Still, it was his space—his territory—where all of his work was carefully piled up. He didn't want to share it with Lumie or Alloy.

He flipped open the folder for the Mitchell case so he could finalize his notes. Mrs. Mitchell seemed like the type to demand a full write-up so Nickel wanted to be prepared. It took a while to handwrite his findings. Once he was done, he flipped open his laptop and composed an email with all of that information to send to her. She lived a few towns away and didn't want to arouse her husband's suspicion by traveling the distance to Dane's office every few days for information. She had given Nickel her email address to use instead. He explained what he had found and then insisted she look at the picture he had also attached, which would clarify any confusion she had. The picture Nickel chose was one of Mr. Mitchell intimately holding hands with the man Mrs. Mitchell had also been seeing.

Alloy was frowning at his fingernails, sitting on the floor and looking utterly bored, when Nickel finally closed the laptop and stood from behind his too-small desk with a groan.

"I was going to walk through town, see if anyone's heard something about whoever is mucking with the weather," Nickel began. "You want to come with?"

Alloy jumped to his feet eagerly and nodded.

Nickel dropped the Mitchell folder into Becky's inbox, which she immediately pulled in front of her with a smile, and then headed to the door with Alloy at his heels. The front door opened onto a small street filled with shops. There was a supermarket to the left of Dane's office and a nail salon and pizza parlor where Nickel had stopped for lunch earlier to the right. There was an electronics store, too, but the other three shops a little farther down the street were empty. Parking was on the street in front, although the grocery store did have a small lot around back. It was a typical small-town block of Main Street, Nickel knew.

For years, Nickel had tagged along with Dane whenever he came to the office. There was no need to walk outside because Dane magically transported them wherever they needed to go. It had been a bit of a shock the first time Nickel had ventured outside and realized the reason he could only see a few buildings whenever he looked out the window was because there really were only a few buildings. Dane had chosen a quaint, one-stoplight town to set up shop in.

The sidewalk wasn't crowded as Nickel led the way past the pizza parlor and nail salon toward the one stoplight. Main Street intersected with Mountain Road there, and the only gas station in the town was tucked into one corner. They turned left at the light, away from the gas station, and continued down Mountain Road toward the park.

Both streets were aptly named. Main Street was the main route through the town. It began at the highway entrance a few miles away and continued through the town and beyond until it turned into Route 23 as it traveled toward the next nearest town twenty miles away. Mountain Road led further up into the mountains. Dane had never confirmed his office's location, but Nickel was pretty certain it was located in one of a dozen small towns scattered throughout the Berkshires.

They were walking downhill, away from the mountain. Now that they were out of the commercial area of the town, houses began cropping up. They were old structures with peeling paint and dated architecture, but they had charm. Well, sometimes they had charm. For as many houses that looked like Grandma had built them and passed down the property to be tenderly cared for by her children and grandchildren, there were just as many that had rusting broken-down cars and the remains of a partially destroyed toilet decorating the front yard. It was a hick town, although Mercury would swat him if Nickel ever said that out loud, but it was also a very nice place to live. Nickel liked walking around and seeing everything.

The park was only a few blocks away. It wasn't as if there was a lack of green space surrounding the town. They lived in the middle of a beautiful, almost totally untouched forest. Despite that, someone had donated the money to build the park. The trees were planted neatly in the park, and each had a wrought-iron fence surrounding it. There were flowerbeds, carefully trimmed grass, a ball field, and a playground. And, most importantly for what Nickel was interested in, there were picnic benches.

After school, kids and parents would congregate in the park instead of going home. During the summer, the park was still the hangout place. Families brought their kids to play, elderly folk found it a relaxing spot to sit, and gossip was tossed around regularly. They spent enough time locked inside during the winter, which could be very harsh in the Berkshires, and therefore spent as much time as they could outside now.

No one looked twice when Nickel and Alloy walked into the park. It was a nice change from five years ago, when Dane had finally allowed the kits he brought to work with him free rein outside of his office too. Dragons, particularly those who lived in wild areas like the Berkshires, weren't educated. Nickel would call them ignorant, but that was a polite description of how little wild dragons had been able to learn about the world outside of their carefully guarded territories. It was a problem when a creature that could use magic, but didn't understand basic currency, came into someone's store to get something. Those dragons shoplifted, and when someone tried to confront them about it, the dragons had been known to get violent in their attempts to escape. The dragons honestly didn't know any better. They survived in the wild, and a wide majority of them would never enter what humans considered civilization.

The humans had been right to be wary of Nickel when he had first started frequenting their shops and walking around the town. Even when he had proved that he had money and paid for everything he wanted, they had still watched him closely. Realizing that he was working for Dane had eventually eased some of their fears, and his continued good behavior had cemented him in their good graces.

Alloy wandered off further into the park, and Nickel let him go.

"Weird weather we're having," Nickel groaned as he sat down on a wooden picnic bench next to two elderly women who Nickel knew were happy enough to gossip with anyone about anything.

Mabel twittered. "It's the Berkshires. Sure, it's never snowed in July, but May or October? Plenty of times."

"It's global warming!" Louise declared.

"Is not!" Arthur yelled from the next picnic bench over. He was supposed to have been playing chess with Charles, Mabel's husband, but he apparently had his hearing aid turned up to max. "It's some spell, I tell you. The government's just hiding their machinations with magic by calling it global warming."

"You're a crazy old fool," Mabel hissed. "It's not magic; it's just where we live!"

"It's magic," Arthur repeated. "Mark my words, ladies! We'll be struggling through knee-high snow before we know it, and the government stooges will shrug and send the snowplows, and then increase our taxes to pay for their own magical messes."

Mabel slowly pushed herself to her feet, her old bones creaking as she moved, and stomped over to Arthur. "You listen to me, you conspiracy-theory-nattered fool!" She continued yelling, attracting plenty of attention, but nothing she had to say helped Nickel, so he tuned her out.

"Are you seeing anyone, dear?" Louise asked gently, smiling eagerly at him as she waited for him to share in the gossip fest with his own news.

Nickel shook his head. "I'm not."

"Haven't found the right girl?" she asked, her grin growing. "Or guy? We may be a backward town," she added when Nickel couldn't help blushing at her words, "but we're not stupid. Anyway, if you're still single, I think you should call on this new boy that just moved in. I've only seen him a few times, but he's cute as a button and about your age. Bought one of the old places high up Mountain Road and only comes down when he needs to go shopping. He's got this long white hair he keeps braided to the top of his head; you can't miss him." She fluffed her own permed gray hair with one hand.

"He recently moved to the area?" Nickel asked, wondering if there was such a thing as a coincidence. The strange weather starting at the same time that a new person moved to the area? Nickel would have to pay the newcomer a visit, although doing so without Louise making the wrong assumptions would be difficult. To be perfectly honest, he was more interested in figuring out why the weather was screwy than finding a date. Maybe Becky could dig up some information for him so he didn't have to ask Louise anything else.

"Oh yes," Louise agreed. She opened her mouth to say more, but was interrupted by a panicked scream from the other side of the park. Two dogs were also barking and a little girl was crying. Nickel jumped to his feet as Louise gasped. Even the argument between Mabel and Arthur paused as they looked over with worry at the noise. Alloy added his voice to the melee, and Nickel started jogging across the lawn toward the disturbance.

"Go away!" Alloy yelled, waving his arms at the two barking dogs. His hands dripped sparks that fell harmlessly to the ground, but the lights scared the dogs. They backed away with rumbling barks as their owner rushed over.

"Sorry! Sorry!" the owner said as he grabbed both dogs by their collars and pulled them farther away from Alloy and the little girl he was standing protectively over. A pair of leashes hung uselessly from his hands.

Nickel joined Alloy in standing between the crying girl and the dogs. Another young boy, maybe a few years younger than Alloy, with the exact same shade of brown hair as the girl, came running over from where he had been playing with a group of other boys.

"Jilly! Are you okay?" the boy gasped, scooting around Alloy and falling to the ground at his sister's side. Another man was helping to hold the dogs back so the owner could safely get the leashes on, so Nickel turned his attention to the girl Alloy had saved.

"I think so," she sniffled. "But one of the kitties ran off." She uncurled, revealing a kitten with his claws imbedded in her sparkly shirt. It was a tortoiseshell kitten, a mishmash of colors ranging from white to black and multiple shades of brown. It mewled softly.

There was a crushed sign under Jilly's knee, Nickel noticed. It was covered in sparkles and rainbows and read "Free Kitties." The idiot dog owner obviously hadn't noticed Jilly or her sign before letting his dogs off leash.

Nickel heard a second meow from overhead and looked into the high branches of a nearby tree. The kitten there was bright orange, his fur sticking out in all directions as he hissed after the quickly retreating dogs. Nickel jumped, grabbing onto the high branch easily. He reached for the kitten, got his hand scratched, and growled. The kitten froze in place for long enough that Nickel could grip it gently around the middle, and then he jumped down.

"Guess we don't have to call the fire department," one of the many bystanders stated as Nickel held out the cat toward the little girl. Her hands were empty, Nickel noticed, but the tortoiseshell kitten wasn't in her brother's arms. She reached out to pet the orange cat's head, but didn't take him from Nickel.

Alloy sighed happily and Nickel looked over to see him with his cheek pressed against the tortoiseshell's side. The kitten was purring furiously.

"We can take them home, right, Nickel?" Alloy asked. He looked so eagerly hopeful, and the kitten looked so contented, that Nickel couldn't say no.

"Only if Dane says we can," Nickel said, trying to compromise while knowing that once Alloy had brought his kitten to Dane's office the kitten was coming all the way home with them. "Wait," Nickel added with a pause to look at the orange kitten glaring in his hand, "we're taking both home?"

Alloy nodded happily. "That one's Lumie's. He told me so."

And that was why Lumie had gone to the extra effort of coming to the office today. The little brat wanted a kitten and knew Alloy would be able to get him one.

Jilly giggled and nodded, her fright forgotten over the happiness of adopting out both kittens. Nickel couldn't say no to her or to Alloy. Dane would no doubt grumble, but it wasn't the worst thing Alloy or Lumie had done. Alloy had melted Dane's oven just hours after hatching.

"Fine." Nickel sighed. "We should return to the office now." Alloy nodded agreement and waved goodbye to Jilly and her brother. Nickel took a more secure grip on the orange kitten and led the way back through the park to Mountain Road. He walked quickly, unsure of how long the kitten would be content with him holding it. His hand already stung from getting scratched earlier; Nickel didn't want to know how bad it would hurt if the kitten clawed his way out of his arms.

Luckily, the office wasn't far away. They turned the corner onto Main Street and hurried up the sidewalk. Nickel pushed the office door open and held it so Alloy could get inside; then he shut it firmly behind them. Lumie was waiting impatiently in the middle of the room, no doubt driving Becky nuts, and he hurried forward to take the orange kitten from Nickel. He cradled the kitten close, rumbling softly at it. The kitten immediately started purring. Lumie wandered back into Dane's office.

"The hell?" Nickel heard Dane swear, followed by an imperious meow. Dane, apparently evicted from his own office, stomped into the main room. "Cats? Really?" he grumbled to the room as a whole.

Becky hid a grin in the Mitchell folder she was still transcribing. Alloy, on the other hand, proudly held out his mottled kitten for Dane to see.

"This is Turtle," Alloy declared happily. Dane looked at Alloy's smile and then opened his mouth—but then sighed and shut it before he could say anything to erase that smile. He shot Nickel a look to which Nickel could only shrug. It wasn't his fault Lumie and Alloy had schemed together to get themselves kittens.

"It was Lumie's idea, apparently," Nickel said by way of explanation.

Dane shot a disgruntled look over his shoulder at his occupied office, and then his shoulders slumped. "I'll go buy some supplies before they pee all over my office," Dane said with a groan without voicing any arguments. Lumie wouldn't actually listen to Dane's words, and Alloy would follow Lumie's less-than-stellar example. Instead, Dane patted his pocket to double-check that his wallet was still there before heading out the door.

Once the door was closed, Becky let out a snort of laughter. "You kits have him wrapped around your little fingers."

"More like he's learned that the word 'no' and Lumie aren't synonymous." Nickel sighed. "Anyway, when you've got a moment, I need some information looked up."

"No problem. Give me a second to save this, and then I'm all yours," she replied.

Alloy took Turtle and vanished underneath Nickel's desk again while Nickel waited for Becky to finish up. Nickel gave her all the information Louise had told him once Becky was ready; then he waited again while she ran a search.

It only took a few minutes of clicking and typing before Becky turned to Nickel with a frown on her face. "I'm not doubting you or your source," she began with, which didn't exactly buoy his hopes, "but there's no record of anyone purchasing property on Mountain Road or any of the side streets up there. Either your young man is squatting illegally, or he's camping in the woods."

Damn. "Thanks, Becky." There went his easy lead.

She shrugged. "I'll see if I can't find a picture of him on a local camera feed."

"Until then, I'm going to have to search the mountain on foot." She nodded, and Nickel sighed again. A glance at the clock on Becky's computer screen told Nickel that he would be better off waiting until tomorrow morning to go hunting through the heavy forest and steep hills. The firm closed in half an hour. Dane would be back any minute with the cat paraphernalia, and he would want to get them all home as quickly as possible before Lumie decided he wanted a dog too.

Tomorrow, then, Nickel thought resolutely with a mental reminder to wear jeans and walking shoes. It was going to be a long day.

Chapter Two

Platinum was running. His bare feet hit the ground, and dry clouds of dirt erupted with every step. His breathing was loud and panicked, more of a wheeze than an actual breath. Everything hurt, but that wasn't strange. Platinum's body had been one constant ache for longer than he could remember. This time was different, though. This time, he hurt because his naked feet kept stumbling on rocks and sticks. His knees and palms were bleeding from all the times he had needed to catch himself after a fall and throw himself back to his feet so he could keep moving. Platinum wasn't used to running either. Most of his life had been spent inside a cell or a lab, and he had never accumulated the muscle needed for running; his legs were yelling in pain with every step. Still, Platinum couldn't stop. This was his only chance at escape.

He didn't know what had gone wrong this time. The scientists and the guards had led Platinum to his normal operating table. They had been as vigilant as always to ensure that he wouldn't have a chance to try to fight back. Fighting was futile, Platinum knew. He had been living with the bastards for nearly twenty years now; he knew that fighting back wouldn't garner him anything but more pain. He was a docile fool, and they knew it.

The gas mask had fit on Platinum's face like it had been molded specifically to adhere to his cheekbones. It had been stuck there for so many hours of his damned life that it had conformed to his shape. Platinum had felt the rush of air as knobs were turned and sleeping gas was sent deep into his lungs. Then, as usual, he had fallen deeply asleep.

Waking up was always difficult after an operation. It wasn't something he would ever get used to no matter how frequently it occurred. There was some relief now that Platinum knew he wasn't going to wake up next to a destroyed dragon egg. There were plenty of those nightmares in his past, but the scientists moved around too frequently now for that to happen. They couldn't keep the eggs alive in their incubators as they changed facilities over and over again, sometimes multiple times every week. Eventually, all the eggs had died, and they were left with only Platinum.

Platinum blinked open his eyes to find that the examination room was empty. The mask slipped sideways off his face. The hooks that were supposed to be behind his ears slid down his chest with the rest of the mask as he slowly sat up. Platinum was in one piece, so they hadn't left his body cut open while they went to lunch. He also wasn't tied down while they waited for the guards to return to cart him back to his cell. There was still air blowing through the mask, Platinum realized as he pushed it off his lap and onto the table next to him. The mask had come free, which had allowed him to wake up unsupervised.

He jumped off the table quickly, stumbling slightly in the oversized scrub pants hanging low around his *waist. When Platinum didn't hear any startled exclamations through the one-way mirror across the room, he felt pretty safe in assuming he was unobserved. The lab door was unlocked when he tried it, and the hallway outside empty. Platinum crept along, ready to startle at the slightest sound. He kept his hands held in front of him, and the tingle of magic flared over his fingers. He was fairly well practiced at calling the wind. The guards didn't mind his using it to keep himself occupied during the long hours Platinum was alone in his cell—there was some sort of spell on the door that kept him from attacking the guards—so it came easily to his call. Anyone who tried to stop him would get pushed out of the way by his winds. Platinum was fully prepared, yet no one came into view.*

Platinum passed one room where he heard a lot of voices and the clink of cutlery on dishes, and it made his legs move even faster. The bastards had left him lying on a gurney, breathing in sleeping gas to keep him docile, while they stopped for a meal.

For the briefest moment, he thought about going into that room and unleashing his wind on them. Platinum could kill them for what they had done to him and still make his escape, but the lure of being outside for the first time in a very, very long time drew him farther from his jailors. The door leading outside was unguarded. It had fanciful panes of glass in the center as if he were in someone's house instead of a lab. The glass let him look outside and see that there wasn't anyone guarding out there either.

Platinum took a deep breath as he turned the lock and put his hand on the door handle. Then he threw the door open and started running.

And he hadn't stopped since. He was their last dragon. The eggs had died, as had the other kits. Platinum was the only one they had to run their terrible experiments on, and they would want him back. They would chase him until they caught him. Platinum could hear dogs barking behind him and the yell of men and women as they called to each other while searching for his trail. He had to find somewhere to hide before they caught up with him.

Splashing through a shallow stream sent unpleasant, aching chills through his bare feet. When he reached the other bank, Platinum changed directions, following the water downstream. The stream grew into a river that slowly got larger and larger. He could hear the splash of falling water ahead. It drowned out the baying of the dogs and people behind him.

Then Platinum reached a high cliff. The river fell over the cliff and into a deep pool below. He didn't hesitate before jumping, and if the fall killed him, then at least the scientists would still be down one dragon.

The water came up quickly, and he hit it hard, all the air forcing out of his lungs as he flailed around.

*

Platinum woke up gasping for air, his hands waving around his head as if he were still swimming. He hastily stilled in the blankets, listening hard to make certain he was alone in the small cabin even as his own heartbeat tried to drown out any sounds he might hear. Every crack and creak as the house settled around him while the wind blew outside made him jump and his heart rate ratchet up again.

The house wasn't Platinum's. He had chosen it because the owners had left the electricity and water on. There were skis and heavy coats in the closets, snowmobiles in the garage, and snowshoes hanging from the walls. It was clearly someone's winter getaway, and Platinum desperately hoped he could continue squatting for a few more weeks before he had to return to running.

The blowing wind outside died down as he pushed the covers back and climbed out of bed. Platinum headed to the heavy curtains he kept pulled over the windows and carefully twitched one small corner back so he could look outside. Early morning sunlight shone through the trees, but the only movement he saw was from the leaves dancing in the wind. There were lots of shiny spots on the ground, and he had to look closer for a few moments before he recognized melting balls of hail dotting the lawn here and there. That must have been some storm. The clouds overhead were skittering away, revealing clear blue sky as the sun slowly rose over the trees.

Platinum let the curtains fall back into place and walked to the bathroom. He had an hour to get ready and get into town before he was late. Today was stocking day at the local grocery store. Although the store restocked every night, today was the day the big trucks drove in—a difficulty considering the location of the town in the mountains—and the owner, a man who insisted Platinum call him Ryan, needed all hands on deck. Platinum was one of a dozen locals Ryan had hired under the table, glad for the help unpacking the trucks and then the dozens of boxes so the merchandise could be properly put away.

Platinum had only gotten the job due to luck. Three of Ryan's usual helpers had been out sick a few weeks back, and Platinum had been standing on the sidewalk contemplating how he was going to steal a couple candy bars from the store so he could eat something for the first time in days. He doubted Ryan knew what he was thinking, but he had offered Platinum money and food for a few hours of work. That Platinum then spent the money on groceries didn't faze Ryan at all. He had invited Platinum back the next week too.

Which was one of the reasons Platinum was so reluctant to leave the town. He knew that if he squatted too long in one place, the scientists would find him. He had to keep moving, but the lure of borrowing someone's soft bed and having money to eat real food kept him stationary.

The bathroom light flickered on when he flipped the switch, and Platinum hurried to the sink to splash some water on his face. He dried himself off and then looked into the mirror. The braids Platinum had plaited his long white hair into after his shower the night before had held. He took the ends and wrapped them around his head, holding them in place with some bobby pins he had bought from the store. Most people assumed Platinum's white hair was either an unfortunate genetic problem or a bad dye job, and they were polite enough not to ask him about it. He refused to dye it even though it might help him hide better. He was an air dragon, and air dragons didn't have ordinary brown hair. It would feel demeaning to alter his hair color like that. His eyes were gray, a shade that could be construed as human. As long as he kept his scales carefully covered by his clothing, no one would suspect him of being a dragon. He had perfected staying hidden like this over the last few weeks, and it helped to keep him safe.

Once his hair was in place, Platinum returned to the bedroom. He changed out of his pajamas into real clothes, made the bed, and packed everything he owned into his backpack to take with him. The last thing he wanted was for someone to come home and find his things everywhere. Platinum had worked hard to earn enough money for a few changes of clothes and the backpack itself, and he didn't want to lose it by leaving anything behind.

Platinum left the house without bothering with breakfast. The storeowner usually provided something, and Platinum needed to shop anyway. A little brush of wind pushed the deadbolt into place, locking it behind him as he headed through the forest and down the mountain toward the town below. He avoided the road so he wouldn't be seen, only stepping into view when the town's sidewalk began to parallel the road. He turned at the intersection and passed a number of smaller stores before heading around the back of the grocery store to the loading dock.

"The trucks are running a little late this morning, Platinum," Ryan called. Platinum had little doubt that he thought Platinum had given him an alias based on the color of Platinum's hair instead of his real name, but Ryan had brushed it off. According to the often wild-sounding stories about living in New York City he sometimes told while they were working, Ryan was used to eccentricities. "Come have some pizza while we wait."

Six large pizza boxes were piled on the loading dock near where Ryan was sitting. Three boys and two girls had already helped themselves. Platinum hurried over, too, glad for the chance to eat before he started lifting heavy things.

Small talk flittered around as they waited. One of the girls was flirting desperately with one of the guys, who was ignoring her. Another one of the guys was hoping to buy the newest gaming console this afternoon with his earnings, and another guy had already made plans to come play. It was inane talk, but it passed the time, and Platinum learned a lot from it.

Platinum's first week of freedom had been spent in the woods, running almost constantly. He had eventually stolen someone's clothes and shoes from a cabin that had a drying line outside and ditched the scrubs. And then he had stumbled into a small town not too dissimilar from this one. Platinum had quickly learned that everything he needed, like food and water, cost something called money, and that Platinum didn't have any. He kept moving, and at the next town, he knew enough to offer to wash dishes at a local restaurant in return for a few meals. Every town Platinum stopped at offered a little more knowledge of how the world outside his cell worked, and these other youths helping with the stocking provided even more insight every day.

The trucks eventually pulled up long after the pizza was gone, and they all got to work. It was a sweaty job, but every box Platinum lifted made him a little stronger. It was better than lifting weights, one of the guys had explained a few weeks back. Platinum was thin from hunger and strong from all the running, but this added a different sort of strength to his body. He would need to buy a shirt in a larger size after a few more weeks of lifting the boxes to accommodate the new muscle he was slowly putting on.

They were fed a lunch of prepackaged deli sandwiches halfway through the day, but by the time the last truck had left, Platinum was exhausted and starving again. Ryan ambled over and handed him a wad of rolled-up twenties, about two hundred dollars, which was very generous for a day's work. Platinum pocketed the money, walked around to the front of the store, and walked inside as a customer.

He filled his basket with the essentials: milk, cereal, and pasta. Then he browsed for a little bit. Platinum liked to try something new, something he wouldn't have been served at the lab. They fed him healthy salads with cut-up chicken or tuna on top. Platinum had discovered that adding pasta to just about anything made it into a meal, and he wanted to break free of the damned scientists, so he picked up something different each time he shopped. Platinum wandered back into the dairy section and spotted a small cartons of eggs. He knew they had to be heated and that the inside would be creamy if he cooked them correctly. Platinum grabbed a half-dozen carton and added it to his basket. Eggs over pasta might be good. He would have to try it.

Spending as little money as possible was Platinum's goal. He had a stash of it in his backpack so that when he had to run again he could afford food without needing to steal and run the risk of being caught by the local authorities. He had little doubt the police would turn him back over to the scientists quickly. The scientists had clout. Platinum knew they did, because otherwise how would they get away with killing so many dragons for their experiments? He paid and took his bag of food with him, then headed up the sidewalk and back into the mountain.

Platinum started sniffing the air as he approached the house he had commandeered. There were plenty of the usual scents around from trees, flowers, bugs, and birds. The occasional acrid whiff of car exhaust from the road nearby made his nose wrinkle in distaste. He couldn't sense any intruders around the house. There weren't any fresh smells of the humans who owned it, and all the lights were still out and the blinds down, just as Platinum had left them. Still, he circled the house cautiously.

Dragon, Platinum's nose informed him the second he stepped onto the gravel driveway leading from the road up to the house. It hadn't stayed, just walked up the drive to the front door before turning around and leaving again.

There were dragons in the town below. Platinum wasn't ignorant of that fact, but he had managed to stay out of their territory so there hadn't been a confrontation. Platinum had only smelled them a few times, particularly around the consulting firm next to the grocery store. Guilt informed Platinum that he would need to warn them to run should the scientists track him here—the scientists wouldn't hesitate to grab more dragons—but Platinum did his best to stay out of their territory. It was safer that way.

Platinum was growling, he realized as he followed the scent of the dragon down the driveway and back to the road. The dragon had continued walking farther up the mountain, Platinum's nose informed him, and then it had eventually doubled back to return to town. Platinum didn't know what the dragon was looking for or why one of the town's dragons had decided to venture up the mountain now, but Platinum had a sinking suspicion that it was his fault and that it was probably time for him to move on to another town. Dragons were very territorial, and the last thing Platinum wanted to do was start a fight because he was accidentally encroaching on another dragon's territory.

The wind came to Platinum's call, and he let it blow his scent off the road and out of the forest. It was a trick he had learned to keep the dogs away, and he hoped it would work just as well on fellow dragons. Once Platinum was certain his trail was covered, he let himself into the house, locked the door again behind him, and went to make dinner.

Platinum would get ready to leave in the morning, he decided as he measured out a serving of pasta. First on his list would be stopping by the grocery store to stock up on things that wouldn't go bad to eat on the way. He would also have to tell Ryan he was leaving so the man didn't expect Platinum for the trucks next week. Once that was done, Platinum would be gone, back into the woods and on his way to a new place to hide.

Chapter Three

Nickel walked back into the office tired, achy, and covered in sticks and leaves. He was also frowning as he thought about his day. He had been wholly unsuccessful at finding the white-haired boy Louise had described, and yet there was definitely something odd up there. Every once in a while he would catch a scent on the wind that didn't quite belong. It blew away too quickly for him to be able to tell what type of creature had caused it, and he hadn't been able to track it to a physical source.

There had been hail on the ground in the morning, and there was something in the woods. It was like the start of a bad horror movie, Nickel joked to himself, except that he was the one in the center of it all, which meant he would probably be the first to die. Nickel rolled his eyes at his melodrama and started brushing the leaves and sticks stuck to him into the trashcan.

"No luck?" Becky asked sympathetically.

"Nothing," Nickel groaned, working a particularly stubborn stick out of his hair. He lost a few strands, but the stick finally came loose.

Becky hummed and then turned her computer monitor for Nickel to see. "Could this be your guy?" she asked, pointing one manicured nail at a fuzzy security video. A young man approximately Nickel's age walked in and out of the camera frame carrying boxes from a large truck. The picture was grainy so Nickel couldn't tell if the young man's hair was blond or white, but it was a possibility.

"When was this taken?" he asked.

Becky grinned at him. "This morning. It continues into midafternoon."

"So while I was tromping through the woods looking for him, he was in town?" Nickel sighed.

"He was next door unloading trucks for the grocery store," Becky added cheekily.

"Of course he was. I wonder if he's still there?"

Becky shook her head. "The trucks left an hour ago. You probably just missed him."

Nickel growled. "At least I can talk to the store owner." He double-checked that he had gotten all the leaves and sticks off and then turned around to head back out the door.

The store was crowded with people coming to shop for their dinner groceries after work. Nickel stopped the first uniformed employee he saw that didn't look too harried and asked to speak with the owner. It took a few minutes for Ryan to appear, but he hurried over to Nickel with a welcoming smile.

"How can I help you?" he asked. "Dane was over just yesterday buying out our cat supplies. We haven't been able to restock yet, but I can give you a call when we do if he needs anything more."

Nickel laughed, remembering the three cat trees, plethora of toys, two litter boxes, food, and other supplies Dane had stumbled back to the office with. Lumie and

Alloy were spending most of today helping get Turtle and Cinnamon acclimated to their new home and had decided not to come to the office. Thank goodness; Nickel didn't think he could deal with them two days in a row, especially after a long day trekking through the woods.

"I think we'll be good with cat stuff for the next decade," he joked. "Actually, I came to ask you about a boy Dane's having me check up on. I think he was helping you unpack the trucks today? He has white hair?"

Ryan was nodding before Nickel even finished his description. "He calls himself Platinum," he began, and Nickel felt the bottom drop out of his stomach. "Comes down from the mountain once a week. I'm pretty sure he was looking to steal some food from me a few weeks back, so I hired him instead. I've a soft spot for runaways, and he looked like he'd been running for a while."

"You're certain he called himself Platinum?" Nickel asked desperately.

Ten years ago, Nickel, Dane, and Mercury had raided a warehouse where some of the evil government-funded scientists had been conducting experiments on air dragons. Mercury had rescued Nickel from the water dragon compound, Chrome and 'Ron from the earth dragon lab, and Lumie, Copper, and Alloy from the fire dragon lab. At the air dragon warehouse they had located Zinc, a female air dragon Nickel's age, and she had told them that the scientists had left her as bait in a trap and taken another air dragon, a boy named Platinum, with them. Despite everyone's best efforts, they hadn't been able to locate and rescue Platinum. It was something that had been driving Dane a little crazy because despite all of his strength and resources, he hadn't been able to catch the scientists and stop their experiments. Apparently,

Platinum had escaped on his own and had somehow landed in Dane's town.

"I'm positive," Ryan said. "Is everything all right with him?"

"I need to speak with him, that's all. He's someone important to Dane." Nickel forced himself to smile and thank Ryan politely.

"He comes by again and I'll point him in your direction," Ryan said helpfully. "He's a good kid, if a bit quiet."

"Thanks," Nickel repeated. He headed outside and walked quickly back into the office. Dane needed to know Platinum was around.

Luckily, Dane was sequestered behind his desk, enjoying sitting in his plush chair for the first time in a while. He was on the phone with a client, so Nickel settled into one of the guest chairs to wait. It took a few minutes before Dane finished. He stood up to run his handwritten notes over to Becky first before returning to Nickel.

"What's up?" he asked once he was back in his seat.

"Platinum," Nickel stated flatly. "Apparently, he's been working to unload the trucks next door once a week for at least a month."

Dane's eyes widened comically and then narrowed as he thought. "Interesting that he would end up in my town. A dragon supposed to be so important to the evil scientists that they've managed to keep him hidden from me for over ten years and he inadvertently ends up on my doorstep? It's too much of a coincidence." Dane had made it perfectly clear to the supernatural community that any dragon in need of aid could come to him for help, and yet, once free, Platinum hadn't come directly to Dane's office. Instead, Platinum was still hiding as if he didn't know about Dane's offer, but then why would he have come to this town specifically out of the dozens of small towns in this mountain range unless he had been sent here?

"I went hiking in the woods looking for a guy who appeared at exactly the same time as the weird weather and found Platinum instead," Nickel added. "That's a lot of coincidences."

"An awful lot," Dane agreed slowly. "You find his den today?"

Nickel shook his head. "He's supposed to be living up the mountain, but I couldn't find any sign of him."

"Air dragons are notoriously elusive and hard to find. I'm not surprised you couldn't locate his trail, especially if he's on the run."

"Do you think he's running or that he's still being controlled?"

Dane frowned and then sighed. "There's no way to tell. Be very careful with how you approach this case, Nickel."

Nickel nodded solemnly. That much was obvious.

The phone rang in the outer office. Becky answered it, and a few minutes later, the phone on Dane's desk lit up. Dane picked up the handset and held it to his ear. Nickel could hear Becky speaking in an odd echo of her voice in the main office and more faintly on Dane's phone.

"Director Stockton on line two," Becky said.

"Thanks, Becky," Dane replied. He waited a moment for Becky to hang up before he poked the button for line two. "This is Dane, your local Supernatural Consultant. How may I help you?" He listened for a few long minutes during which Nickel couldn't hear more than a murmur from the other half of the conversation. "Chatter?" He sounded like he was repeating something Stockton had said. "You're certain?" Another couple minutes of silent listening. "Nickel will be happy to find out." And now Nickel was being volunteered for something. Nickel sighed in exasperation. They spoke for a few more minutes, mostly just exchanging pleasantries from what Nickel could hear, before Dane hung up.

"What did you rope me into now?" Nickel asked sharply.

Dane smiled. It wasn't a friendly sort of grin, meaning that Dane had something up his sleeve and Nickel was about to regret agreeing to work for him. Nickel just scowled in reply and waited somewhat impatiently for Dane to get on with the explanation.

"You remember O'Simmons from five years ago? The corrupt police officer that had captured two precious dragons?" Dragons whose magic wasn't confined to an element, unlike Nickel. There had been other raids and other dragons saved in the five years since, but that raid had also included the Secretary of Defense in the planning, and since then Nickel had gotten official legal status as a US citizen because he had been born in the country. That included a Social Security number and the requirement that he pay his taxes properly. Outwardly, that wasn't a big change, but it brought a strange sort of security into Nickel's life, which was probably helped because Dane and Mercury had both been able to legally adopt all the kits in their care.

"I remember," Nickel answered, wondering where Dane was going with his explanation.

"Well, one of O'Simmons's cohorts revealed the location of some of their safe houses during interrogation. At the time, all the safe houses were searched and then put under surveillance. A little over a month ago, one of them showed signs of life. A team was dispatched, but within twenty-four hours the occupants had moved on. According to Stockton, a few members from the strike team decided to stop for lunch on the way back to headquarters. They went to a restaurant in one of the small towns only about sixty miles from here. The gossip that day was about a very polite young man awkwardly asking to wash dishes in return for a meal and how diligently he worked just for a hamburger and some fries."

Nickel nodded along with Dane's story, still wondering where it was going and why Dane looked so interested in it.

"Then two men at a nearby table started asking some very pointed questions. Was his hair very long and white? Was he about eighteen years old?"

Was he an air dragon? Nickel added to himself. Was he, perhaps, the air dragon calling himself Platinum currently haunting the woods up Mountain Road?

Dane nodded as if he could read the direction of Nickel's thoughts on his face. "They repeated the story to their supervisor, who sent them to ask some questions of their own at some of the other towns. At the town closest to the safe house, they heard a story of a white-haired teen stealing a few granola bars. Then there was the town where they had lunch. After that, there were two more towns where a young man matching the same description offered to wash dishes."

"He was slowly moving closer to us?" Nickel asked.

"Or being herded," Dane contradicted. "I've never made a secret of where a dragon needed to come to get my help. What if it's another trap planned by the enemy to catch us?"

"Then why send Platinum our way? All they would need to do was come to your office themselves to corner us." Nickel was frowning as he tried to figure out that contradiction. "Maybe he did escape and they're trying to catch him too? It could just be luck that he came in this direction."

"We're missing one important fact," Dane said after a moment of thought. "If Platinum really is manipulating the weather with his powers over air, there's no way the enemy would allow him to escape their clutches."

"If they even know what kind of power he has," Nickel countered. If it was even Platinum causing the bad weather, too, as there was no guarantee that coincidence was fact either. All they had was a lot of speculation. "You said something about chatter?" Nickel asked when he couldn't think of another avenue to take their current discussion.

Dane frowned and rubbed his chin absentmindedly with one hand. "Stockton thinks he's found an online chat room where the scientists from various separated hiding spots get together to share information. One group is claiming they're about to get their hands on the most powerful dragon they've ever seen. They apparently call it the philosopher's stone dragon."

"Are they trying to change lead into gold?" Nickel scoffed. Outwardly, he was trying to brush it off as just another crazed fantasy, but the mere idea that those evil scientists might get their hands on a dragon that powerful was extremely frightening.

"More like turn the least magical race on earth, humans, into the most magical race," Dane replied scathingly, his scowl completely focused on those damned scientists. "It's pretty much the same level of impossibility."

With modern science, it wasn't impossible to turn lead into gold, Nickel knew, just as it was also possible for those evil scientists to somehow use dragon magic. Nickel didn't doubt they would be happy to increase the limited spool of power they had managed so far into something far greater—and a philosopher's stone dragon might give them that.

"Stockton's got his own people looking into it, of course. Mercury included," Dane continued. "But he's emailing you all the information so we can work together on it. The URL for the chat room should be included. Why don't you introduce yourself?"

Nickel nodded and pushed back his chair. He stood and walked from Dane's office to his own little desk in the corner. His laptop let out a soft beep when he opened it. Nickel settled carefully in his own chair so he didn't bump his knees and waited for his email to load.

Was there a philosopher's stone dragon? Not that Nickel could think of. There were elemental dragons like him. Those dragons could manipulate just one element. Maybe the enemy was focusing on a precious dragon, like Mercury. Precious dragons weren't confined by the elements, able to do whatever spell they wanted within their personal power restraints. Some precious dragons were stronger than others, but the enemy had already experimented on both precious and elemental dragons and hadn't been nearly as excited about the prospect.

If Nickel had to guess, he thought one of the dragons the enemy had experimented on in the past might have been genetically altered enough to cause that kind of excitement. Nickel had certainly never heard of an elemental dragon able to manipulate the weather, if that was even what Platinum was doing. Perhaps they had conducted a new type of experiment on Platinum that had given him such advanced powers. He had been able to escape using them, but the enemy knew that once they caught Platinum again they would have a wealth of power at their fingertips to exploit.

Nickel's resolve to find Platinum before it was too late only doubled. If Nickel hadn't been able to find his den in the woods, the enemy shouldn't be able to either. Still, Nickel thought he might spend the night camping out on the mountain just in case.

The first email that popped up was from Mrs. Mitchel. Nickel read through it quickly, but she hadn't said much. Just a simple thank-you, a confirmation that she would handle the rest, and a note that she would put a check in the mail.

Stockton's email was much longer. Dane had already told him all the salient information, Nickel saw as he read. At the end of the email was the URL link with a username and password already created for him. The username was Scienceguy1965, and Nickel hoped it would hold up to inspection. He clicked the URL and waited while his web browser opened.

According to Stockton, Scienceguy1965 was named Marcus Quillian. He was a microbiologist who had been working for the research arm of a big-name pharmaceutical company, but had been fired when his experimentation went a little too far into the illegal range for the company to feel comfortable with. He was someone the evil scientists would be happy to hire: a man with loose morals and a big brain. That he had been entirely fabricated by the US government in order to catch the bad scientists was another matter entirely.

The page that finally loaded was a plain black screen with two fields for username and password. Nickel signed on and found himself in an active chat room. There were three other people there. HaikuMu was typing up a storm. Petridish1000 appeared to be interjecting every once in a while. ThatGuy wasn't saying anything, and a closer glance at his status said he had been present, but inactive, for over three hours. Nickel decided to follow ThatGuy's example.

It was agony sitting in front of his too-small desk, reading HaikuMu blathering on about how her most recent accommodations didn't even have running water. How could she conduct any experiments when she only had antibacterial wipes to keep her hands clean? It didn't sound like she had any actual live dragons, just specimens, but Nickel still kept track of everything she was saying just in case she gave away her location. Petridish1000 was entirely unsympathetic. Apparently, he had been camping out in the woods for three and a half weeks, waiting for an opportunity to strike. The bastard was probably waiting for a dragon to wander into his path and fortunately hadn't had any luck yet.

After an hour of their bitching, Nickel was ready to pull out his hair. He wanted to be back on the mountain, searching for Platinum. He knew he wouldn't find Platinum no matter how hard he tried—an air dragon couldn't be found if it didn't want to be, as Zinc had taught Nickel many times—but that didn't mean Nickel didn't want to try anyway.

You don't say much.

The private message popped onto the lower right-hand corner of his computer screen. ThatGuy apparently hadn't fallen asleep at his computer after hours of watching HaikuMu and Petridish1000 gripe at each other.

There's not much to say, Nickel typed back after a moment of thought.

Then why are you still here? ThatGuy asked. There was no way to infer tone from a few words on a computer screen, so Nickel didn't know if ThatGuy was merely curious or whether he was testing Nickel. Everything was a test, Nickel reminded himself. ScienceGuy1965 was fake, so everything Nickel typed had to fit the correct persona or ThatGuy would shut Nickel out.

I was promised science and the next big breakthrough. I'm waiting for that to start.

You just have to be patient, ThatGuy insisted. *Everything is in place. Give it a few more days and the philosopher's stone will fall directly into our hands.* Nickel suppressed a wide grin. The SupFeds had really done a good job integrating ScienceGuy1965 into the enemy's trust if they were willing to tell him their plans in a private chat.

I'm looking forward to it.

As am I. We may have also located the soldier in our search for the philosopher's stone. Two dragons of immense power should be coming your way soon.

Nickel frowned at ThatGuy's last sentence. Who was the soldier?

How invigorating, Nickel wrote. He was trying to sound evilly excited. *I should make extra preparations.*

I will contact you again when we have made the capture.

ThatGuy didn't sign off, but his status returned to inactive. Nickel did sign off. He flipped windows to Stockton's email and hit the reply button.

A user named ThatGuy has confirmed their search for the philosopher's stone dragon, Nickel wrote. *He also indicated that they had located a dragon they're calling the soldier. I would appreciate your sending me any information you have regarding the soldier. ThatGuy also appears to be a leader of some sort. He knew everything that was going on. Have you been able to track him down?*

A crack of thunder sounded, shaking the building and echoing through the mountain. Nickel jumped, and he might have also let out an undignified squeak. Dane swore in his office, and Nickel heard something clatter off his desk. Becky continued blithely typing on her computer. Lightning flashed as Nickel got up to look out the window. The sky was dark with heavy thunderclouds, and wind was whipping through the trees. Another crack of thunder sounded, strong enough that the window shuddered in its frame.

"Shut the computers down before the storm fries them!" Dane called from inside his office.

The surge protectors the computers were plugged into were supposed to protect them in bad storms, but it was still safer to shut them down entirely. Nickel hurried back to his laptop, sent the email, and shut down.

"It's almost time to close up anyway." Dane sighed as he walked into the main office. "Let's head on home."

"I was going to keep an eye out for Platinum tonight," Nickel said with an apprehensive glance out the window as another bolt of lightning flashed and thunder followed.

"Not in this weather you're not," Dane disagreed sternly. Becky was pulling out her purse as he was speaking and getting ready to head home too. "Look, no one's going to want to be outside in this weather. I'm certain Platinum will be safe from any dragon snatching tonight."

Nickel felt like a child being reassured that there weren't any monsters under the bed, but like that child, he trusted Dane to know what he was talking about. Platinum would be safe in his mountain den until Nickel could return in the morning.

Becky smiled at them both and waved goodbye before activating the spell circle that would take her home. Dane called on his magic, sending a shiver through the air, and Nickel felt his wards go up around the office. Nickel put his hand on Dane's shoulder, and Dane's magic pulled them both away.

Chapter Four

Thunder woke Platinum from a late afternoon nap. It rolled through the mountain range like drums beating through the heavy trees. Lightning flashed. He rolled off the couch and brushed his hair out of his face. It had come loose from the braids he had tied it in, but he had to wash it anyway.

The window in the kitchen was small, but it was big enough that he could see well into the woods in the back of the house. All the trees and their large leaves blocking out the sun made it seem later than it was. Platinum splashed water on his face at the sink and dried himself on a dishtowel while watching the heavy rainfall. He had been having a nightmare, Platinum remembered. The rain beat against the kitchen window while he frowned at his reflection. He couldn't remember all the details, but there were more than enough terrible things in his memories to amount for an entire lifetime of nightmares. And dragon lifetimes weren't short as long as they didn't run into any evil scientists killing them off in droves.

Knowing he was going to live forever and ever with only his nightmares for company was a lonely feeling. There was a time when there had been other dragons around him when he woke from a nightmare. He remembered Zinc calling through the bars in her cell so he could hear her comforting words. But then the scientists had taken him to a new facility and left her behind. He only found out later that she was dead thanks to overhearing some gossip.

Platinum knew he was better off away from the scientists. He never wanted to be put under for some unknown experiment again, not knowing if he would actually wake up or slip off into the realm of death with some bastard's scalpel still inside him. At the same time, he missed the sound of voices as the scientists and the guards spoke around him and the touch of another person's hand, even if it was only a guard dragging his half-conscious body back to his cell. Platinum was all alone in the forest, running and hiding without hearing a voice outside of his own except for the times he worked unloading the trucks at the grocery store. He knew he had to live like that, and he wasn't under any illusions that he would find a kindred spirit willing to run through the woods at his side. Maybe he would run into Zinc's ghost, but it was safer to be alone so he didn't get anyone else tangled into his mess.

The rumbling thunder sounded like the storm was slowly moving away, heading east. Platinum thought he might follow the storm in the morning and see what a big city was like. He knew there was one on the coast called Boston thanks to an old map decorating the wall of a diner he had stopped at in one town.

Platinum spun away from his reflection in the window and sighed. He might as well shower and get ready for bed, even though he would only have more nightmares waiting for him. He wished the storm would return—the thunder booming overhead was better than having to listen to his own thoughts—laughed sadly at his foolishness, and went to wash his hair.

*

The leaves overhead were still dripping when Platinum packed all of his things into his backpack. He threw his garbage into a neighbor's can—his one bag hopefully wouldn't be noticed amid the rest of their trash—and headed down the mountain one last time. The ground was springy with excess water and squelched under his shoes as he picked his way around the puddles. The storm hadn't abated until very early in the morning. Every time Platinum had been woken up by a nightmare, the thunder had been there to greet him.

It took longer than usual to walk into town. He had to take a serpentine route in order to keep his shoes dry, which added time. He didn't really want to be wearing soaked shoes while walking the miles and miles it would take to get to Boston. Plus, Platinum didn't need to rush to get to the grocery store before the trucks arrived. He was on his own time and could move at his own pace.

He could see a construction crew moving into one of the vacant lots along the shopping strip as he turned the corner by the gas station and headed toward the grocery store. They were busy pulling out whatever fixtures the previous tenant had left. Platinum briefly wondered who would be moving in, then pushed that thought away. As much as he liked the sleepy town, he was only an interloper stealing a bed. It didn't matter how much he liked the town or how interested he was to know who was opening a shop. He was moving on, and that was final.

The consulting firm that smelled like dragons was dark as he walked past. They would be arriving any minute, Platinum guessed, given how early it still was. He should leave a note warning them that the scientists chasing him would snatch any dragon they came across along the way. Maybe the grocery store owner would take a message over there for him. Platinum didn't want to encroach on their territory, but leaving a note was better than letting another dragon get hurt.

Platinum reached the grocery store and walked inside. The automatic doors closed quickly behind him as he headed to the nearest associate that didn't look too busy.

"Can I talk to the owner?" Platinum asked the young woman standing idly in the bagging section of a checkout line. There wasn't anyone in her line, but she still took a few seconds to double-check before she nodded.

"I'll go get him." She waved to the cashier to tell him she was leaving for a minute and headed to the back of the store.

It took a long time for Ryan to arrive. The woman working the bagging station returned with a smile and was followed by Ryan a few minutes later.

"Platinum, just the guy I was looking for!" Ryan said with a happy smile. "I've a friend who wants to meet you. I just called, but it seems he's not in his office yet. Do you mind waiting a few minutes?"

"Looking for me?" Platinum repeated warily. Had the scientists found him? Ryan was a good guy, but he wouldn't know a corrupt cop if one approached him about locating Platinum.

"Nothing bad," Ryan reassured Platinum, no doubt seeing Platinum's wariness on his face. "It's Dane from next door. He runs a Supernatural Consulting Firm, and he would like to have a few words with you."

Platinum took an involuntary step back. "You can tell him that I'm not encroaching on any dragon's territory. I'm planning to leave as soon as I stock up on some travel supplies, so he doesn't have to worry about me any longer."

"Dane's not a dragon." Ryan paused, looking thoughtful. "No idea what he is, to be perfectly honest. He's got at least one dragon kit helping out at the firm, but as far as I know, they haven't claimed any territory. Look, Dane's a nice guy. You really should think about staying to speak with him."

"I'm moving on," Platinum said firmly. He had made his decision, and he was sticking to it. "Warn Dane that his dragons might be in trouble thanks to the bastards following me." His conscience made him add that part in. Platinum nodded politely to Ryan and then hurried away to the snack aisle where he could get some cheap nonperishables that would fit in his bag.

It didn't take him long to make his choices. There wasn't any sign of Ryan when Platinum moved to the nearest checkout line. He paid and packed up his backpack, then strode from the store. He took one last look at the little town he had inadvertently grown to love, sighed heavily, and turned his back on it. He walked down Main Street away from the mountain. Platinum would stick to the sidewalk until he was out of town, and then turn into the woods and allow himself to get lost amid the large trees.

"You're not going to get very far with the tracker they put in your shoulder, you know," a young boy's voice said from Platinum's left. Platinum jumped and a whip of wind surrounded him.

The boy didn't even blink as he was buffeted in the face by Platinum's power. His eyes were red, and his now-windblown hair was equally as vibrant. There was no doubting that he was a dragon kit. He was probably one of the kits that worked at the consulting firm. Then his words penetrated through Platinum's surprise.

"What tracker?" Platinum asked sharply, wondering what the boy was talking about.

The boy shrugged and reached through Platinum's swirling wind to grab Platinum's arm. "They've been following you all month," the boy stated like it was common knowledge. "Nickel says it's because you're the philosopher's stone dragon. That's not true. Zinc says if you're still alive after all these years, then they'd want to keep an eye on you at all times if they let you out for some plot."

"They didn't let me out; I escaped," Platinum insisted. Inwardly, he was reeling at the boy's audacity. Zinc was dead, and no matter what this boy said or how the boy had been able to slip past Platinum's defenses, there wasn't anything he could do that would convince Platinum otherwise.

The boy just smiled knowingly, his red eyes slightly piercing as if he were seeing more than just colors and shapes in the world around them.

Platinum looked away. He started walking again, pulling the boy along when he refused to let go. Tires squealed behind them and a car door slapped open.

"Lumie!" a frantic voice yelled.

Platinum turned slightly to see what was going on. A young man approximately Platinum's age with short blue hair was running at them. His hands were outstretched and water was coalescing between them. On the road, moving faster than the blue-haired boy could run, was a large white van. The side door was open, and a person wearing a black mask was leaning out over the sidewalk.

Platinum spun and sent his magic at the car. It hit a shield of some sort and rebounded, sending Platinum sprawling. Lumie landed on top of him, and a force of some kind yanked them both up into the air and then sideways into the car.

"Lumie! Platinum!"

The door slammed shut on the blue-haired boy's yelling, and with a screech, the car took off. Platinum growled and flung his magic outward, trying to hit anything or anyone that would get the car to stop. His magic had zero effect. It was like he was back behind the cell door with the guard laughing on the other side while he screamed and threw his magic ineffectually at the door over and over again.

A hand came into view and patted him gently on the head.

"You did well, dragon," the man Platinum only knew as one of the bad scientists said pleasantly. He had taken his mask off, and his sneer was both familiar and frightening. Platinum could still move, and he sat up and batted the hand away.

"What are you talking about?" he whined, trying not to scream or burst into tears. He had escaped! He had gotten out of the lab and survived the forest. He had learned about humans and figured out what he needed to do to live among them. Never had he imagined that it had all been part of some plan by the scientists.

The scientist shifted past Platinum in the limited space of the van and crouched next to Lumie, who had been sitting quietly off to one side simply listening. "You were our bait in a trap, and you netted us an amazing prize. The philosopher's stone dragon is going to revolutionize our research. Right, little red?" He turned his attention solely toward Lumie, who grinned up at him.

"The dragon soldier is going to drown you," Lumie said happily.

The scientist laughed. "The dragon soldier is about to fall directly into the second part of our trap. He's not someone I'm worried about."

Lumie just shrugged. "So, where are we going?" he asked. "We can't drive too far. I have to be home before lunch, or Cinnamon will start clawing the couches and Daddy will get mad."

Both the scientist and Platinum stared incredulously at Lumie. Didn't he understand that a crazy person who was going to lock Lumie away and conduct cruel experiments on him for the rest of his life had just kidnapped him? There was something very wrong with this kit. The scientist's lips twitched upward a bit. Platinum had no doubt he was probably happy for the fact that Lumie was clueless. It would be much easier to take advantage of Lumie if he went along with anything done to him.

There wasn't anything Platinum could do to escape. He didn't understand the wall his magic was stuck behind or how it had been switched from his cell door to a moving car with ease. All he knew was that he had tasted freedom and a life not behind bars. It was probably the cruelest thing they could have done to him, letting him go and then reeling him back in once they had gotten what they wanted. With the return of his personal hell, he wanted to lash out and start screaming and crying. At the same time, he didn't want to give the scientist the satisfaction of seeing him break down. Platinum sat quietly and sullenly as the van drove off into the mountains.

They drove for about two hours. Lumie was smiling and humming to himself the entire time. There was almost a sense of smugness about him; there was definitely something wrong with the poor kit. The scientist sat between them. He also looked smug, but at least he had a reason to. The car never got on the highway, but the roads were so winding and hilly that it would be difficult for someone to follow them.

A roll of thunder sounded overhead, and a flash of lighting lit up the car. Through the front window, Platinum could see the sky darkening with heavy clouds as another thunderstorm built overhead. Branches swayed alarmingly as the wind picked up, but the car pulled up a long driveway and into an enclosed garage before any rain could start falling.

"Out," the scientist said forcefully as the driver got out and opened the side door. Platinum didn't want to obey, but he didn't have any other options. Lumie cheerfully hopped out of the car, and Platinum followed. They were led into a barren house. There wasn't any furniture Platinum could see, and the kitchen looked unused as they were herded to a basement door off to the side of the empty pantry.

The basement was dim. There was only one bare light bulb hanging from some wires overhead. The floor was cold concrete. On one side of the room, a line had been chiseled into the concrete. Platinum and Lumie were led to the other side of that line, and then the scientist backed away.

"That's the boundary," he said sharply to the dragons. "The bathroom's through there." Platinum could see a small room within the boundary line with a toilet, sink, and standing shower off to one side. The door had been removed to eliminate them being able to hide behind it. "Be good," the scientist finished with a cold laugh as he left them behind in their improvised cage. Luckily, he left the light on, but Platinum didn't trust that mistake wouldn't be rectified soon.

Platinum sank down onto the cold concrete. He half expected himself to burst into tears now that the scientist was gone, but he felt too raw. He knew that if one tear escaped, he wouldn't be able to stop for a long time. It was still hard for him to believe that the scientists had engineered his escape attempt with the goal of using him to catch other dragons. It was infuriating, and maybe that anger was enough to keep the tears at bay. Platinum had never thought back on the day he escaped with anything other than relief. He had never thought it had been too easy, and the horrible cuts and blisters his bare feet had accrued while running from pursuit had only cemented the idea of his success in his mind.

He hated the scientists. Absolutely hated them! Another crack of thunder shook the house.

Lumie walked over to Platinum with a wide grin. He held out his hand for Platinum to take, and since Platinum didn't have anything better to do than wallow in misery, he allowed Lumie to pull him back to his feet.

"The driver guy just left to go pick up supplies," Lumie explained as he led the way toward the line carved in the cement. Platinum put his hand out, already knowing what he would find. An invisible, impenetrable wall pressed against his fingers. He had never been confined out in the open like this before, but they had used that damned wall plenty of times.

Lumie stepped over the line and through the wall without pause, and then he turned to frown at Platinum and tug impatiently on the hand he was still holding.

"The other scientist guy just logged onto his laptop upstairs. We have ten minutes before he comes down to taunt us some more."

Platinum watched incredulously as his hand clasped in Lumie's passed through the impenetrable barrier. He stepped forward, following the tug on his arm, and the rest of his body slipped through the barrier as if it weren't even there.

"How..." He paused, looking down at Lumie as they walked to the staircase. This was one of two dragons Platinum's faked escape was supposed to capture. The philosopher's stone dragon, he thought the scientist had called him. Platinum didn't know what a philosopher's stone was, but giving what appeared to be an ordinary dragon a special name must mean something. Platinum had only ever been called "that dragon" for his entire life.

Still... "How do you know all of that?"

Lumie shrugged as he pushed the basement door open into the kitchen. "I have dreams," he said vaguely. The kitchen was empty and the back door within easy reach. They were outside before Platinum had the chance to register what Lumie had said.

It was pouring. Platinum was soaked in seconds and shivering. The forest was lit eerily for a moment as lightning flashed and a roll of thunder echoed, bouncing around the mountain peaks before fading. Lumie took a tighter grip on Platinum's hand and continued leading him farther away from the house.

Trees surrounded them within moments. The rain slowed thanks to the covering of leaves above them.

Platinum glanced behind them, but he couldn't see the house or anything but more trees. They were only a few minutes of walking away from the house, but Platinum didn't hear any yelling or the start of a search. In fact, if he didn't know better, he would have said they were nowhere near human habitation.

Rain continued to pour, but it was easing off with every step. The amount of trees around them was lessening as well. Lumie pulled him between two large, looming pine trees, and they stepped out into a wide, grassy clearing. The sky was blue and almost totally cloudless overhead. A large house sat in the center of the field, and Lumie picked up his pace as he headed toward the front door.

Platinum let himself continue to be dragged along. He had no idea where they were or how Lumie had known somewhere safe was only a quick walk away. He was honestly still reeling over the fact that he wasn't still stuck in that horrible basement with pain and suffering, combined with the terrible knowledge that he had led Lumie and at least one other dragon to the same doom.

Lumie opened the front door of the house as if he lived here and had every right to simply walk inside. Maybe he did. He let go of Platinum's hand for the first time since their escape and yelled, "I'm home!" into the spacious foyer.

There was a crash from somewhere just ahead, and the sound of a door banging into a wall; then a set of footsteps pounded closer. Platinum flinched back. He was almost ducking behind Lumie, a boy quite a few years younger than him, but Lumie seemed to have this perfectly in hand while Platinum was still horribly lost and confused.

A woman with brilliant green skin dashed into view. She skidded to a halt in front of them and gasped into the phone she was holding to her ear.

"Lumie's here. He just walked in the front door with another dragon kit in tow. You're Platinum, I assume?" she asked Platinum gently. Platinum nodded wordlessly. She ended the call, crossed her arms over her chest, and glared at Lumie. "Do you have any idea how worried we've been?"

"I have a feeling he doesn't," another voice said from directly behind them. Platinum hadn't heard the door open and close, but when he jumped in surprise and spun around, a bronze dragon was standing behind them with his arms also crossed. "Lumie, you scared us very badly today. I don't care that you knew how to get to safety. Dane, Nickel, and I have been very frightened."

"I told you I would be home in time for lunch!" Lumie insisted pointedly.

The bronze dragon growled. "But you neglected to mention that you would be kitnapped and would be able to safely find your way home afterward! Lumie, you need to share those details with us so we don't worry ourselves to death trying to find you!" He was near tears as he scolded Lumie, and a second later, he bent down to pull Lumie into his arms.

"I'm sorry, Daddy," Lumie replied, his voice low and sad. "I didn't mean to make you sad."

"I know you didn't, Lumie, but you have to think about these things before you act."

"I will, Daddy," he said earnestly.

His father smiled slightly, just a small upturn of his lips, and he looked down at Lumie wryly. "You had better," he said. "You're still not getting any Cinnamon

Bombs for the rest of the week. To help you remember why you're supposed to tell us these things," his father explained sternly when Lumie whined.

"Platinum?" a girl asked very softly, shock in her voice.

Platinum looked around. He was utterly tired of this day. Tired of surprises and being yanked around every which way by people he didn't know. He wanted desperately to go back to the little cabin in the woods he had commandeered, climb under the covers, and let the world fade away around him.

He matched face to voice when he saw a young woman descending the stairs. She had the exact same face as him right down to the arch of his eyebrows and the length of his nose. He had seen his face in the mirror plenty of times since his first escape, but it had been years since he had seen his face mirrored on his egg-twin.

"Zinc?" he breathed. They had told him she was dead! He had always assumed it had been an experiment gone wrong, and it had never crossed his mind that they had lied to him.

She flung herself across the room and into Platinum's arms, sobbing loudly. "They've been trying to find you for ten years!" she babbled into his shoulder. "Ten years!"

Platinum was crying too. He had never thought he would see her again, but to know she had been safe and alive all this time was... Well, it was amazing. He was so damn happy.

Another half-dozen kits flooded the foyer, asking questions about what was going on at the top of their lungs. It was a madhouse that the green-skinned woman, Lumie's father, and another man who appeared to glow slightly were all working to calm. Platinum didn't care. He had his egg-sister back. She was alive and safe and doing well in this crazy family of dragons. It was almost worth all those years he had been held captive to know she had been saved.

He couldn't jeopardize her now.

Platinum slowly pulled away. He studied Zinc's tearstained face at arm's length for a long moment, taking in the changes ten years had made. She was older, of course, and her features had grown with the rest of her body. The only real difference Platinum could see between them, aside from the fact that they were a different gender, was that she kept her long white hair in one thick braid down her back. He kept his in many smaller braids pinned to the top of his head. That, and the fact that he was gaunt while she looked muscular and healthy. Zinc was beautiful, and he was so glad to see her again. Platinum had to remind himself to let go and take a step back.

"They put some sort of tracker in me," he said to the room as a whole. "I need to keep moving before they find you too."

The man who glowed slightly laughed. "They've known about my house for as long as I've had kits trying to bring the building down around their own ears. They've tried and failed, and I won't give them an opportunity to try again. You're safe here, Platinum."

Platinum looked around at all the dragons gathered in the foyer. He had absolutely no doubt the scientists would love to get their hands on any one of these dragons, especially if they were all as magically strange as Lumie.

"I'm sure I can get that tracker out of your body if you like, but for right now let me make introductions," the shining man finished with a very disarming smile.

Platinum didn't like the idea of someone he didn't know poking around in his body, but at the same time, getting that tracker out would be amazing. "You know Lumie and Zinc, obviously," he continued. Platinum didn't miss the way his eyes paused for a second on Zinc's identical face as a touch of surprise kicked in again. "I'm Dane. I'm the Supernatural Consultant whose office you've been walking by for weeks."

Platinum forced himself not to stare at Dane incredulously. Was he trying to say that all those weeks ago when Platinum had stumbled into that town, all he'd needed to do was stop by that firm and Dane would have been ready to help him? Then again, if Platinum had heard a rumor of that sort, he would have been just as likely to think it was a trap set by the scientists and would have run as far as possible in the other direction.

"This is Mercury. We're mates," Dane said with a gesture to the adult bronze dragon. He introduced Copper, a red dragon the same age as Platinum, 'Ron and Chrome, two brown dragons a few years younger than Platinum, and then he introduced Alloy.

Platinum couldn't help staring at the two different colors that Alloy sported. He was both a red and a blue dragon, fire and water combined into one creature. It was unnatural and very awful. It was... Platinum swallowed hard. Alloy was an experiment gone wrong. So was Lumie. In fact, all the dragons in this house were rescued from the evil scientists.

"Daisy is our housekeeper and babysitter," Dane finished with a gesture toward the green-skinned woman.

Platinum looked around at the assembled dragons and couldn't help thinking back to the blue dragon that had so frantically been chasing after the van that had taken Lumie and Platinum away. He wasn't present. Maybe he wasn't part of this family? Platinum felt a pang of disappointment in his chest. That boy had looked so desperate as he had reached out for the van with his hand and with his magic. Platinum wanted to apologize.

"Is there a water dragon?" he asked hesitantly.

Mercury laughed. "You met Nickel, huh? He's still at Dane's office doing some research on the guys that grabbed you."

"I'm going to bring him a sandwich when I head back," Dane explained. "Daisy, if you wouldn't mind my using the kitchen really quickly?" The kits all looked excited at the prospect of lunch and started babbling again. They began walking as a herd down a nearby hallway. Platinum got caught up with them and was led into a spacious kitchen.

"Lunch is in the oven. Baked mac and cheese," Daisy said. "You've got plenty of time before I have to start heating up the vegetable soup." Several of the kits groaned at the mention of vegetables, but Platinum had never eaten mac and cheese or soup and would love a chance to try them both.

Dane headed into the pantry and fridge to start pulling out everything he needed to make sandwiches. Platinum saw three different kinds of meat and all sorts of vegetables he had seen at the grocery store, but he had no idea what to do with them so hadn't bought them. Lumie climbed up on a stool next to Dane and directed him.

"You need to make one more," Lumie said when Dane pulled out four pieces of bread from a bag and began twisting the opening shut again.

"Becky has her own lunch," Dane disagreed. "I only need to make a sandwich for me and Nickel."

"And Platinum. He's going with you," Lumie insisted.

Dane paused to look at Lumie; then he bent over slightly so he was at Lumie's height on the stool and could firmly catch Lumie's gaze.

"You're not withholding information again, are you, Lumie?" Dane asked warningly.

Lumie started to shake his head, but then his eyes caught on a basket of candy sitting on top of the fridge and his head stilled.

"It's not my secret to tell," he said after a long moment of staring at that basket. He popped his thumb in his mouth as he climbed down from the stool. Lumie went over to the kitchen island and climbed onto another stool next to Alloy. The conversation was apparently over.

Dane frowned, but he opened the bag of bread again and pulled out two more slices without arguing.

"It looks like you're coming with me," Dane said apologetically to Platinum. "Maybe I can take a look at that tracker in your shoulder while we're there."

Platinum nodded. He didn't want to argue with Lumie either. He turned toward Zinc, who was standing at his shoulder. "I'll be back," he reassured her, hoping he was telling the truth. "I want to try mac and cheese and soup sometime."

"I'll save you a plate," Zinc reassured him tearfully. She also didn't appear to have anything to gainsay Lumie's claim that Platinum needed to go.

Dane finished assembling the sandwiches quickly. He filled a few plastic containers with sides and grabbed a jug he filled with juice, and then he turned to Platinum and held out one hand.

Platinum hugged Zinc before taking Dane's hand. He felt magic settle around him for a moment, and the kitchen vanished from sight. A generic office appeared around him moments later. There was an elderly woman sitting in a wide chair behind a desk in the center of the room. Off to one side was a doorway leading to what appeared to be a private office. There was a child-sized desk in the corner covered in papers and a closed laptop.

"Where's Nickel?" Dane asked the old woman. She looked up and Platinum blinked. The old woman was gone, replaced by a middle-aged one with a pleasant smile.

"He stepped out for a few minutes," she replied. "Who's this?"

"This is Platinum. He's Zinc's twin brother. Platinum, this is Becky. She runs this office," Dane explained. "I'll introduce you to Nickel when he gets back. Come into my office and tell me your story while I see what I can do about that tracking chip."

Becky smiled at them both before turning back to her computer. Platinum followed and took one of the guest chairs on the closer side of the desk. Instead of walking around the desk to take his own chair, Dane bent closer to look at the back of Platinum's shoulder.

"They just shoved this in here, didn't they?" he sighed. "It's going to twinge a bit. Why don't you start with after you and Lumie were taken?" He placed his hand on Platinum's shoulder.

Telling what had happened would at least take his mind off of how overwhelming everything else around him was. Maybe Dane would even help explain the parts that Platinum didn't understand.

"Lumie just sat there when the scientist gloated," Platinum began slowly, his voice just above a whisper. It was easier to talk about how Lumie had acted than to focus on how unbelievably scared he had been. "I guess it's because he already knew he could walk us right out of the house the scientist led us to. We were in the car for maybe two hours. The scientist had his shield up, so I couldn't stop him with my magic."

"A shield?" Dane asked curiously.

Platinum nodded. His shoulder was itching; Dane must have been doing something. "I can't walk past it, and my magic can't penetrate it. It's awful. But they called Lumie the philosopher's stone dragon, and he walked right through the shield like it was nothing! Sometimes... sometimes when they left me alone in a cell for days and days, I would send an entire hurricane of wind at that shield. It never cracked. Not once. And Lumie just walked right through it!" He was sobbing, gasping for breath, and unsure what words were actually coming out of his mouth. "They let me go. I thought I had finally escaped from behind that shield, but I was just bait for their trap. To catch two dragons. And once they had that, they threw me back behind that shield again."

A sharp pain made him cry out through his tears. It felt like a needle shoved deep into his shoulder. Dane pulled his hand away with a curse and dropped a smoking bit of metal barely the size of a grain of rice onto the desk in front of Platinum.

"That's it?" Platinum gaped, shocked that something so small could keep track of him so well.

"That's it," Dane confirmed. "I'm sorry that hurt so much, but they added a touch of magic to it to make it difficult to remove. So they wanted two dragons?" he continued, changing the subject swiftly. "You and Lumie?"

"And the dragon soldier," Platinum added. "Mostly they wanted Lumie, I think, but the scientist and Lumie both spoke about the soldier too."

"The dragon soldier?" Dane swore and spun around on his heel. He rushed into the outer office. "What did Nickel say when he left?"

Platinum slowly followed Dane and saw him crouched next to the child-sized desk with the laptop open and running in front of him.

"Just that he wanted some air so he could think," Becky said. She looked worried as Dane flipped through different windows on the laptop. He froze suddenly at one window, reading it with a quickly deepening scowl on his face.

"He knew Lumie and Platinum had come home," Dane mumbled to himself. "He was standing right next to me when I was on the phone with Daisy. Why would he...?" Dane stopped talking for another minute, then swore loudly and colorfully. "Because he wanted to catch the person behind all this and stop the dragon hunting once and for all."

Platinum inched closer to read over Dane's shoulder. He had no idea what he was looking at, but he read the words slowly. The text inside was short and pointed. It almost sounded like a conversation to him.

We have the dragons ready for you. They are waiting at the address below. Can you be there in two hours?

The address didn't mean anything to Platinum. He didn't know where he was on a map. He barely knew how to read, but one of the friendlier guards had given him a children's book once and explained what the different letters meant before vanishing one night.

Below that someone else had written: *Yes.*

Chapter Five

Nickel had been the first person downstairs for breakfast that morning. It hadn't been storming over Dane's house, so Nickel had no idea whether the storm had held through the night. He was hopeful that Platinum was still safe wherever he had hidden up in the mountain. Lumie wandered downstairs just as Nickel was fixing himself a bowl of cereal, so Nickel helped Lumie fill his bowl too. Dane was only a few minutes behind them, but by the time he was finished eating, Nickel was starting to get antsy.

All the dishes were put into the sink. Mercury would dump them in the dishwasher before he went to work in an hour. Dane would be at his office much earlier than normal, but Nickel didn't care. He needed to be there to help Platinum, and something told Nickel that today would be the day he would finally have that chance.

The office was still dark when they arrived. They had beaten Becky there, which didn't happen very often. Nickel took his hand from Dane's shoulder and hurried to the front door to unlock it and turn on the lights. Lumie let go of Dane's hand and went to the nearby window to look out at the street.

Nickel moved to his too-small desk next. He opened his laptop cover and hit the button to start it up. The phone's message light was blinking.

"There's a message on the machine," Nickel called into Dane's office where he was also getting set up for the day.

"Go ahead and listen to it. Take notes for Becky," Dane replied quickly.

Nickel picked up the handset and held it to his ear, then hit the button for the messages.

This is Georgetown Electric with a great deal on solar panels!

Nickel hit the delete key. The machine beeped and moved to the next message.

Hey, this is Ryan next door at the grocery store. Platinum, that kid you asked me about, is here right now. I snuck a glance at him just now, and he looks to me like he's getting ready to skip town. I'll try to convince him to head your way first, but you might want to come over here...

Nickel hung up before the message had finished playing. "Platinum's at the grocery store right now!" he yelled excitedly to Dane.

Lumie was already outside and halfway down the sidewalk. He was heading straight for a young man with white hair braided and pinned to his head, who was walking along the sidewalk away from the consulting firm. Nickel jogged after them.

A large white commercial van with no windows surged past Nickel, driving much faster than most cars bothered in the sleepy town. A side door popped open, and a man leaned out and reached for Lumie and Platinum.

"Lumie! Platinum!" Nickel shrieked, sending a jet of water at the truck. His magic didn't rebound, exactly. Nickel wasn't entirely certain where his magic went, just that it vanished before it could hit the van. Platinum spun and sent a wave of air at the truck. His magic vanished too, and some sort of force knocked both him and Lumie to the ground.

For a startling second, Nickel thought Zinc was lying on the ground, but she was safely at home and he was definitely looking at a male dragon trying to scramble to safety. Another force yanked Platinum and Lumie up and into the van. The side panel closed, and the van took off with a screech of tires. Nickel sent another plume of water after it and watched in disbelief as his magic dissipated on impact. The van vanished around a curve in the road.

Nickel wanted to change shape and fly after it. He could keep track of it from the air and help Platinum and Lumie escape once the van reached its destination. He snarled in fury and was about to shift when Becky's arm slid through his.

"I have the make and model of that van as well as the license plate number. No need to go chasing after it. We'll find it on our own." She dragged him back to the office and handed him over to Dane, who was standing at the office door with a pinched look on his face.

"Lumie," Dane grumbled. "That little brat!"

"I can fly after them!" Nickel insisted. "I'll carry a cell phone and report back when I've found their hiding spot."

"You will do no such thing," Dane disagreed immediately. "It's bad enough Lumie's gone haring off. I won't have you disappearing too."

"Someone's got to save them!" Nickel yelled. "They've been taken by the enemy!"

"I know," Dane said in a voice far too calm for Nickel's liking. He growled loudly at Dane to emphasize that fact. "You think I'm happy one of my kits and another dragon we've been hunting for years just got snatched on my front doorstep?" His words thundered with power. "I'm pretty damned pissed. But think for a second, Nickel! Lumie is with Platinum. Remember that. By the time you reach them, Lumie could already have gotten them both free, and then you'll be infiltrating an empty lair. What we need to do is contact our allies, alert the proper authorities, and start making a plan. The enemy has shown their hand, so we need to respond stronger and more forcefully to shut them down for good."

"And what if Lumie can't get free?" Nickel whispered, his fears taking root now that his frantic anger had diminished.

"Lumie is the philosopher's stone dragon. I have absolutely no doubt of that," Dane said. "A few years ago, when Mercury first started working as a field agent, he caught a copycat Quicksilver bombing case."

"I remember," Nickel said, wondering where this conversation was going.

"He made a mistake and got caught in a spell that was trying to force him to change shape. Mercury thinks the spell was supposed to draw me out and keep us both busy while the enemy caught three dragon kits and their mother running in the woods. Except I brought Lumie with me, and he popped Mercury free in seconds. One of the enemies snapped a photograph of Lumie and probably told a superior about what Lumie had done. Someone must have guessed that he's one of the dragons Quicksilver rescued and that one of their experiments had gone right."

"And you think they've been aiming to capture Lumie ever since?"

"I think that's very possible," Dane agreed. "You remember Jessica, the territory leader that tried to grab Alloy? She went after Lumie first, couldn't catch him, and grabbed Alloy instead. But I don't think they have any understanding of what Lumie can do. Lumie can walk through my wards like they don't even exist; he'll have no problem escaping the enemy." It sounded like Dane was reassuring himself along with Nickel.

Nickel growled and stomped over to his desk. He couldn't just stand around and wait while Becky and Dane made phone calls. Nickel needed to do something, too, anything that might help locate the enemy and stop them for good. Maybe there would be someone in that chat room running their mouth.

Becky hung up her phone at her desk. "An all-points bulletin is out on that van," she announced, which meant that all the local and state police officers would be on the lookout for it. Without Nickel tracking the van from overhead, it was all they could really do. Nickel was worried and upset, but he was also still angry that Becky had stopped him from chasing after that van and that Dane had agreed with her. Sitting behind his too-small desk while staring at a blank chat room screen was infuriating.

Some of the things Nickel remembered reading from the last time he had logged into the chat room were starting to make a bit of horrible sense. Petridish1000 had been camping in the woods, probably following Platinum around and waiting for him to finally make contact with any of Dane's dragons. Well, the bastard had what he wanted now, at least until Lumie made his move. Dane was probably right about that. Petridish1000 had no idea what he had actually caught. If Lumie could walk through a half-god's shields, a human's stolen magic wouldn't be able to touch him.

Although, the shield that had stopped Nickel and Platinum's magic had been decidedly odd. Nickel had sent a very strong wave of water magic at it, which would make even Dane's shields creak with strain when they practiced combat. The enemy's hadn't budged in the slightest. In fact, if Nickel had to make a guess, he thought that maybe instead of trying to block Nickel's magic or force it to rebound, the shield had, instead, absorbed his magic.

What if—and even in Nickel's mind it was a radical thought—what if it was a self-sustaining shield? He had actually read about them in one of Dane's catch-all magic books back at the house. It made sense the more he thought about it. The humans had such a limited amount of magic, and keeping a shield up against the combined onslaught of Nickel and Platinum's attacks should have flattened the magic user in an instant. All the other battles Nickel had fought against the enemy had ended similarly with him popping whatever personal shield they had and then ending them swiftly. But what if the shield absorbed whatever magic was attacking it and used that extra magic to continue powering itself? Platinum could control the weather—he was probably even more powerful than Nickel. There was no way a mere human could contain him unless Platinum's own magic was used against him.

That was actually a very saddening thought. The idea that Platinum had involuntarily kept himself confined for all these years was heartbreaking. All he had needed to do was wait patiently for the human's magic to run out. The shield would have fallen, and he would have been free much sooner and without the tracking chip implanted.

ThatGuy signed in about an hour after Lumie and Platinum had been kitnapped, but his status immediately went to unavailable. Nickel wanted to demand the whereabouts, but he knew he couldn't blow his cover yet. The SupFeds had worked hard to set up his fake online persona, and blowing it before ThatGuy had the chance to divulge everything would be a terrible waste. Besides, ThatGuy could log out of the chat room and Nickel wouldn't be able to contact him for information ever again.

Nickel waited for another hour and a half, impatiently tapping his foot against the side of his desk while Dane and Becky made phone call after phone call to try to organize some sort of help. After two and a half hours, Petridish1000 logged in. Nickel froze in place, waiting for the bastard to type something. He didn't have to wait long.

I have the philosopher's stone dragon and the bait.

ThatGuy's status changed to active milliseconds before he replied. *Well done.*

Almost simultaneously a private chat room opened between ThatGuy and Nickel. *The mission was a success. Are your experiments prepared?*

Nickel took a slow, deep breath to steady himself before typing his reply. *As long as you have my dragons ready and waiting for me, I'm ready to go.* Nickel hoped he sounded like a scientist whose lab rats had finally been delivered after what seemed like an endless wait.

Dane strode into the main office, his cell phone pressed to his ear. "Wait, Daisy. Repeat that?" He listened for a long moment, then grinned. "I'll be right there." He snapped the phone shut and bounced excitedly in place for a moment. "Lumie just walked in the front door at home with what sounds like Platinum in tow," he announced to the room. "I'm going to call Mercury to let him know and head home to make sure they're both all right. Do you want to come, Nickel?" Dane asked.

ThatGuy was typing something. He and Petridish1000 couldn't know their prey had escaped yet. Nickel wanted to milk them for whatever information he could get before they had to run off to attempt to retrieve the dragons. Lumie and Platinum were beyond the enemy's reach at home. They were safe, Nickel reminded himself in relief, but that didn't mean the battle was over. Someone had to confront the enemy and make them pay for their crimes.

Nickel shook his head to Dane who was already dialing Mercury. Dane didn't think twice about it, more interested in telling his mate about their safe kits while popping home.

We have the dragons ready for you. They are waiting at the address below. Can you be there in two hours?

ThatGuy sent the first message and then almost immediately sent the second with the address in it. He had queued the messages, typing them both before sending them, which was why it had taken him so long to respond.

Dane left with a soft pop of displaced air while Nickel stared at his screen. Two hours was a long time during which any number of things could happen. He couldn't miss this chance to confront the enemy inside their lair. Dane had other things to worry about, as did Mercury. Besides, ThatGuy was expecting a scientist. A dragon falling from the sky to capture him would be unexpected. It just might work.

Nickel put his fingers on the keyboard keys and typed, *Yes.* He did a quick online search with some aerial maps to find out where he needed to go as his plan solidified in his mind.

"I'm going to get some air," Nickel told Becky as he closed his laptop and casually strode to the door.

"Don't stray too far, dear," Becky said kindly.

Nickel didn't want to lie to her again, so he didn't answer. He let himself out of the building and walked quickly toward the edge of town. It was ironically the same direction Platinum had been planning to go before he was kitnapped. Once Nickel felt he was far enough from the office that Becky wouldn't notice, Nickel jumped. He shifted to dragon form in midair and let his wings pump him up above the tree line.

It didn't take him even an hour to reach his destination. Dragons always knew which direction they were flying, so it was just a matter of him covering the distance and finding the right spot from the air. The satellite image Nickel had found online showed a decaying house high in the nearby mountains. The road leading up to it was long and curving as it slowly traveled to a higher elevation around the many trees and rocks. There was a carport out front, and a small blue sedan was parked inside. Nickel didn't see any sign of the white van, but they were probably going to dump it now that it had been used in a kidnapping in broad daylight. The address number matched the numbers nailed into the wall next to the front door, so he knew he had found the right place.

Nickel moved a little farther away from the house to a small clearing where he could land and shift forms. He approached the house on human feet from the back.

ThatGuy couldn't be expecting any visitors yet. There was still at least forty-five minutes before Marcus Quillian was supposed to arrive, and the long driveway meant

ThatGuy would be able to see any cars well before they reached the house. He was probably sitting in a front room with a window that overlooked the drive, waiting for someone to come.

Or he was probably frantically rushing around, trying to figure out how Lumie and Platinum had escaped. ThatGuy would have to be desperate to find the dragons before Marcus Quillian arrived. He wouldn't expect Nickel to sneak in his back door and take him down.

Nickel hesitated at the edge of the tree line to take one last look at the house. He didn't see any movement inside. There weren't any lights on that Nickel could see either. Maybe no one was home? Had the white van taken them somewhere—probably to search nearby for Platinum and Lumie—presumably with the intent to return before Marcus Quillian was supposed to arrive? If that was the case, Nickel had no problem breaking into the house and lying in wait for their return.

Nothing jumped out at him as being out of place, so he stepped out of the cover of the trees and strode across the lawn. He was halfway across when the back door opened and a man stepped outside.

Nickel froze in place. Magic sparked between his fingers, but he held it in until he knew who the man was. The stranger was pale, almost sickly looking. His head was balding and shiny, and he had a good amount of paunch hanging over his belt. His legs were thin as sticks, but his shoulders were thickly muscled.

"I suppose two hours was far too generous," the man sighed. "I hadn't calculated the distance it would take for you to fly here. Silly of me."

Nickel didn't bother trying to pretend in order to trick his way out of what he was quickly realizing was a trap.

He had the blue hair of a water dragon; the man knew exactly what Nickel was. The chat room must have been a setup. He had been skillfully drawn here because he thought he was the one with the successful subterfuge. It was the exact opposite, Nickel now knew as the man slowly walked closer.

The worst part of it was that Nickel had fallen for it hook, line, and sinker. He had trusted Stockton's information and his own strength. Nickel didn't think Stockton was the traitor; it was probably someone who had helped set up Marcus Quillian's false identity. Nickel had been so certain he was the one springing a trap that he hadn't bothered arranging backup or even telling Dane what he was doing. He was caught with no escape route, and it was his own damned fault.

What he wouldn't do was allow the enemy to think Nickel had fallen into their trap. He would remain confident even as his stomach was roiling with defeat. Besides, Nickel knew he was strong. He would fight his way free or die trying. The bastard wouldn't get a speck of Nickel's magic.

Nickel reached out one hand and was unsurprised when he found an invisible wall a foot in front of his nose. The shield felt firm and impenetrable under his fingers even though he couldn't actually see it with his eyes. Nickel had no doubt he was enclosed inside it.

"I suppose you've heard by now that the philosopher's stone dragon and the air dragon you used to bait your trap have both escaped." The man's face tightened briefly in upset at Nickel's words, but it cleared a moment later. "I bet you have no idea how they managed it, but I know how and it's the reason that this"—Nickel tapped on the shield with his knuckles—"won't hold me either."

The man laughed. "This shield was perfected just for you! You defeated three of my best when you were just a child and then a few years later defeated the men and women I had specifically trained to fight dragons with advanced precious magic. I knew I had to find some way to contain you in order to capture you, and this shield is the result."

He was talking about two of the times Nickel had fought at Dane's side to free dragons captured by the enemy scientists. The first had been when he was only eight years old. Dane and Mercury had descended into an underground warehouse to free any captured air dragons. That was when they had rescued Zinc and discovered that Platinum was still held captive. It had been a trap set by the enemy, but before they could spring the earthquake spell that was supposed to have buried Dane, Mercury, and Zinc into early graves, they had sent three men and women to try to capture Nickel.

Their magic had felt amateurish to Nickel, and he'd fought them off with ease. It had still been early in the scientists' studies at the time. Nickel had more difficulty with the second attack, defeating the men in the warehouse where a corrupt police officer was hiding two precious dragons. The enemy had used precious magic, which had more versatility than water magic, but Nickel had proven himself to be stronger when he took out those scientists too.

Nickel was a fighter. He went into battle at Dane's side and held his own against what might appear to be uneven odds. He was a soldier, Nickel realized with an internal jolt of surprise. He was the dragon soldier ThatGuy had been convinced he was about to catch along with the philosopher's stone dragon.

"The shield has a fatal flaw," Nickel disagreed immediately. "And that flaw is you." The shield fed on magic. If Nickel attacked it with his water magic, his powers would be absorbed by the shield and then used to sustain it. As long as Nickel didn't use any magic, the shield was fed from ThatGuy's spool of power, which was finite. The man would run out of power soon enough, and Nickel would be able to get away.

It would be simple enough to hasten the process too. Nickel grinned and shifted forms, his teeth elongating into sharp points in his snout. His larger body hit the shield as he took on his dragon form, pushing the shield back and forcing ThatGuy to grit his teeth and commit more of his personal magic into keeping the shield active. Nickel backed up a step and then rammed his body against the shield. It creaked, but held, so he did it again.

"You think you'll escape that way?" the man laughed. "I have been preparing for this day for years!"

The shield flexed around Nickel's body as he rammed it again, but not as if he were putting a dent into the side. It continued to ripple, and then suddenly it started shrinking. Nickel locked his legs in place as the shield tried to force him to the ground. A roar escaped him as the shield continued to shrink, compressing around his body. He fought back, trying to stay on his feet even as his spine was bending under the pressure.

Nickel staggered and fell to one knee, then twisted into a ball. His lungs and head were screaming as the shield compacted around him, and even curling up protectively didn't stop the shield from continuing its onslaught.

With a shudder, his body involuntarily shifted to its smaller human form, desperately trying to find relief from the shield, but the shield only accelerated its shrinking to fit his new shape.

Nickel was going to pass out. He couldn't breathe, and there were spots running across his vision. That wasn't an acceptable outcome, however. Passing out meant the enemy had won. He would be their guinea pig forever now that they had a proven way to subdue him. Nickel just had to hold out. ThatGuy's magic had to be nearing the end of its spool. Nickel needed to be conscious enough to escape when that happened.

It was the only way to survive this. He desperately held on to that thought, but even his ability to think was diminishing with every second.

He was going to lose and suffer for it. Nickel cursed himself for his stupidity as blackness flickered at the edges of his vision and his body used up the last of his strength to keep fighting. In another moment, it would be over. This was the end for him.

Chapter Six

Platinum grabbed for Dane's arm when he started to shimmer in place. Dane could transport from place to place without a spell, and Platinum wanted to be with him when he went after Nickel. His reasoning was purely selfish, of course. Platinum had spent all of his life under the thumb of the scientists, and doing something, anything, to make those scientists pay for what they had done excited him. Zinc would also be devastated if anything happened to Nickel. From everything Platinum had seen about this family so far, he could tell that Zinc and Nickel had grown up the past ten years as brother and sister, and he didn't want to do anything to that relationship. Besides, he remembered Nickel running frantically after the van, after Platinum and Lumie. His short blue hair and wide blue eyes were something Platinum knew he wanted to see again.

The office vanished around them. They reappeared in the middle of a forest. A small house was nestled in between the trees. It might have been quaint if they were there for a friendly visit, but they weren't. Platinum immediately started sniffing the air for signs of occupancy. The house was dark and appeared to be empty—however, Platinum would recognize the stench of the lead scientist anywhere, and the entire place was saturated in it. Platinum also smelled water and dragon on the wind.

"This way," Platinum said softly, creeping to the corner of the house and peeking around the edge toward the backyard where the scent of water dragon was coming from. Nickel was curled on the ground in a ball. His blue hair was visible underneath the arms he had wrapped around his head. He was growling, but otherwise he looked beaten. Platinum called on the wind, ready to send it streaming around the house and against the lead scientist. He had to do something to save Nickel before it was too late.

"Don't," Dane hissed. He clamped his hand on Platinum's shoulder, and Platinum's magic dissipated without him telling it to. "Look at Nickel. It rained all morning here. The trees are still dripping and the grass is damp, but Nickel didn't even try to harness any of that water."

Which meant he hadn't used any magic against the enemy. "Maybe his magic was blocked somehow?" Platinum asked. Now that he was looking, he could see deep gouges in the dirt and grass from claws trying to find purchase there. Nickel had fought with only his strength. Nickel was the dragon soldier, so Platinum didn't doubt that he was very strong, but Nickel was used to fighting with magic. He probably didn't have a chance against the enemy with strength alone.

"Or he was smart enough not to use it," Dane replied. His face was pinched as he stared at Nickel's body. He seemed to glow slightly, and to Platinum's surprise, his ears grew to points, and his hair got even blonder. "We need to help him, now. Don't use any magic. That shield around Nickel will only absorb it and grow stronger."

He dashed around the side of the house, his steps silent on the wet grass. Dane ran straight for Nickel. Platinum followed, but slowed when he got into the backyard to look around.

The lead scientist was standing in the shade cast by the house. He looked surprised and slightly afraid as Dane and Platinum came into view, but his chin firmed a moment later. He gestured, and Nickel writhed on the ground.

At first, Platinum thought Nickel was growling, but after a moment of listening, Platinum realized that Nickel was screaming as loudly and as painfully as he could. He didn't have the air or the strength to scream louder.

Platinum rushed the scientist. This was the man Platinum remembered every time that awful gas mask was placed over Platinum's face. He wore a weird crooked grin whenever Platinum was getting experimented on that featured in many of Platinum's nightmares. Now the scientist was trying to capture Nickel and do the same terrible things to another dragon. Platinum wanted to hit the scientist with a fist encased in a terrible whirlwind, but Platinum remembered Dane's warning and suppressed his magic. He didn't have to suppress his fist, and it caught the scientist satisfyingly hard in the chin. Something cracked, and a stab of pain radiated in Platinum's knuckles. The scientist went sprawling, and Platinum let out an involuntary shout of glee at the sight.

Nickel's gasp was loud in the silence as the scientist fell to the ground, and then Nickel slumped over, unconscious. The scientist scrabbled along the grass, trying to get as far away from Platinum as he could. His mouth was bleeding, and his legs didn't seem to be moving normally. They were twitching on the ground as if he was trying to get them underneath his fat body and get to his feet, but they weren't obeying his commands. Before Platinum could advance on him again, he vanished in a swirl of stolen dragon magic.

"Damn!" Dane snarled. He was kneeling at Nickel's side, one hand gently pressed to Nickel's back. "Damn! If I could have used magic, that bastard wouldn't have been able to go anywhere." Platinum didn't doubt that; Dane was definitely very strong for all that he wasn't a dragon. Dane pulled a cell phone out of his pocket with the hand that wasn't holding Nickel and hit a few numbers. He held it to his ear for a moment while it rang. "Dr. Krantz, Nickel was attacked. He's unconscious, and I'd like you to take a look at him." He paused to listen for a moment, then nodded. "I won't move him physically. I'll transport him as is to my house." He listened for a few more seconds, then hit a button on the phone to hang up. Dane put the phone back in his pocket. "Come over here, Platinum. I'm going to very slowly transport us back home before that bastard returns with reinforcements."

Platinum nodded and hurried over. He reached out with his right hand to grab Dane's shoulder, then had to stifle a gasp of pain when straightening out his fingers sent a bolt of agony through his knuckles. Platinum quickly grabbed Dane with his left hand. Getting Nickel to safety was more important than stopping to figure out what he had done to himself.

Dane's magic swelled around them. Platinum expected the forest and the house to immediately vanish to be replaced by Dane's home. That didn't happen this time. Dane was being extra careful of Nickel. The trees blurred and faded away. An odd sort of blank space, a nothingness that must exist between places, replaced them. After a few, very long seconds where Platinum was beginning to worry that Dane had gotten them stuck, he realized that the blank space was taking on a form. The walls of a room slowly appeared, and Nickel's unconscious body settled down into a soft bed. It took a few more seconds for the magic to fade away.

They had appeared inside what Platinum guessed was Nickel's bedroom since the bedspread Nickel was lying on was a brilliant shade of blue. The transportation magic had only faded away for a half second before the bedroom door was flung open. Mercury hurried inside, followed by a human man Platinum didn't recognize.

"Dane, my boy, what have your kits gotten into this time?" the stranger asked sharply. He didn't wait for an answer, instead pushing Dane out of the way to lay his hands gently on Nickel's curled form. Platinum backed away from the bed and found a space on the wall where he would be out of the way. Mercury took his spot at Dane's side, kneeling next to the bed with Dane while the stranger tutted and hummed to himself.

"Nickel got himself into this one, Dr. Krantz," Dane sighed. "I got him out, and now I need you to patch him up again."

Dr. Krantz grunted. "Easier said than done, I'm afraid," he grumbled.

Platinum couldn't help swallowing hard at that admission. What if Nickel was hurt really badly? It was Platinum's fault the scientists had been able to goad Nickel in the first place. Nickel was lying in bed, terribly hurt, all because Platinum hadn't been able to properly escape and run from the enemy.

"It looks like someone put your boy into a vise and tried to squeeze him to death," Dr. Krantz continued. "His head and lungs took the brunt of the damage." Dr. Krantz must have some sort of magic since he hadn't pulled out any instruments to verify his statements. He only had his hands pressed against Nickel's side.

"Is there serious damage? Brain damage?" Mercury gasped, his voice barely above a pained whisper.

Dr. Krantz frowned. "If Nickel were human, we would be having a different, less hopeful conversation," he said thoughtfully. "A dragon's superior healing abilities combined with my magic should mean that Nickel will make a full recovery. There shouldn't be any permanent brain damage or reduced lung function. Still, I'm going to put him in an induced coma for a week to give him a chance to heal properly. Don't you go messing around with my spells either, Dane, my boy. I'll be back to check on him tomorrow. Now give me some space while I get these healing spells set in."

Mercury and Dane both stood quickly so they could get out of Dr. Krantz's way. Mercury had his arms crossed over his chest, and his face was very blank as he looked down at Nickel's curled and unconscious body. Platinum thought he might be holding off tears. Dane turned around, caught sight of Platinum hovering by the wall, and held out one hand.

"Come downstairs with me," Dane said. "I need to call Becky to tell her we found him. I bet Daisy still has the mac and cheese out."

Platinum took one last look over at Nickel. Dr. Krantz was carefully straightening Nickel's body, and Platinum could see pinched lines of pain between Nickel's brows. A moment later, Dr. Krantz put his hands over Nickel's cheeks, and those lines faded away and were replaced with a serene look. Platinum swallowed hard and tore his eyes away so he could follow Dane out of Nickel's room and downstairs to the kitchen.

Daisy hadn't put the mac and cheese away. In fact, the kits were just clearing their plates and bowls when Platinum walked into the room. Platinum paused, surprised. Had so little time passed since he had left the house? Dane had made sandwiches that they hadn't eaten, and after he cleaned up, the kits had begun setting out their own lunch plates. Yet it hadn't taken too long to realize that Nickel had run off and even less time to actually rescue him.

Platinum settled into the stool next to Zinc around the kitchen island. A full plate of food appeared in front of him. Platinum picked up his fork with his left hand and speared a bit of curved noodle covered in gooey yellow cheese sauce. He popped it in his mouth and couldn't stop a happy moan. It was creamy and cheesy and utterly delicious. Platinum opened his eyes, unsure of when he had closed them, and caught Daisy rolling her eyes as he went for a full scoop.

"I can see we have another convert to the 'mac and cheese is the only food I'll eat for lunch' religion," Daisy grumbled good-naturedly. "Dane, have you bought any stock in the mac and cheese industry? Because your kits are going to single-handedly raise its shares."

Dane was putting his phone away in a pocket when he walked into the kitchen. He looked at Platinum's full mouth and grinned. "I bought those a long time ago," he joked. Platinum had no idea what they were talking about, so he ignored them both and scooped up more mac and cheese onto his fork.

"Is Nickel going to be okay?" Alloy asked softly. He was peering around the edge of the counter up at Platinum. The rest of the kits froze in place so they could hear Platinum's answer.

Platinum swallowed, the food suddenly tasteless in his mouth. "This doctor said so," Platinum replied.

A collective sigh breezed through the kitchen. The clanking of dishes as they cleaned up lunch continued as everyone returned to their chores.

"I hope I won't be returning because any of you decided to follow Nickel's example," Dr. Krantz said sternly as he walked into the kitchen.

"I don't want to get poked with another needle," Alloy said while sticking his tongue out and making a face. Platinum put his fork down slowly. He got off his stool and inched his way toward the door. Dr. Krantz was supposed to have helped Nickel. That was the only reason Platinum hadn't said anything against him being there, but a doctor that, instead, experimented on the kits with needles wasn't someone Platinum wanted to be around.

Mercury's hand came down on Platinum's shoulder. He steered Platinum back to the kitchen island. He was gentle, but firm, as if he knew and understood where Platinum's fears were coming from and didn't want him to run from them.

"Dr. Krantz was just giving Alloy his immunizations. The needles had drugs in them that keep him from getting sick," Mercury explained, interpreting Platinum's blank look. Platinum had no idea what immunizations were.

"We all got them," Zinc said reassuringly. She picked up Platinum's fork and pressed it back into his hand. "Honest, Platinum. He's a good person, nothing like those scientists."

Zinc would know what she was talking about, and he trusted her, but there was only one real way to find out. Platinum's right hand was shaking as he lifted it into the air toward where Dr. Krantz was patently waiting. Dr. Krantz took one look at the swollen and red flesh around his knuckles and sucked in air through his teeth.

"When did you do that?" Dane gasped.

"I punched the lead scientist in the face to get him to stop hurting Nickel," Platinum said softly. Zinc let out a loud giggle at his words. Platinum didn't take his eyes off Dr. Krantz, who was very slowly holding out his own hands to take Platinum's mangled one. Dr. Krantz's hands were dry and his grip gentle.

The pain had been persistent and sharp. Platinum had been doing his best to ignore it—this wasn't the first time he had a broken bone that he had to live with until the scientists decided to finally put the bone back in place—but the second after Dr. Krantz took Platinum's hand in his, the pain faded away. The fork fell from his other hand as he sagged in relief.

"Luckily it's only dislocated, my boy," Dr. Krantz said after a moment of studying Platinum's hand. "I'm going to put some healing on it so you'll be able to use it, but wait at least a week before you punch anyone again."

"I also took a tracking chip out of Platinum's shoulder," Dane said before Dr. Krantz could let go of Platinum.

"I noticed," Dr. Krantz replied with a frown at Dane. "I'm fixing that mess too. You could have left it for me to remove properly, you know," he grumbled at Dane. "Platinum, my boy," he added after Dane had shrugged sheepishly at him, "you're also missing a kidney. They really mucked around with your insides."

"Anything serious?" Mercury gasped, echoing Zinc's squeak of fear.

"His magic is certainly acting oddly. He's causing unseasonably bad weather wherever he goes," Dane added.

Dr. Krantz hummed for a long moment, then smiled. "The physical issues just need some time to heal. I prescribe a combination of good food, good rest, and a good family, all of which you'll find here. I can't speak about the magic issues, but I could recommend someone I trust to take a look."

Dane thought his magic was causing the storms? Platinum didn't want to believe him, yet at the same time something told him that was true. He remembered the thunderstorm that had sprung up his last night in the cabin and had continued the entire night. Every time he had woken up from a nightmare, the thunder had rumbled overhead as if to say, "I'm here and you're safe." Though he was an air dragon, and air dragons didn't have power over the weather. He could make the wind blow to varying degrees, but calling down an actual thunderstorm was well outside his magic's parameters. At least, it was supposed to be.

When Dr. Krantz let go of Platinum's hand a moment later, the pain didn't return. The horrible red swelling was gone and his hand looked normal. Platinum carefully flexed his fingers and felt only a residual stiffness in his knuckles.

"Like I said, refrain from punching anything for the next week or so. The magic I used and your own healing abilities need time to work." Dr. Krantz sounded stern, yet friendly. Platinum's fears that Dr. Krantz was similar to the scientists that had used him for their experiments faded away under the overwhelming evidence that Dr. Krantz was a good and trusted doctor. "I will be back in tomorrow to check on Nickel's progress, and I'll bring a full round of immunizations for Platinum. I assume you want to register him in the local school system, so I'll also bring the doctor's paperwork you'll need to submit."

"Thank you, Dr. Krantz," Mercury said as he and Dr. Krantz headed out of the kitchen and toward the front door.

Platinum looked down at his healed hand once more, but before he could ask any questions—not that he was entirely certain which question he should be asking first—Daisy bustled over. She handed him a clean fork and picked up the one he had dropped.

"Eat your vegetables too, Platinum," she admonished. She gave his shoulder a gentle shove toward his half-eaten lunch and then hurried back to the counter where she had another plate made up. Dane took the second plate when she held it out to him and sat at the kitchen island to eat.

Platinum swapped his fork for a spoon and dipped it into the soup. He brought it up to his nose to sniff. He had always been dubious of the vegetables in the grocery store. He didn't know how to cook them, and they hadn't looked particularly appetizing anyway. The soup smelled like those vegetables. It was lightly orange in color with big chunks of cut-up vegetables swimming in it. Platinum put the full spoon in his mouth, chewed, and swallowed. One glance at Daisy told him he had better eat more, so he quickly slurped up half the soup before pushing it to the side so he could finish the mac and cheese slowly, savoring each bite.

Daisy whisked his plate off the table the second he had finished the mac and cheese. She looked around the room with a frown. "Who is supposed to be in lessons right now?" she asked sternly. Every single kit, even Zinc, groaned. One by one they filed out of the kitchen. Zinc gave Platinum a quick hug before she followed.

"Should I be going with them?" Platinum asked.

Mercury settled into Zinc's abandoned stool at Platinum's side. "We need to talk about that, actually. I'm going to speak with some people I know about getting you legally into the system."

"What does that mean?" Platinum asked warily when Mercury paused to take a breath.

"It means the government will give you a social security number. You'll be able to vote and have to pay taxes, and if you ever vanish for more than three days, Mercury and I can put out a missing person's report and have the entire country search for you," Dane explained.

"It also means you can go to school and get a job where the storeowner doesn't have to pay you illegally under the table," Mercury added.

It sounded nice to Platinum. He had no doubt Zinc had taken Dane and Mercury up on it. Nickel had, too, yet Nickel hadn't been stuck in a classroom all day. He was working at Dane's consulting firm instead.

"What did Nickel choose to do?" Platinum asked.

Dane rolled his eyes. "I'm never going to live down the fact that I made promises to Nickel that the other kits took to include them as well, am I?" he grumbled to Mercury.

"Nope," Mercury said with a laugh.

"Nickel wanted to help me hunt down the people experimenting on dragons. In return for completing his schoolwork on time, he was allowed to accompany me to my office to aid in my investigations. He recently passed his GED exam—General Education Development test, the equivalent to taking classes in school. He submitted his paperwork for a private investigator's license last week. The rest of the kits," Dane continued quickly before Platinum could make up his mind about what he wanted to do, "are homeschooled. They take classes with a tutor and will graduate from high school the same as if they were in regular school. Zinc and Copper are less motivated than Nickel and will need a few more years to complete their education, but afterward, I'm hoping they'll find jobs or think about colleges."

Platinum already knew which option he would choose. "I want to help Nickel," he said firmly. "I want to help the rest of the dragons and stop the scientists. What do I need to do to get a private investigator's license too?"

Dane sighed, exasperated, but he didn't look upset, just resigned. "You need at least three years of experience working with a private investigator before you're eligible for a license. Nickel is going to need a secretary when he becomes a full-time investigator. I'm willing to hire you if you prove you can read, write, and do math at a high enough level to handle the job."

Platinum bit his lip in worry. He could sound out words well enough to read, but he had never had the chance to learn to write and math was a completely foreign concept.

"You can work with the tutor that teaches the rest of the kits until you catch up," Dane offered, interpreting Platinum's expression correctly.

Dane was offering him a home and a job, two things Platinum had never had before. It felt like the first light of the sun breaking through the sky after a heavy storm as relief surged through him. His constant fear of being caught, not just by the scientists but also by the police since he had been squatting illegally and periodically stealing food, could fade away. He felt as light as a gentle breeze.

Platinum nodded his agreement, since he really liked that idea, but before he could open his mouth to agree verbally, Dane's phone rang. Dane frowned and dug it out of his pocket, and his frown only increased when he saw the caller ID.

"Stockton, how can I help you?" Dane asked after hitting a button to accept the call. He listened for a moment; then his eyebrows shot up in surprise. "We'll be right there," he said, then hit another button on his phone to end the call. "The white van that took Platinum and Lumie was spotted parked in the lot in the back of the grocery store next to my office," he explained quickly. "Local police called it in. Stockton wants you to take lead on it, Mercury."

"My tracking chip is still at your office," Platinum gasped. The scientists had probably followed it, thinking they could at least grab Platinum and not have their trap be a total failure. "I'm coming with you," Platinum added when Mercury held out his hand for Dane to transport them away. Platinum hurried forward to put his hand on Dane's shoulder before Dane could argue.

Dane didn't argue. Instead, he called on his magic, and the kitchen vanished from around them. They reappeared near the familiar gas station at the crossroads of the little town Platinum would still like to call home. A car was sitting in one of the parking spots, and the front doors opened so two uniformed officers could hurry over to meet with them.

"We have officers watching the van," one of the police officers began. "We believe they've broken into your office and are searching the building." They glanced down the street where the front entrance to Dane's office was completely visible.

"How the hell did they get into my office?" Dane snarled. "I sent Becky home when it looked like I wouldn't be returning for the rest of the day, and she knows to set the wards. She has never forgotten."

"Their shield spell," Platinum gasped. "Nickel didn't use any magic against it even when it was crushing him. What if it absorbs magic?" It was a horrible thought because it meant that every time Platinum had sent even the slightest breeze at the shield spell holding him captive he had only been further ensuring his own captivity. He had sent an entire hurricane's worth of wind against that shield! Platinum shuddered and forcefully shoved that horrible thought away. This wasn't the time or place to melt down sobbing over his helplessness.

"If it were strong enough, it could have absorbed my wards," Dane said thoughtfully while scowling in the direction of his office. "I had a good look at the shield while it was hurting Nickel. I think I might be able to do something about it. That damned shield isn't the only thing that absorbs magic around here," Dane finished with a grin that was even scarier than his scowl.

"We need to set up a perimeter," Mercury interjected. "Neither of you have magic, correct, officers?" he asked. They nodded, so he continued. "I'll need you to stay out of the danger zone until we have the situation under control; then you'll need to come in and make the arrest. Dane, I need you to get rid of that shield spell so you and I can go in and stop them."

They were going to go in headfirst, directly into the line of fire. Mercury was a bronze dragon, a precious dragon. Platinum had little doubt that he could hold his own. Dane was... Dane was something very powerful, although Platinum couldn't say what. Together they probably stood a chance, but it would be easier for them if they had the element of surprise. Charging in blindly might do more harm than good.

"Let me be bait," Platinum said. "Only this time, I'm bait for the good guys to catch the bad guys." He looked at Mercury as he said it, trying to sound confident. "I'll distract them while Dane gets the shield down and Mercury can get into position."

Mercury didn't look happy, but he nodded sharply. "Fine."

Things moved quickly after that. The police officers got back in their cruiser and drove through the intersection. They parked in the middle of the road to block any traffic from coming down Main Street. A moment later, a second police car pulled out of the parking lot behind the grocery store to block traffic coming from the other direction. Dane and Mercury took up a position across the street where they were partially blocked from sight by the trees. Platinum walked down the sidewalk like it was any other afternoon, except this time he was heading to Dane's office instead of the grocery store.

The front door was open slightly when Platinum reached it. He pushed it open even more with one hand and stepped inside. He only made it a few feet into the front room before his toes hit an invisible wall while trying to take another step forward. The room had been utterly trashed, he saw with dismay. The top of Becky's desk had been cleared, all of her papers and folders scattered around the desk on the floor. Her desktop computer had been dumped in a heap next to her overturned wastebasket. The glass screen had giant spider-web cracks running across it. Nickel's small desk had been entirely overturned, and all of his papers and his laptop were also on the floor. The desk drawers had been yanked out and tossed across the room.

Platinum recognized the two men who ran out of Dane's office as he walked inside. One was the driver of the white van. He had one of Dane's file folders open in his hand. The other was the familiar scientist.

"You think you'll find any information about the rest of the dragons here? The Supernatural Consultant wouldn't be so stupid," Platinum taunted them. He lifted one hand and pressed it against the shield.

"Maybe not," the scientist sneered, "but it brought you back. I hope you enjoyed your moment of freedom, dragon, because you'll never have the opportunity again."

Platinum let his anger over their words bolster his anger over what they had done to the office, to Nickel, and to him for his entire life. That anger translated to power, and he let his magic unfurl. It built around him slowly, a gentle breeze that increased in size and speed until a cyclone encircled his body. He didn't allow a single breeze to touch that shield, holding his magic tight to himself.

"You're not taking me anywhere," Platinum insisted.

The scientist laughed cruelly. "You really can't be that stupid."

Platinum's fingers flexed as the shield faded away beneath them. Platinum didn't need Mercury's yell of "Now!" to know it was safe to attack. He sent his cyclone directly at the scientist and the driver, releasing all of his pent-up magic into the attack.

With a crack of thunder, the cyclone roared toward the enemy. It was pouring in the office, rain coming down in sheets as lightning flashed and the walls shook with thunder. Platinum had sent everything he had against the scientist, apparently including a terrible thunderstorm. It was a buoyant feeling to experience his magic being used at full force for the first time in his life. He held nothing back; he couldn't have even if he wanted to.

It was impossible to see. The whipping wind and driving rain felt pleasant against his skin, but Platinum had to close his eyes. He jumped in surprise when a pair of hands landed on his shoulders. He turned to direct the wind to attack whichever enemy had caught him and felt the wind shut off like someone had hit the light switch that controlled it.

Platinum blinked water out of his eyes and looked up to find Dane standing behind him, Dane's hands on Platinum's shoulders.

"That's enough," Dane said kindly. He was grinning, almost laughing, as he looked down at Platinum. There was standing water halfway up Platinum's calves, and even though his magic had been cut off, there was still water raining down from the ceiling. Mercury waded past them to the front door, which he shoved open, and then stood back as a wave of water rushed through the opening and out onto the street.

With a guilty start, Platinum saw Nickel's laptop caught in the current. It didn't take long for the water to empty out, and once it did, Mercury waved to the police officers. One of the cars and an ambulance pulled up in front of Dane's office. The EMTs from the ambulance rushed inside, heading straight to two bodies that had been revealed by the shrinking water level.

The scientist's face was blue, and the EMT checking his pulse shook his head. The woman kneeling next to the driver nodded and started breathing into the driver's mouth and pressing on his chest. Water bubbled out of his mouth with every press.

Platinum leaned back against Dane, suddenly realizing that Dane's hands were the only thing holding him upright. The room was shimmering slightly, as if it were still covered in water and the sun was hitting it just right.

"I don't feel so good," Platinum gasped. His knees buckled and Dane caught him.

"Of course you don't," Dane said firmly. "Your body was already weak from starvation and overexposure, and you just overextended your magic. I'm shocked you're still conscious. Let me get you home and into a warm bed."

Platinum leaned against Dane's side and felt Dane's magic swirl around him.

"Did I drown him?" he asked, hoping Dane understood that he meant the dead scientist.

"There's no way to know without an autopsy," Dane hedged as the wrecked office vanished from around them.

"But Lumie said the dragon soldier would drown the scientist. Nickel's the soldier, not me," Platinum insisted.

They reappeared inside Nickel's darkened bedroom. Someone had added a second bed against the far wall while they had been gone. It was neatly made, but Dane yanked the covers down unceremoniously with the hand he wasn't using to support Platinum. He stripped off Platinum's wet clothes, gently batting aside Platinum's weak and fumbling attempts to help with the buttons. Dane helped Platinum sit carefully on the edge of the bed before disappearing into the hall for a quick moment. He returned with a soft towel and a pair of blue pajama pants. Once he had Platinum dry and dressed, he helped Platinum get under the covers.

"You should sleep," Dane insisted.

Platinum's thoughts were swirling, but his brain kept landing on the one about Lumie. "But Lumie said..."

Dane frowned at him, but sighed and nodded when he saw that Platinum wouldn't let himself succumb to sleep until he had his answer. "Lumie was probably right. The dragon soldier did drown the scientist."

"But Nickel..."

"What is a soldier?" Dane asked. He didn't wait for an answer, which was good because Platinum didn't think he could formulate one at the moment. "A soldier is someone who is strong and brave, who jumps into dangerous situations to save others. But to become a soldier, one individual must join with other individuals in an army. One soldier, surrounded by dozens of other soldiers. You and Nickel are both dragon soldiers, part of the dragon army whose mission it is to save the dragon race."

He smoothed Platinum's damp hair off his forehead from where it had come free from one of his braids. "Don't put too much stock into what those scientists call you guys. You are Platinum, and whatever that means to you is what is important. Now, go to sleep."

Platinum obeyed. His eyes slid closed, and he drifted to sleep with Dane's last words the only thing in his head.

Epilogue

The primer was elementary level, which was Platinum's reading, writing, and math level. He was working his way through it, learning each letter properly this time. He traced the letters on the oversized lines with a pencil, getting the correct shape for each curve and point. He was learning to write numbers, too, by tracing the dotted lines, which were set up as math problems. It told him that two plus two equaled four—he didn't need to figure it out on his own—but that was more math than he had known before.

Dane and Mercury had created a wonderful schoolroom with fancy tables, a whiteboard, and more in the largest bedroom of this wing of the house. The rest of the kits used it every day when the tutor came and even did their homework there after the tutor had left. Platinum got private lessons in the afternoon, but otherwise he didn't use the schoolroom much.

Someone had pulled a chair up to Nickel's bedside, and more often than not Platinum found himself occupying that chair with his schoolbooks. He was still sharing the room with Nickel, so it wasn't too strange. Copper and Alloy shared a room, 'Ron and Zinc shared, and Chrome and Lumie shared when Lumie could find his bed underneath Chrome's mess. Lumie usually ended up bunking with Alloy instead. That left only Nickel without a roommate, and Dane and Mercury had moved Platinum in without worrying what Nickel would think about having his space invaded. Platinum did hope Nickel would be okay with it when he was awake and able to protest.

Platinum had a bed of his own with a bedside table he could work from, and he had tried for an hour or so to do that, but he had eventually gravitated to Nickel's bedside. He didn't spend all of his time there. Platinum had his lessons with the tutor in the schoolroom. He was also trying to get reacquainted with Zinc. Ten years apart was a lot of time for each of them to grow up differently. They might still look the same on the outside, but their insides, their likes and dislikes, had changed drastically. Platinum was also trying to figure out Zinc's convoluted relationship with Copper. Sometimes he thought they were courting, and other times he was certain they were going to kill each other before the end of the day. It was very confusing.

Most of Platinum's morning was spent with Dane at Dane's office. Dane was showing Platinum how the consulting firm had worked before Platinum had destroyed the office. He was helping Becky and Dane pick through all the soaked paperwork and destroyed computers to see if anything was salvageable, and then he was going to help Dane move his entire office over to the new location he had purchased. Dane had been the one to buy the empty store just down the street. He was expanding his office space to give Nickel his own private office as a partner in the firm deserved.

Once they had made some progress with cleaning, Dane put Platinum through his paces magically. He was teaching Platinum how to use his wind effectively and how to manipulate the weather so that the next time he drowned the enemy, he did it on purpose.

Platinum's days were very busy, but they were busy because that was how he wanted it. He could have the entire morning off like the rest of the kits, playing and lazing around under Daisy's supervision until the tutor came, but he wanted to help Dane and to learn how his magic worked. He had chosen his daily activities, and that was a novel and wonderful opportunity to have. The scientists had kept him locked up unless they wanted to experiment on him, and running had necessitated he keep himself safely hidden. Now he could openly and eagerly decide what he was going to do each day, and he loved it.

Yet at the end of every day when he sat down to do his homework, he still ended up at Nickel's bedside as if under a compulsion to do so. It was soothing somehow. When he was learning a new letter or number, he could hear Nickel's slow breathing. When Platinum looked up to rest his eyes, he could study Nickel's calm, sleeping face.

Nickel's blue hair had lost some of its luster thanks to not being washed for a few days. There were circles under his eyes from the induced sleep. He looked like he was losing weight, too, even though it had only been a few days. Dr. Krantz said it was because Nickel's body was using up all of its stored resources to heal. If it got really bad, Dr. Krantz said he would increase Nickel's IV fluids, which would help. Until then, all Platinum could do was sit and watch.

The bedroom door opened. Platinum looked away from Nickel's face and found Mercury walking into the room.

"Come down to dinner," Mercury said softly. "You can finish your homework afterward."

Platinum nodded and stood up. He went over to his own bedside table to put his schoolbooks away and then followed Mercury to the door. Platinum couldn't help pausing in the doorway to take one last look at Nickel's sleeping face before he headed downstairs.

There was something on his stool, Platinum noticed as he stepped into the kitchen. The rest of the kits, Zinc included, were ignoring it. Platinum walked closer to see what it was and found his backpack. It had gone missing when he and Lumie had been kitnapped, and Platinum hadn't thought he would ever see it again. He gaped at it, then hurried forward to double-check what was inside.

"The police took it in as evidence, but when I explained to them it belonged to one of the kitnapping victims, they let me have it," Mercury said. "It smelled like you."

Platinum's spare change of clothes were inside, as was half a box of pasta, the rest of his traveling food, and his roll of money. He began to carefully repack the bag, then paused. Platinum was wearing a new shirt, pants, and shoes. He had enough changes of underwear to last two weeks if he was lazy and didn't do his laundry. Plus, he now owned three pairs of shoes. Dane and Mercury were also providing food and a warm bed.

Being Zinc's egg-twin might have something to do with why Dane and Mercury had decided to make room for him inside their own home. Platinum had heard some stories over the last few days about other dragons they had saved that were living safely somewhere else, but from day one he had been made to feel like part of this family.

The backpack was full of all the things he had needed while he was running. That terrible part of his life was over now. Platinum knew he would never have to run from something or someone without Dane, Mercury, and the rest of the kits running at his side and supporting him. The backpack was superfluous.

Platinum could put the extra clothes in his dresser drawers, the food in the kitchen pantry, and the money... After his next magic training session with Dane, Platinum thought it might be nice to pop over into the grocery store and buy Nickel some sort of get-well gift. Platinum didn't need to save the money for life essentials any longer.

"I'm going to put this away really quick," Platinum told Mercury.

Mercury smiled and nodded. "I'll make sure there's still food left," he said while gently batting Chrome's hand away from one of the bowls Dane had put on the island.

Platinum jogged out of the kitchen and back upstairs. Nickel's bedroom was unchanged, not that Platinum had expected it to be any different. He was keeping his presence as low key as possible until Nickel woke up and gave him permission to share the room. There were empty rooms in the other wing of the house where Mercury and Dane shared the master bedroom, but none of the other kits had rooms over there, and Platinum honestly didn't want to be singled out like that.

It only took a moment to stow his backpack in the closet. Platinum would go through it later. Despite Mercury's claims, Platinum knew that if he didn't hurry, there wouldn't be much food left for him. Still, he couldn't help detouring past Nickel's bed to take one last look at Nickel's face.

Platinum didn't know why he was drawn to a person he had never spoken to. The only interaction with Nickel he'd had was when he had seen Nickel running after the van about to kitnap him and Lumie. Nickel had probably been worried about Lumie—his brother—getting hurt, not Platinum.

Yet, the most comforting sound Platinum had ever heard was Nickel's soft and even breaths. It was the sound Platinum went to sleep to every night and woke up to every morning, and he loved it. Platinum needed Nickel to wake up so they could actually talk, so Platinum could figure out what all of his swirling feelings actually meant, but Dr. Krantz wasn't coming back until tomorrow to see if Nickel was healed enough to be woken from his induced coma.

So maybe tomorrow Platinum would finally get the chance to speak with Nickel. He hoped it would be tomorrow. With that thought in mind, Platinum pulled himself away from Nickel's bedside and left the room. Dinner was waiting.

DRAGON

SOLDIER

Chapter One

Nickel fought to open his eyes. The lids felt like they were weighted down or as if someone had sewn them shut. He struggled with them for a few long minutes, then, exhausted, gave up and drifted off to sleep.

The second time Nickel woke, most of the weight had vanished. His eyes slid open easily enough, and then he had to blink away tears as the bright light from his bedside table lamp almost blinded him.

"Sorry!" Someone whose voice Nickel didn't recognize gasped. There was a thump as something hit the floor, and the light snapped off a second later. Footsteps ran away from him, heading toward the door. More light flooded into the room as the door was flung open, but Nickel's eyes had finally adjusted. "He's awake!" the stranger yelled into the hallway.

A series of familiar thumps, bumps, squeals, and exclamations sounded as Nickel's family literally dropped whatever they were doing and ran toward Nickel's bedroom. The door was flung open wider, and a small stampede rushed to Nickel's bedside.

Alloy reached Nickel first. He climbed onto the chair pulled up next to Nickel's bed where the stranger had been sitting moments before. He leaned over Nickel's head to see him better.

"Yup, he's awake," Alloy chirped happily. Alloy's hair was rumpled from playing, and the bright red-and-blue strands that matched the colors of each of his wide eyes hung over his forehead. A pair of hands wrapped around Alloy's middle and gently lifted him off the chair. Alloy was happy to settle into Mercury's arms so Mercury could bend closer to Nickel.

"How are you feeling?" Mercury asked. His voice was soft, almost as if he was afraid of startling Nickel, which was silly after all the yelling from just a moment ago. Mercury's bronze-colored hair was long on his neck, and his bronze-colored eyes looked concerned. Mercury was still wearing the button-up shirt he wore to work, so it must be late afternoon.

Nickel blinked slowly, trying to figure out what he had done to deserve the fanfare. Had he been sleepwalking? No, he didn't feel strong enough to sit up, let alone get out of bed and walk around. He must have been sick, yet that answer didn't jive either.

The rest of his family had lined up behind Mercury. Lumie was standing next to Copper, their bright red hair and eyes an exact match for the shade in Alloy's hair. They were fire dragons, but Lumie was only ten years old while Copper was eighteen, the same age as Nickel. Next to them were 'Ron and Chrome, the two earth dragons. Chrome looked like he had been digging outside again; half of his face and his clothing were covered in dirt the same color as his and 'Ron's hair. They were both thirteen years old, but 'Ron was considerably cleaner than Chrome. Dane had his hands on 'Ron's shoulders, no doubt to keep her from jumping onto the bed to give

Nickel a hug. That would be painful, but Nickel still couldn't remember why his body ached so much.

Dane was the tallest person in the room. His blond hair seemed to glow, and his ears were pointed at the moment, which meant the glamor he used to hide his otherworldly appearance was down. He was unbelievably beautiful, but then he was the child of a god.

Zinc was next in line. Her long white hair, distinctive of air dragons, was loose from the braid she usually kept it in. It hung in a wave down her back. Her gray eyes were earnest as they looked at Nickel, except her face seemed thinner than Nickel remembered. She also seemed to be taller, almost Dane's height.

Nickel blinked in surprise, and then saw the hand clasped in Zinc's and gaped. Zinc, with her hair still in its distinctive white braid, was standing next to herself. Only, now Nickel was realizing that the first version of Zinc was actually male. They were egg twins, identical dragons except for their gender, hatched out of the same egg. He was Platinum, the dragon who Nickel and the rest of his family had been searching for ten years.

Like a spark had been lit, a fire erupted in Nickel's head. He winced at the sudden pain, only it didn't exactly hurt. Memories flooded back, each a little video that connected with the others to give him the whole story. There were a lot of them, the sheer volume overwhelming him and causing the pain-mimicking feeling.

Searching the woods for the person mucking with the weather. Finding out that Platinum had escaped from the enemy scientists. Watching Lumie and Platinum get kitnapped. Flying off to defeat the scientists once and for all. Losing the battle. And then nothing. He didn't know how he had gotten home, only that he was safe now.

"How long am I grounded for?" Nickel asked. His voice was thick and scratchy and his throat dry. How long had it been since he had last spoken? Surely it couldn't be more than a few hours. A day at most.

Mercury let out a growly snort. "For the foreseeable future. And don't even think the word 'candy.'"

Nickel sighed, but at the moment he honestly just wanted a glass of water. Begging for candy could wait until he could sit up properly again.

His eyes drifted almost involuntarily back to Platinum. Nickel had only seen Platinum once, and only briefly as Platinum and Lumie were yanked into the kitnapper's car and driven away from him.

"Are you okay?" Nickel couldn't help asking and was surprised when his stomach filled with what felt like butterflies when Platinum's cheeks turned pink at the question.

Platinum nodded and grinned shyly. "You're the one we've all been worried about," he rumbled.

His voice was the strange one Nickel had first heard when he'd woken up. Platinum had been sitting at his bedside, waiting for him to wake up? Why? And why did that thought only increase the butterflies?

"You've been in a medically induced coma for a little over a week, Nickel," Mercury explained. "Dr. Krantz was worried about brain damage."

Nickel's gaze was yanked away from Platinum as he turned to stare incredulously at Mercury. "A week?" Nickel gasped even as he was thinking *brain damage!*

"Dr. Krantz wouldn't have let you wake if you weren't healed," Mercury continued, "but it's been a long few days for us all."

If Dr. Krantz and Mercury were no longer concerned about brain damage, then Nickel wouldn't be either. He let that worry go and instead focused on more immediate concerns. A lot could happen in a few hours, let alone a full week. Both sides in the war had won decisive battles, but it appeared Nickel's side had won this skirmish. Lumie, Platinum, and Nickel were all home and safe; the evil scientists hadn't succeeded in capturing any of them for use in their cruel experiments. Had Dane and Mercury been able to press their advantage, or had the enemy vanished into their rabbit holes again? That was the main thing on Nickel's mind.

At least, that was all that should have been on his mind.

For ten years, his entire life had been focused on finding the enemy so he could save the dragons. Nickel spent his days working at Dane's side, learning everything he could about investigations so he could find the enemy with only the slightest clue. He had honed his magic to a knifepoint and spent almost all of his free time on whatever he had come up with that week to make him better able to accomplish his goal.

His entire life had one purpose, which was why he couldn't figure out why his eyes kept straying away from Mercury and Dane, who could give him the answer to his question. Yet he wasn't surprised at all. From the very first moment Nickel and Mercury had partnered with Dane to save the dragons, there had been one name fixated in his mind. They had to save Platinum, Zinc's brother. The last ten years had been failure after failure. Even with all the dragons they had saved, poor Platinum had remained elusive.

Now Platinum was standing in front of Nickel, mixed with the rest of Nickel's family like he belonged there. It was where he should have been all along.

That must be why Nickel's gaze kept straying back to Platinum and why those damned butterflies weren't going away. Nickel forced himself to refocus.

"Were you able to catch the man I was fighting?" he asked. The man, who Nickel only knew as *ThatGuy* from an online chat room, had been informed about the enemy's entire operation including the plan, the people involved, and the desired final outcome. That was a first.

Most of the people they had confronted throughout the years had known their specific task, their role in whatever plan the enemy had concocted, and not much else. That was why Dane, Mercury, and Nickel had been having so much trouble tracking their movements and stopping them entirely. They would capture one person who would give them one small piece of the puzzle. It was just enough to make Nickel think they were making progress, only for them to find out after digging a little more that the puzzle piece was missing the connecting bit that matched it to another piece. Jacobson, their first lead, had only led to a trap. Jessica, the territory leader who had succumbed to the enemy, had led to yet another dead end. It was infuriating.

Dane and Platinum were the ones who shook their heads.

"I punched him," Platinum said proudly, a wide and slightly smug grin eclipsing his blush. "But we didn't want to use magic around the shield holding you, so he ran off, and we couldn't stop him."

"Damn," Nickel swore. "Did we get anything?"

"We got you back, idiot," Dane replied sharply. "Until Dr. Krantz gives the okay, you won't be returning to work. Take this time to relax and heal, Nickel."

"But, Dane!" Nickel yelped, shocked that he was being sidelined. For ten years, he had been the dragon

Dane trusted at his side. Dane trusted Mercury too, but Mercury usually remained behind to protect the rest of the kits who couldn't fight. The house had previously been attacked while Dane and Nickel were out, and Mercury had been there to save the day. It was Nickel who worked with Dane, who fought at Dane's side. He couldn't be tossed to the side so easily.

"No buts! Nickel, you took a risk that didn't pan out. Now you're on medical leave until you heal. Think of it this way," Dane said, his voice softening as if he understood where Nickel's panic lay. "You've been badly hurt. Any soldier would go on leave for a few weeks to ensure they could return to the field at full strength. Nickel, I need you at your best. The work will still be waiting for you when you're better. I promise."

Nickel relaxed slightly, unaware that he had tensed, but he felt the strain on weakened muscles now that he was loosening up again. Dane's words made sense, especially now that he could feel just how weak his body was. His magic was a mere puddle where an ocean should reside. Nickel didn't have to like it, but he did need to heal before he would once again be of any worth in the fight. He would get better, and the next time he confronted the enemy, he would destroy them.

"Okay, let's let Nickel get some rest," Mercury called. 'Ron groaned and Alloy pouted, but everyone obeyed. Chrome ran off, probably back to whatever he had been doing that had gotten him so dirty. The rest of the kits were more reluctant until Daisy's voice echoed up the stairs.

"I'm making dinner," she yelled, which immediately got everyone's attention.

"Who is supposed to be helping her?" Dane asked, which got the kits moving. In seconds, only Mercury,

Dane, and Platinum were left. Dane closed the door as the last kit scurried away, and then moved to Nickel's bedside.

"Confronting the enemy on your own wasn't just stupid; it was suicidal," Dane said. He wasn't yelling or even scolding; instead, he was speaking as if he was simply stating a fact. It hurt more to hear Nickel's mistakes stated so baldly, yet at the same time Nickel couldn't disagree with Dane so he didn't argue. He deserved the dressing down. "It was the action of someone blinded by rage and ambition. Logic, teamwork? There was nothing that I've taught you to rely on in your attack. If Platinum and I hadn't realized what you had done and hadn't come after you..." He trailed off while shaking his head, as if he couldn't speak the words.

After a moment of painful silence, Dane continued. "Dr. Krantz wants you on bed rest for the next week or so. You leave your bed to use the bathroom and only with someone there to ensure you don't collapse on the way. I want you to spend your time recovering and thinking about how you could have acted differently and what the outcome might have been if Mercury or I had been with you when you confronted the lead scientist."

"He got away because of me," Nickel forced out, the realization running through him like he had stuck his finger in an electrical socket. If Nickel had had backup, they could have taken out the enemy while Nickel was distracting the scientist by fighting with the shield. The war could be over, but because of Nickel's childish stupidity, the enemy had gotten away.

"Maybe, maybe not." Dane shrugged. "He ran as soon as he realized he was outgunned. If you'd had backup, we may have never even seen him, let alone had the chance to fight him. Besides, we were all woefully unprepared for that shield of his. Now we will be ready for it in the next battle. I'm more concerned with the fact that you could have died or could instead be cut open on a gurney somewhere while idiots stole your magic for themselves. You are a soldier in the war, yes, but, Nickel, you're also a commodity. Dragons are the poker chips here, and you almost handed the enemy a straight flush."

Nickel swallowed hard and nodded. The mistakes he had made were a lot to come to terms with, but Nickel wasn't stupid. Dane was giving Nickel a chance to grow, to become a better fighter in the war. Nickel was confined to a bed by doctor's orders; a better time wouldn't come for Nickel to have the opportunity Dane was offering.

"When the week or so is over and Dr. Krantz gives the go ahead, we'll decide together where you go from here," Dane finished.

"I am sorry," Nickel had to say.

"Oh, kit." Mercury sighed. He knelt at Nickel's bedside and reached out to gently clasp Nickel's shoulder. "We're honestly just glad you're okay. Get some rest. You deserve it." He leaned forward to press his lips against Nickel's cheek.

A crash and an exuberant yell sounded from downstairs, and Nickel caught Mercury rolling his eyes as he got back to his feet.

"At least with you awake we can return to dealing with the rest of the kits," Dane joked. He reached out and took Mercury's hand in his, softly pulling Mercury out into the hallway. They left the door open, but Nickel's eyes almost inevitably wandered back to Platinum instead of staying on the door.

"I'm glad we finally found you," Nickel said.

Platinum turned slightly pink again, and that shy smile reappeared. "I'm glad too."

Chapter Two

Platinum could see Nickel's struggle to stay conscious, but he had a feeling Nickel wasn't even aware he was having any difficulty. Nickel had a strong will that clearly didn't allow distractions like the fact he had been in a coma for a week take him out of the game. If Nickel had the strength, he would already be out of bed and working to locate the enemy. There was no stopping Nickel from his goal, even illness.

It was remarkable, but it was also sad. That single-mindedness didn't leave room for much of a life.

Nickel had looked so bewildered when he'd woken. Those bright-blue eyes popped open and stared at the ceiling for a brief moment as if Nickel had no idea where he was or why. They were beautiful eyes framed by blue lashes and set in a face that had gotten too pale and thin over the last week.

When Platinum slept, he had a lot of nightmares, a lifetime's worth of horrors for his consciousness to bring back to life, but lately there had been one pleasant dream. He didn't remember all of it, just Nickel's blue eyes staring at him. And now they were looking at him again.

Nickel blinked, and it took him a few very long seconds before his eyes opened again. His body was finally starting to take over to get the healing rest he needed.

"Let me get you some water," Platinum said finally.

Nickel nodded, but his head moved sluggishly. Platinum left the room quickly. He filled a glass at the sink in the nearby bathroom and hurried back. By the time he reached Nickel's side again, Nickel had fallen asleep. Platinum left the glass on the bedside table. He gathered his schoolbooks from the floor where they had fallen during his scramble to let the rest of the family know Nickel was awake and moved them to his own bedside table. There would be time to finish the chapter he was working on in the morning.

The last week of his life had already made up for the previous eighteen years. Platinum didn't remember living in the wild before being captured. He knew he hadn't hatched in one of the scientist's facilities, but he and Zinc had been taken from their mother's den too young for him to know what life on the outside of a cell door was like. The first eight years hadn't been too bad. There had been many dragons in captivity, which spread out the terrible experiments. Platinum had been taken from his cell only once every few weeks, and when he'd returned, Zinc had always been in the cell next door to offer whatever comfort she could.

He had been horrified when his captors had moved him to a new facility and left Zinc behind. Learning that Zinc was dead had left him crying and alone for weeks. Platinum didn't know when he had fallen into a sort of depression of inevitability, but as the dragons around him died and the eggs were cracked and broken, he'd sunk into a stupor. The experiments were conducted daily, and the apathy that filled his brain and body as he lay alone in his cell afterward hadn't faded. Only that one fateful day when he'd awoken on the operating table and been able to escape the facility had changed all that.

Platinum had survived in the wild. It was lonely and depressing, particularly having to watch over his shoulder every second for the scientists trying to take him back, but he lived his life on his own terms for the first time. Meeting his new family eclipsed even that moment. From the first second Lumie had dragged Platinum into the house and introduced him to Dane and Mercury, Platinum's life had gotten better in leaps and bounds. In only a week, he was laughing and smiling, had put on five pounds of needed weight, was learning to read, write, and do math, had found Zinc again, and now Nickel was awake. He had a family and a real home. It was everything he hadn't known was missing from his life, alone in his cell, and he wouldn't give it up for anything.

There was no denying he was completely overwhelmed. The sudden influx of having seven siblings, two parents, and actual responsibilities was staggering, and he was struggling to keep his head above water. He was loving every moment of it, but sometimes he missed the house where he had been squatting in the woods where there was quiet and solitude. A life of being alone meant that he now didn't know how to handle it when people surrounded him. His time sitting by Nickel's bedside was the only solitude he had found over the last week.

"Dinner's ready," Mercury said from behind Platinum, who jumped in surprise and spun around to see Mercury standing in the open doorway. "Come down and eat with us. I called Dr. Krantz, and he said Nickel would most likely sleep on and off for the next few days while his strength recovers. He'll be by tomorrow morning to check on Nickel." And Platinum knew Dr. Krantz wouldn't be pleased to find out that Platinum was wasting away, staring at Nickel helplessly instead of eating and getting stronger like he was supposed to be doing.

Platinum went to grab a hair tie from his bedside table and took a few seconds getting his long hair pulled out of his face. Mercury dropped a bendy straw into the glass of water Platinum had left for Nickel and put a small handbell onto the table next to the glass so Nickel could alert them if he needed help. With Nickel taken care of, they both left the room and headed downstairs to the kitchen.

The kitchen island was just barely big enough for all of them to sit comfortably around, but when Nickel was back on his feet, there wouldn't be enough room. Though it wasn't an issue they needed to worry about just yet, Platinum had caught Dane perusing kitchen-remodeling websites in some of their downtime between getting the consulting firm back up and running.

Zinc was already sitting in her spot, and Platinum felt another rush of relief at the sight. He wasn't sure he would ever get used to the fact that she was alive and well. It was a shock every time he saw her that tightened his throat with unshed tears.

Dinner was chicken and rice with a steamed vegetable on the side. Platinum sniffed the vegetable skeptically. He had never eaten cooked green beans before, and the other kits were avoiding the round green strands for as long as they could.

"Eat your vegetables," Dane scolded. He said it to the entire table, but Platinum didn't miss the sidelong look

Dane sent him. Platinum speared a bean on his fork and stuck it in his mouth. He chewed, tasting the butter and tarragon the bean had been coated with. He also tasted vegetable. Bleh.

"Carrots aren't too bad," Zinc said when Platinum took a big gulp of water from his glass to clear his mouth. "They're best when they're mixed with something, not on the side like this." A glance at Zinc's plate showed only one or two missing beans. She didn't like them either.

Platinum ate a few more bites of chicken and rice, but the beans were still taunting him on his plate. Mercury hadn't given him a large scoop—he hadn't given anyone except Dane a lot of them—but he would expect Platinum to eat at least half of what he had been given. Platinum refilled his water glass first and then speared three beans on his fork. He shoveled them into his mouth, chewing as quickly as he could and swallowing hard to get it all down. Then he took a big gulp of water. Platinum repeated that process two more times until the pile of beans on his plate was acceptably reduced. He finished his water and happily returned to his chicken.

Nickel probably ate all of his beans without complaint.

Platinum pushed that thought aside. This was dinnertime, his chance to experience having a family moment. He shouldn't let thoughts of Nickel all alone in his room intrude. Still, Platinum couldn't help keeping an ear trained for the ringing sound of the bell left for Nickel. It was hard to hear over the constant chattering going on around him, but it was a much better thing to listen for than trying to decipher and follow what everyone else was saying.

He hadn't helped get dinner ready, so Platinum couldn't escape back to the quiet solitude of Nickel's bedroom when his plate was empty. He waited somewhat impatiently for everyone else to finish. The candy basket was passed around quickly when dinner was over. Zinc preferred colored lollypops with sticky chocolate centers, but Platinum didn't really like those. Nickel liked the blue rock candy, Platinum knew. They came in packs of blue and green, and no one else was eating any of them. Platinum had started eating the green rock candy and was fairly certain he was going to stick with it. Finally, dinner ended and Platinum cleared his plate and started putting dishes into the dishwasher. The other kits, except Lumie and 'Ron, who were helping him clean up, ran off to play again. Mercury and Dane slipped away as well.

It took a while to get all the dirty dishes put in the dishwasher properly. Platinum, as the oldest, was in charge of the handwashing. It was summer, so the sun was still visible on the horizon by the time he was finished. Lumie and 'Ron were quick to run off. Platinum heard the front door slam behind them as he followed at a much more sedate pace.

Platinum hesitated at the foot of the stairs. Zinc had dragged him outside a few times, so he knew a good bit about Dane's property and the air currents that surrounded it. She insisted that, on top of all his studying to get a high school diploma, he should also practice his flying. She knew the cells where Platinum had been kept were far too small for him to change into dragon form. It had been years since Platinum had shifted form, and he was afraid he didn't know how. He certainly had never flown.

He wanted to learn everything, math and flying included, but it was so much piled on at once. Plus, he was scared. What if he couldn't fly anymore? What if he couldn't even change shape?

Platinum swallowed hard on that thought and resolutely turned toward the stairs. This wasn't the right time to find out.

He was running away and he knew it, but he preferred the safety of reading the next chapter in the book he had been assigned, to growing intellectually, than focusing on something else the scientists might have stolen from him.

Mercury and Dane had settled down together on one of the couches in the sitting area at the top of the stairs. They were cuddled close and deep in discussion, but they both looked up with welcoming smiles when Platinum approached. He was planning to walk past them to the bedroom he was sharing with Nickel, but Dane waved him over toward a nearby armchair.

"Mercury was just telling me that the lab results for the samples they took from the house where Nickel fought with the lead scientist came back," Dane explained once Platinum was settled.

"They weren't able to positively identify him, unfortunately," Mercury added with a sigh. "The tainted magic he uses apparently warped the samples too much. I wish there was something we could do to track him down!"

"What about the chat room?" Platinum asked. Director Stockton, the Director of the Federal Bureau of Supernatural Investigations, or the SupFeds, had sent Nickel to an online chat room where the enemy was allegedly talking about their terrible plans. It had turned out to be a trap for Nickel that Nickel had fallen into, but luckily it had also provided Dane with the information he needed to then save Nickel and bring him home safely. Stockton had been livid when Dane had told him the chat room was a trap because, according to Mercury, it meant that someone working for him within the SupFeds was dirty. Stockton had promised to find that person.

"Nothing," Dane snarled. "We have nothing but my vague description of the lead scientist and another dead end. These people are far too good at covering their tracks. I'm hoping when Nickel is more coherent, he'll be able to give us something."

Why was their description of the lead scientist vague? Platinum had punched him right in the face. The scientist featured in some of Platinum's worst nightmares. He knew exactly what the bastard looked like.

"The scientist was fat and bald. His smile looked like this," Platinum explained. He pulled the left side of his mouth upward in a rictus of a grin.

Dane and Mercury stared at him for a long second with their mouths hanging open, and then Dane swore.

"You were with them for over a decade," Dane said before swearing again. "I can't believe we never thought to ask you if you knew anything!"

"We're idiots," Mercury agreed. "I should turn in my badge right now."

"I should shred my PI license," Dane said.

Platinum couldn't tell if they were joking, but a moment later he had their undivided attention.

"Why don't you start from the beginning, from after you and Zinc were separated?" Dane asked. "Tell us everything."

Platinum nodded, but his palms were getting sweaty with fear. The memories with Zinc were at least tolerable, but after he and Zinc had been separated... He really didn't like thinking about it. At the same time, he had to if he wanted to help stop the scientists from hurting any more dragons.

"It was just me and a crazy dragon Zinc and I called Babble," Platinum began slowly. He pulled in breaths evenly as he spoke to help him stay calm. "The scientists broke Babble a long time ago, and all he did was talk, constantly, but his words never made any sense. Zinc had been left behind, and I later overheard them saying that she was dead. Babble kept on babbling, except one day the scientists took him away, and he never came back. Then it was just me."

"Do you know where they took you?" Mercury asked.

Platinum shook his head. "They never said, and I never saw the outside. They would sedate me whenever they moved shop. The first time I had ever been moved was when they left Zinc behind. The facility with Zinc was where they used to keep us after they captured us from the wild. After the move, I was at this second facility for a long time. Then they suddenly started moving me around almost constantly. Until I escaped"—and Platinum was going to continue thinking he had escaped rather than that they had let him go to be bait—"I had no idea where I was."

"Okay, so that wouldn't help us. What about the people around you? The scientists. Do you remember any of them?" Dane was leaning toward Platinum as he spoke, hanging on to Platinum's every word. Platinum had known perfectly well that Dane had been working incredibly hard to help save the dragons, but, even though Platinum had seen Dane at work, he had never seen anyone look so intently earnest about anything. Dane wanted Platinum's answers very badly. That was all the reason Platinum needed to delve into the darkest of his memories.

"Most of the scientists came and went frequently. Some were there for a while before vanishing, and some were there only once and I never saw them again. There were only a few who were there every time. I'll start at the beginning like you asked.

"Soon after they moved me and Babble was gone, a lady appeared. She had blonde hair, but she was always darker up here." Platinum touched the top of his head where her hair had been dark brown until the blonde started. "She started stopping by every week and then every day. I didn't like her. One day she stopped coming, and I overheard them saying she had failed. They moved me again right after that."

"Could that be?" Mercury asked Dane, who frowned and nodded.

"Let me grab my laptop, Platinum. I want you to look at a picture, and tell me if you recognize that woman."

Dane jogged off down the hallway and returned a few minutes later with his laptop in hand. It took a few moments for him to pull up the image he wanted. When he turned the screen around so Platinum could see, the woman's face was all too familiar. He nodded wordlessly.

"This was Jessica," Dane explained. "She was the territory leader of the Midwest with her base in Chicago. It sounds like she offered her territory as a sanctuary for the scientists in return for power. We killed her when she tried to kitnap Alloy."

"But, Dane, remember that Jessica tried to grab Lumie first," Mercury added. "We're pretty sure her main target was Lumie, and she just grabbed Alloy to ensure she didn't totally fail when Lumie escaped."

"So their attempt to take Lumie last week was not their first," Dane agreed immediately.

"All from that damned photo," Mercury growled. Platinum must have looked very confused, because

Mercury grimaced and explained. "I made a mistake on my first field assignment and got myself trapped in a spell. I called Dane, who brought along Lumie since Lumie can crack through spells like they're a cinnamon bomb, and the enemy managed to get a photograph of Lumie doing something no ordinary dragon should ever be able to do."

"We're assuming that's why they're calling him the philosopher's stone dragon," Dane agreed. "Jessica snuck into my house under the guise of a territory leaders' meeting, apparently to take Lumie, and we stopped her."

"You said they moved you, which means the SupFeds were just a hair too slow getting into Jessica's compound in Chicago." Mercury sighed.

"It was rushed. They didn't sedate me all the way. It's the first time I saw the head scientist. They moved around a lot after that. We never stayed in one place for more than a few days. They still had some eggs and me, but the eggs couldn't handle all the moving around. They died, and the scientists soon only had me."

Dane and Mercury were both nodding. "They needed more dragons, quick, but they didn't want to start from scratch with new dragons caught in the wild and lose decades of work," Dane theorized. "So they hatched the plan to set you loose and see if you could reel in any of their escaped dragons, Lumie and Nickel in particular."

"Although if they could have gotten Alloy or any of the other kits, I'm sure they would have been happy," Mercury growled.

Dane grunted back in apparent agreement. "So they're definitely on the run again, and they don't have any dragons that we know of. They do have their research and can always go to a forest where they can snatch more dragons, but we've given them a blow it will be hard to recover from."

"You think they're going to try to take some of your dragons, and they're going to attack again." Platinum gasped as he connected some of the dots.

"They're arrogant," Mercury said in agreement. "Otherwise they wouldn't have brazenly attacked Dane's consulting firm. We need to figure out their next move before they act, and for that, we need everything you know."

"We have your description of the leader, but there's still an enemy spy buried in the SupFeds that we have to find. Do you remember any other people?" Dane asked intently.

Platinum nodded and delved into the worst of his nightmares. These were the faces that terrified him, waking him in the middle of the night in a cold sweat with tears staining his cheeks. The woman with the cinnamon-colored skin and the dead black eyes. The guy who giggled every time Platinum was escorted into the surgery. The man with the long fingers and wide green eyes who always snapped his latex gloves on his wrists while he was waiting for the sleeping gas to knock Platinum out.

He told Dane and Mercury everything. They very kindly ignored his shaking and his wet eyes. He was utterly drained by the time he ran out of faces. Mercury stood with a gentle smile on his face. He bent over Platinum and pressed his hands into Platinum's shoulders.

"Go take a warm bath," Mercury said softly. "Take some time to relax and get the bad memories out of your head again."

Platinum nodded and got to his feet. The bad memories wouldn't go away with just a relaxing bath, but at the very least, his face wouldn't feel tight with tears afterward. Mercury stepped back to Dane's side where Dane was still typing furiously on his laptop, as he had been since Platinum had started talking.

A loud crash sounded from outside just as Platinum reached the hallway. The walls shook and pictures rattled in their frames. Dane and Mercury immediately ran to the window that overlooked the backyard with Platinum only a few steps behind.

Mercury let out a very heavy sigh and shook his head in exasperation. Dane muttered something disparaging under his breath as he unhooked the lock on the window and slid the glass upward.

"Chrome, stop destroying my lawn!" Dane yelled. Platinum peeked over Mercury's shoulder and saw a large, leafy tree laying in the grass. Branches were scattered everywhere, and Chrome's dirty face peered up at the window from between two of the larger ones.

"Aw, Dane," Chrome whined, his voice carrying over the lawn just as successfully as the noise from the crashing tree had.

"Leave the trees alone," Dane reiterated with a frown. "Is your bedroom clean?" Chrome winced and ducked his head deeper into the concealing branches. Dane shared a quick glance with Mercury as they both sighed; then Chrome squeaked as his body was abruptly jerked into the air by magic and pulled toward the house. "Finish cleaning your room before you can go back outside."

Chrome beat Platinum up the stairs to the bedrooms thanks to the magic pulling him along. Platinum followed Chrome down the hall and went into the room he shared with Nickel.

Nickel was still sleeping, his breaths even and soothing to Platinum's frayed nerves. Platinum's breathing was labored, thick with tears and phlegm, and the noise of it wheezed glaringly in comparison to Nickel's. Platinum forced himself to take in a deep breath, almost coughing at the abrupt change, and braced his hands on the back of the chair still at the side of Nickel's bed. His head was spinning with everything he had just had to talk about, but it was all in the past. He had to remember that.

Everything in his memories was over. He was here now, in Dane and Mercury's house with Nickel, Zinc, and the rest of the kits. Rescued. He would never have to go back to that ever again. That thought was what finally had his breathing slowing down and his swirling thoughts steadying. His past would be used to catch the horrible people who had tortured him for so long, to ensure his freedom and the end of dragons being captured so cruelly.

He needed a few more moments of watching the rhythmic rise and fall of Nickel's chest and the disheveled mess of Nickel's blue hair before Platinum could step away from the chair and head to his half of the room so he could start getting ready for bed.

Nickel stayed asleep despite the light Platinum turned on and the noise he caused, as he pulled his pajamas out of drawers, before heading to the bathroom to soak away the stress of the evening. When Platinum was snuggled underneath the covers, his brain finally, happily quiet, Nickel's even breaths helped Platinum drift off to sleep just as they had been doing for the last week.

Chapter Three

It took a few moments of lying completely still and silent in his bed before Nickel heard the noise that had woken him repeated. He had no idea what the strange sound was, though. It took hearing it a third time before Nickel could place the noise. Someone was sobbing, and Nickel was hearing their choked whimpers.

Nickel carefully sat up, glad that the combination of his arm and stomach muscles was enough to get him upright. He still felt weak and shaky, and probably would for the next few days, but at the same time, he did feel slightly better now than when he had woken just a few hours ago. Each bit of improvement was a step in the right direction. Pretty soon he would be able to go back in the field, although that would depend on if he was ever ungrounded. Nickel grimaced at that thought and refocused on finding where the crying had come from.

A second bed had been added to Nickel's room sometime while Nickel had been in his coma. The white hair poking out from under the blankets gave away whom he was sharing with, and the reason made perfect sense to Nickel. He was the only kit who didn't have a roommate, so he had the space. Plus, while Platinum could have taken one of the empty guest rooms in the other wing of the house, that would have segregated him unnecessarily from the rest of the family. Nickel didn't mind sharing his bedroom, although getting woken up by strange noises in the middle of the night wasn't pleasant.

Platinum whimpered again and thrashed under the covers. Overhead, a rumble of thunder sounded. The comforter slipped sideways off the bed, revealing that Platinum was only wearing a pair of loose boxers. He thrashed some more, and his whimper became an indistinct cry. Nickel wanted to walk over to Platinum and gently shake him awake, but there was no way Nickel could even climb out of bed. He settled for calling out to Platinum.

"It's just a bad dream, Platinum," Nickel whispered, trying to explain without bothering the rest of the house. "Wake up, Platinum. It's okay. It's just a dream."

With a muffled gasp that might have been a scream had Platinum been awake, Platinum shot upright in bed. His gray eyes were wide and wild, and his hands trembled where they hovered in front of his chest. He caught sight of Nickel looking at him and scrambled out of bed. He hurried to Nickel's bedside and settled into the chair pulled up close. The way he moved through the dark room toward Nickel spoke of familiarity, as if he regularly woke abruptly from an unsettling dream and headed to Nickel's side while he recovered.

"Do you need anything?" Platinum asked earnestly. "I can get you more water." The wildness was starting to fade from his eyes as he looked at Nickel, but there were tears drying on his face, and his whole body was shaking with slight tremors. The thunder overhead had lessened to the occasional rumble.

"You were dreaming," Nickel explained softly. He hesitated for a brief moment, but couldn't stop himself from reaching out to take one of Platinum's hands in his. It was odd to want to comfort someone he barely knew. Giving Alloy or 'Ron a hug when they needed it was necessary, but otherwise Nickel didn't usually touch anyone else. Yet, with Platinum looking so distressed, Nickel had to reach out and let Platinum know he wasn't alone.

Platinum's hand was clammy from nervous sweat, but his fingers clamped around Nickel's involuntarily. When Nickel didn't protest, Platinum continued to squeeze.

"It was a dream?" Platinum asked. His voice was soft and hoarse with unshed tears. "It was just a dream," he reiterated in a much firmer voice. "I'm sorry I woke you. I can go sleep somewhere else if you prefer."

Platinum started to get to his feet, but Nickel didn't let go of his hand despite the slight tug Platinum gave, so Platinum sank back into his chair with a questioning look on his face.

"It's better to have someone with you after a nightmare," Nickel explained. "I've had a few of them myself. You want to tell me about it?"

Platinum shook his head, but a second later he must have reconsidered, because he nodded.

"I was telling Dane and Mercury about all the different people who I used to see when I was held captive, but I didn't tell them that the reason I remember who they are so clearly is that I see them almost every night in my dreams. I guess that's why tonight's nightmare was so loud."

Nickel had a few nightmares of his own. He tried not to think about them, but every once in a while they did creep up. The first time Nickel had killed a man was the one that recurred most often. He had still been a kit, only five years old at his best guess, and had been locked up and experimented on for at least three years. He had seen an opening and had taken it, but that had required putting his claws through a guard's throat.

The guard wasn't a friend or even someone Nickel had liked, but the man had been someone Nickel had seen every day for three years straight. Killing him had left an imprint that Nickel never enjoyed remembering.

Platinum still looked lost, as if half of him wanted to run and hide until all the bad things magically went away. Nickel wanted to pull Platinum closer and offer his own arms and blankets as shelter, yet at the same time he didn't understand where that want was coming from. The strange mix of feelings roiling inside Nickel was making him feel lost too.

The other half of Platinum didn't want to go anywhere. Nickel could tell by the way Platinum still hadn't let go of Nickel's hand. They could just as easily talk without touching, but neither of them was apparently willing to separate. That fact definitely didn't help with Nickel's mixed-up feelings.

He had never felt like this before about anything or anyone, and he didn't know how to handle it. Still, he knew he had to comfort Platinum. One of Nickel's hands was holding Platinum's while the other was helping to keep himself propped up in bed. Nickel tugged on the hand he was holding, pulling Platinum closer.

"You deserve a hug after having to tell them everything like that," Nickel explained as he continued to weakly pull on Platinum's arm.

Platinum hesitated. Nickel could see the divide of want and worry in the twist of his lips, but eventually

Platinum let out a heavy breath of air and practically collapsed onto Nickel's bed. Nickel let his body drop back down flat and used that now-free arm to wrap Platinum in a hug.

"It's all right, Platinum," Nickel said gently. "You're safe here. You don't have to worry about those scientists ever again."

"I do," Platinum mumbled into Nickel's pillow. His own arm had come up to rest around Nickel's waist, but their other hands were still clasped tightly. "We need to stop the scientists forever. They can't have another chance to recapture any of the dragons that escaped them. They also can't be allowed to start over with new dragons they capture from the wild. I'm strong enough to help fight them, which means I have to face them again." He turned his head to look at Nickel, his face tear-stained, but resolute, and only inches away from Nickel's own head.

Nickel nodded. "We have to fight them. Together." That was a lesson he had definitely learned the hard way. "That's why you don't have to worry. Together we're invincible."

Platinum smiled. It was just a slight upturn of his lips and almost lost against the tears drying on his cheeks. Nickel knew then that he would do anything to see that smile again.

Mercury had once said that he had known from their first meeting that Dane could be his mate. It had taken them a few awkward conversations and a bit of dancing around each other before they had decided to see where their growing relationship would lead, but Mercury had always known.

Nickel knew. That smile told him he would do anything to make Platinum his forever. Which finally explained all of the weird twisting emotions that had been twining through Nickel ever since he'd woken up and gotten his first good look at Platinum.

The low-level rumbling of thunder overhead that had been continuing in the background throughout their conversation slowly faded away as Platinum relaxed in Nickel's arms. Nickel felt his own body easing back into the mattress as his exertion to comfort Platinum took its toll on his already exhausted body.

Sleep came quickly for both, and this time there weren't any nightmares to disturb them.

*

"I want to wake them."

"Aw, but they're so cute! I bet Platinum never gets his hair untangled from Nickel's."

"Blue and white are pretty together, but not as pretty as blue and red."

"Can I wake them? I'll only bite a little bit!"

Nickel recognized the three voices whispering at his bedside with a grimace. He had better wake up now, or he might end up missing a large chunk of a limb thanks to Chrome. Nickel also didn't know what Zinc thought about seeing her egg twin in Nickel's bed. Nickel opened his eyes and found he was still facing Platinum on the pillow they were sharing. Platinum's eyes were open, too, and they were wide with worry as if he was equally unsure of how Zinc and the rest of the kits would handle his being in the wrong bed.

"Go away," Nickel grumbled. He rolled his eyes playfully at Platinum, who lost some of his wide-eyed worry beneath another small grin that sent Nickel's heart racing.

"Don't wanna," Chrome griped.

"I want to know why you're sharing the same bed," Zinc added in apparent agreement.

"What's wrong with sharing a bed?" Alloy asked. "I share with Lumie all the time."

"But you're just sleeping with Lumie," Zinc explained.

"What else do you do in a bed?" Alloy sounded very curious, which had Nickel suppressing a laugh at Zinc's mistake. He squeezed Platinum's hand one more time before letting go so he could roll over and see Zinc's red face. It was the exact same shade of bright pink embarrassment as Platinum's. "Beds are for sleeping."

"Maybe they were jumping?" Chrome asked. "And they were so tired when they were done they fell asleep like that?"

"Daddy doesn't like it when we jump on the beds," Alloy agreed. He nodded as if that was the most obvious answer to explain why Zinc was so concerned. "You could get in trouble."

"I'm gonna tell!" Chrome crowed. He turned and dashed out of the room yelling, "Daddy, Daddy! Guess what!"

"Chrome! Tattling is bad!" Alloy yelled as he turned and ran after Chrome.

Platinum slowly sat up so he could look at Zinc over Nickel. "I had a nightmare," he explained.

"I heard the thunder last night," Zinc said. "You could have crawled into bed with me, you know." She sounded hurt. They had only been reunited a week, and Platinum had chosen Nickel over Zinc. That couldn't be pleasant for Zinc, Nickel knew. Her own egg twin wasn't as close to her as he was with another dragon. Nickel would have to tread carefully with her if he wanted Platinum as his mate.

Platinum frowned at her. "I woke up Nickel, so I had to stay in case he needed something."

Zinc let out a growl. "Fine. So stay with him for all I care!" She stomped out of the room.

"What was that about?" Platinum asked. He had never braided his hair back when he went to bed, so as he sat up, it fell in tangles everywhere. Nickel brushed white hair off his face so he could see Platinum better.

While Platinum's hands were busy with his hair, finger combing through the worst of the tangles, his gaze was fixed on the door Zinc had just gone through. He was worried.

"She thinks I'm going to take you away from her," Nickel tried to explain. "You were just reunited with her after being apart for so long, and you're choosing to spend time with me over her."

"Of course I am," Platinum replied as if it were the most obvious thing in the world. Nickel felt his heart lodge in his throat as Platinum continued speaking. "She's my twin, yeah, and I love her, but you're..." He paused as if he didn't have the right words to explain.

"Mate," Nickel whispered. He pressed one hand gently against Platinum's neck where he could feel Platinum's pulse jumping. "You're my mate. It's not better or worse than your tie to Zinc, but I think it means you'll choose me over her when you need a hug."

"Mate," Platinum murmured as if he was trying out the feel of the word for the first time. "Mate," he repeated, sounding much more certain this time. "But you're a water dragon, and I'm an air dragon. I didn't think we were compatible."

Nickel shrugged, unable to really answer that. He didn't know enough about his own species to be able to say for certain. Still, unlike Platinum, Nickel had seen a mating like theirs before.

"I don't know if he's had the chance to show it to you yet, but Dane set up a village just for dragons he's helped," Nickel explained. "When I was younger, we heard about the scientists attempting to nab an adult earth dragon; she was probably one of their first attempts to go after a full-grown dragon, and she broke free. Made a run for it with two earth kits who had also been captured. Word reached Dane that she needed help, and we responded. We got her safely to the village, and she took one look at an adult fire dragon, and wham. Instant attraction. We're expecting her to lay eggs sometime in the next few years."

"We're dragons," Platinum speculated. "It doesn't matter what color we are or what powers we have."

"Not in the least," Nickel agreed. "Look at Mercury and Dane. A bronze dragon and a half-god are a mated pair. Love isn't restricted like that."

Platinum went pink in the cheeks again when Nickel said "love." It was too soon for that, admittedly. They had barely had a chance to get to know one another—just long enough to acknowledge their mutual attraction and the fact that it could grow into something more. Nickel didn't know all of Platinum's likes and dislikes, and he hadn't yet been able to share his with Platinum either. In fact, Nickel wasn't entirely certain Platinum knew what his own likes and dislikes were. Platinum had been free to make those decisions independently for such a short amount of time. The possibility of their deciding to be mates added to everything else he was already going through must be overwhelming.

Nickel still wouldn't take any of their conversation back though. He needed to know Platinum understood what being mates could mean for them both, so if they chose to move forward with this budding relationship, they would do so as equals. And Nickel very much wanted to try and see where a relationship with Platinum would go.

A knock sounded on the open bedroom door. Platinum spun around in surprise, and Nickel startled. He propped himself higher on the bed and saw Dane standing in the doorway.

"Breakfast," Dane said to Platinum, who nodded and climbed off Nickel's bed. Instead of going right to the door, Platinum headed over to his own nightstand, where he pulled his hairbrush out of the drawer.

"I'll be five minutes," Platinum said to Dane as he closed the drawer and finally headed to the door. "I just need the mirror to fix my hair."

Platinum glanced over his shoulder at Nickel one last time, his cheeks going pink, and he ducked his head shyly before slipping past Dane into the hall.

"Been jumping on the bed, have you?" Dane asked cheekily with a wide grin. Nickel felt his own face heat at the admission. "You've still got a bit more healing to do before you're up for that," Dane added pointedly. "But I have the queen-sized bed that used to be in the school room in storage. We could remove the two twin beds and replace them with one big bed instead?"

Nickel realized he was gaping at Dane with his mouth hanging open and shut his jaw quickly. How the heck did he answer that? "Yes" was the answer he most wanted to say, but he didn't want to push Platinum too far too quickly.

"I want Platinum to get settled in first," Nickel finally said.

That made Dane frown. "Platinum is an interesting kit, but I'm not sure he's ever going to settle. He can handle people one on one, but the second a large group descends, he gets completely lost. He has a habit of running away to hide when that happens."

"The whole house is a large group of crazy kits," Nickel pointed out.

"I know." Dane sighed. "I'm thinking of offering him a place of his own in the dragon village, but it can get pretty crazy there too."

"And I don't think he would want to be so far away from Zinc," Nickel added, although he was hoping that not being too far away from him would also be part of Platinum's decision.

Dane's slight smile said he hadn't missed where Nickel's thoughts were going. Thankfully, he changed the subject.

"Dr. Krantz should be by any minute to have a look at you. If you're recovering well, we'll have a conversation about what you're allowed to do while you're grounded."

"Can I return to work?" Nickel asked hopefully.

Dane let out a snort of laughter. "Not a chance. Dr. Krantz needs to give you a 100 percent clean bill of health before we can discuss your returning to work. Since you can't even sit up properly without help, it's not going to happen any time soon. Enjoy the vacation. Take the time to get to know Platinum."

Nickel nodded, but he didn't feel in any way happy about the forced vacation. He knew perfectly well he couldn't get out of bed just yet, but it wouldn't be too much trouble to help him get propped up against the headboard so he could do some research on the computer. Okay, yes, Nickel did want the chance to get to know

Platinum better, but he would prefer to do it without the weight of his letting the scientists get away again hanging over him.

"At least tell him something," Platinum said as he walked past Dane and back into the room. The mass of long white hair hanging all around Platinum's face had vanished. He had plaited dozens of tiny braids into his hair and had managed to artfully pin them around his head. It was adorable, and Nickel couldn't help staring as Platinum put his hairbrush away. "He'll worry if you don't."

"Have you found out anything about the scientist I was fighting with?" Nickel asked, seeing an opening and hoping Dane would be willing to answer, thanks to Platinum's urging.

Dane sighed as he shook his head. "Stockton and I have both hit a roadblock. Platinum's description that he was bald helped, but we don't have enough to go on. We'll find him, Nickel. Don't worry."

Nickel frowned and thought back to the beginning of the fight. He had walked into the backyard of the house where he had been lured, and a pasty-faced bald man had met him. Nickel remembered the thick arms and a rounded stomach, but he also remembered strangely sticklike legs.

"What if the lead scientist is wheelchair bound?" Nickel asked, thinking through the man's body physique out loud. "He had big arms, but tiny legs."

"When he was running out of magic and I hit him, he couldn't get back up!" Platinum added excitedly.

"Dragons have enhanced healing. He might have synthesized it into part of the magic he was stealing." Dane looked thoughtful. "I'll contact Stockton and see what he thinks. Good eyes, Nickel. Platinum, go on down to breakfast. Mercury will bring a tray up for you, Nickel." Dane left the room still looking thoughtful.

Platinum shared a grin with Nickel.

"Go eat. Spend some time with Zinc so she doesn't decide to kill me," Nickel said only half jokingly. Platinum nodded and followed Dane. Nickel lay back down, satisfied that so far today had been a pretty good day.

Chapter Four

Dr. Krantz decided that Nickel had spent enough time lying in bed while he was in a coma and needed some time outdoors. Platinum watched as Nickel, who was still damp from the bath Mercury had helped him with, was carried down the stairs and out the back door. There was a deck set up there with long padded chairs that Nickel could rest on.

The frown on Nickel's face was deep. Platinum knew Nickel had always been the most progressive of Dane and Mercury's kits, taking charge of caring for himself in a way the other kits just hadn't bothered. Having to be bathed and then carried around like an infant had to be grating on him, but other than the frown, Nickel didn't once complain.

He was getting better, though. Platinum had made certain to be close enough to overhear Dr. Krantz's evaluation. In just a week or so, Dr. Krantz thought Nickel might be well enough to move around on his own, although not well enough that he should be returning to work.

"I'm sorry we made you come in on a Saturday," Mercury said to Dr. Krantz after he had finished spreading a soft blanket over Nickel's legs.

"Nonsense," Dr. Krantz replied immediately. His brown eyes were kind over a wrinkled brow, as he glanced from Nickel to Mercury, and his hands were strong whenever they held Nickel in place despite Dr. Krantz's apparent age. "My dear boy, your kits are far more entertaining than the Saturday morning cartoons I would otherwise be watching." He was looking curiously at the large tree laying in the middle of the lawn as he spoke.

The kits apparently took that as permission because they streamed outside around Mercury and Dr. Krantz. Chrome went to his downed tree, and 'Ron rushed to join him. Alloy had grabbed hold of Copper and was pulling him by the hand around the side of the house. Lumie galloped in the other direction, and an orange fur ball rocketed after him.

"That is not an outdoor cat, Lumie!" Dane yelled. He jogged after Lumie and quickly vanished around the corner of the house as well.

"I see what you mean," Mercury said with a sigh. "Would you like something to drink?" He led the way back inside with Dr. Krantz following.

That left Platinum standing awkwardly next to Nickel, who looked like he was about to fall asleep at any moment. Luckily, Dane came back a few moments later looking ruffled and without a cat to bring inside. Copper flew through the air overhead, a giggling Alloy held upside down by the ankle in Copper's claws.

"I give up," Dane sighed as he stared after Copper and Alloy. "You should go see if you can save Alloy before he gets dropped," he added to Platinum.

Platinum shrugged. "I'm sure he'll be okay." Platinum was aware that his voice was a little too stilted. He didn't mean to sound aloof and uncaring, but he was very, deeply afraid of the idea. The last time he had been in dragon form was before he and Zinc had been separated. What if it was gone? What if he couldn't fly? He had never actually tried flying. Platinum wouldn't be surprised if his wings had atrophied and fallen off.

Dane's answering smile was a touch too kind. It was almost as if he could read Platinum's thoughts.

It wasn't Dane who spoke, though. "Have you tried?" Nickel asked very gently. Platinum hurried over to Nickel's side, so Nickel didn't have to strain, but his gut was churning because the answer was no. He hadn't dared for fear of what might happen if he failed. "You have to try sometime," Nickel insisted. He held out one hand to Platinum, who immediately took it in his own.

"I don't know if I can do it," Platinum whispered.

"You're a dragon," Nickel replied firmly. He squeezed Nickel's hand comfortingly. "You can do it. I know you can."

Platinum swallowed heavily and squeezed Nickel's hand for a long, bracing moment, before stepping down off the deck and onto the grass. Zinc was standing beside Dane when Platinum looked up one last time. She was biting her lip and looking just as nervous as Platinum felt, but she smiled when she saw he was looking at her.

Dragon magic was never something Platinum had to learn to use. He had come out of the egg already knowing how to call on the wind. It had taken some trying to access a human form for the very first time. While claws were essential for survival, having access to opposable thumbs was far too useful. Platinum vaguely remembered an adult dragon urging him to find his human form, although he had no idea whether that was one of his parents or another captive dragon at one of the scientists' facilities.

Changing forms was instinctive, and usually once a kit learned how, they never forgot, but Platinum had been hiding away parts of himself in order to survive for so very long. It took a while to remember the pathways his magic needed to take to trigger the change.

For a long moment, nothing occurred, and Platinum honestly believed that was because nothing would happen. He was stuck forever as a human. Dark clouds began to gather on the horizon as his distress called to magic he couldn't quite control yet. Then he felt his body stretch, almost like a balloon filling with air. It didn't hurt. Usually the transformation happened quickly, between one moment and the next, but this one was prolonged for a few extra seconds.

He closed his eyes, feeling both nauseous and exhilarated. It was happening. He could access his dragon shape. When he opened his eyes again, the ground was much farther away. He was considerably larger as a dragon, although he wasn't quite fully grown. He could see his claws on his front paws and the wide gray scales down his chest.

"Oh, Platinum," Mercury breathed. "You're gorgeous!"

Platinum tilted his head on his long neck so he could see himself better and froze in surprise. Air dragons were usually white or light gray. Silver dragons were metallic gray. He was neither. His scales ranged from gray so pale it was almost white to gray so dark it was practically black.

"Like a storm in the sky," Nickel said. He sounded shocked, but not upset. "Your scales look like heavy clouds lying low overhead."

Platinum couldn't see his entire body. He awkwardly spun in a circle, trying to see what Nickel was talking about, but couldn't see enough to get the entire picture. What he did get was the fact that all four of his limbs were working in concert. He had half expected to be immobile and weak as this form had been left to decay.

Zinc had changed forms, too, and now passed her nose along his spine to take a closer look. Without a ladder, being in dragon form was the only way for anyone to see if he had any issues on his back. She was light gray in color without the striations in color Platinum had. They might be egg twins, but whatever the scientists had done to Platinum during the years Zinc had been safe with her family had somehow altered his dragon form so he no longer looked exactly like her.

"What about your wings?" Zinc called over everyone else's exclamations. She was apparently satisfied with her inspection of Platinum as she returned to her human form.

Everyone quieted quickly at her words and turned to look at Platinum. He had changed form, and he could move properly. Maybe he might even be able to fly! Platinum couldn't quite believe it, but he had to try to see whether this one last essential part of being a dragon was lost to him.

His wings were a heavy weight on his back. They were fully grown and large enough to carry his entire body through the air. Flying was something else dragon kits didn't need to learn. It was instinctive from the moment a dragon's body grew large enough to match the oversized wings they were born with. When a kit was ready to fly, they flapped their wings and took to the air.

Platinum rustled his wings. It hurt. He tried only to unfurl them, no flapping or other movements, and the sharp, piercing pain that radiated through his back sent him crashing to his knees with a scream.

"Platinum!" Nickel yelled.

The pain was intense, but as long as he didn't move his wings, it slowly began to fade. Platinum only realized that he was curled on the ground sobbing when the pain finally diminished enough that he could open his tearing eyes. Nickel was sitting on the ground next to him, one hand carefully stroking along Platinum's snout, although how Nickel had gotten from the deck chair to Platinum's side was a mystery. Zinc was standing next to Nickel with her hands held out impotently in front of her, as if she couldn't figure out where it was safe to touch.

"Let me see," Dr. Krantz said gently from Platinum's other side. Platinum turned his head and saw the doctor reach out to touch one half-furled wing. Just the touch sent another spike of pain through Platinum's back, causing him to whimper. "That must be quite painful. Oh dear."

A cooling, soothing balm felt like it was being spread across Platinum's back. He let out another whimper, this one in relief, and his shuddering body slowly relaxed as the pain faded away.

Dr. Krantz only stepped away once Platinum's back was numb. He walked to Platinum's head where Platinum didn't have to strain to see him.

"This healing isn't going to be like fixing your dislocated knuckle. For that, I simply set the joint and used a touch of magic to accelerate your already advanced healing process. I would wager you have not used your flight muscles for well over a decade. That takes a toll on your body, one that will not be easy to rectify."

"But I can walk?" Platinum forced out through a tight throat scratchy from tears and screaming.

"You use your arms and legs in human form, and those muscles correspond to the ones in your dragon form," Dr. Krantz replied. "However, you do not have corresponding muscles for wings in your human form. Together, you and I must remind your flight muscles how to flex and move."

"Will he fly?" Mercury asked sharply, echoing the fear Platinum couldn't find the words to express. Without flight, he wasn't a dragon. He would only be a scaled lizard with some powers. Platinum didn't deserve Nickel's or Zinc's love, or even a place with this wonderful family, if he were only half a dragon. Yet, he also knew that was only his fear warping his perceptions. Lumie and his magic both weren't right inside, and Alloy was mixed up on the outside. Despite that, this family had warmly welcomed them. They would do no less for Platinum, but he was still deeply afraid that he was too broken for them to want to bother.

"A little physical therapy will fix him right up," Dr. Krantz replied simply. "If he's diligent in his exercises, he could be flying within a year or two."

"That long?" Zinc gasped.

"There is quite a bit of damage to repair, but I do believe he will fly again." He leaned closer to Platinum as if Platinum hadn't heard him properly the first time. "Don't fret, my boy. We'll have you back in tiptop shape soon enough."

A shudder went through his body at those words, as if his body were throwing off all of his negative thoughts and fears. He felt like he was filled with a ray of sunshine finally able to pierce through the thick clouds of an afternoon rainstorm.

"What do I need to do?" Platinum asked.

"For right now, nothing," Dr. Krantz replied. "I, on the other hand, will unfurl your wings so we can let the muscles properly align for the first time. We'll get those muscles stretched and warmed up today, and I'll be back every day for the next two weeks to do the same. I'll have you furling and unfurling your wings without pain within the month, never fear."

For the next two hours Dr. Krantz climbed over and around Platinum while Platinum lay on the ground and tried not to move. Most of the kits came and went. They all had to come and see what was happening, but watching Dr. Krantz pull on Platinum's wings until they were fully extended and then carefully push them back into place on his back got boring after a while.

Nickel remained sitting on the ground next to Platinum's head. He had stopped petting Platinum's snout when exhaustion took over, and now he was using the back of Platinum's front paw as a pillow. It was unbelievably comforting to have Nickel so nearby. Even if Nickel wasn't awake to talk to. He had refused to be moved away from Platinum. Zinc had stayed with Platinum, too, and had made herself useful by helping out Dr. Krantz whenever he needed another set of hands. She seemed to be enjoying herself, which was good because Platinum really wasn't.

The spell Dr. Krantz had used to dull the pain wasn't quite strong enough. Platinum began to feel a constant dull ache creeping in within the first ten minutes, and sudden excruciating flares of pain had him gasping or crying out. By the time Dr. Krantz declared that he was done, Platinum felt both mentally and physically exhausted. At the same time, he felt a strange sense of relief. He was so used to being poked and prodded for nefarious reasons that having someone work on him to help make him better was a novel experience.

"Same time tomorrow?" Mercury asked Dr. Krantz when Dr. Krantz stood and dusted himself off.

Dr. Krantz shook his head. "No, I think we should make one o'clock our regular meeting time. Turn back human, my boy," he added to Platinum. "I don't want you to strain something while in dragon form."

Platinum obeyed, calling on his magic to turn human. He shrank slowly, like a balloon letting out air. He ended up sitting on the ground with Nickel curled in his arms. The low-level pain was gone, but he still felt like one wrong move could have it all rushing back.

Dr. Krantz looked satisfied, so Platinum decided it all must have been working. He was completely wrung out, like he hadn't slept in days. It was far too easy to ignore Zinc hovering worriedly, curl up around Nickel, and fall asleep, so that was exactly what Platinum did.

Chapter Five

For the second time in just a few hours, Nickel woke with Platinum in his arms. This time, they were curled up in the grass with a blanket thrown over their bodies. Alloy was sprawled on his back in his dragon form at their side, his arms and legs akimbo and one corner of the blanket thrown over his stomach. He was asleep. So was Platinum, actually. Nickel turned his head slowly so he didn't jostle Platinum, saw a tree had been knocked into their yard, rolled his eyes because he really didn't want to know what Chrome was up to, and then turned to look in the other direction.

Mercury and Dane were sharing one of the long deck chairs up on the patio. They had their heads pressed together comfortably, but they both looked serious as they spoke.

"Any news?" Nickel called just loudly enough so they could hear him. He didn't want to wake Platinum or Alloy.

Dane stood from the chair and walked down to Nickel so he didn't have to yell. "I would say you're not as injured as we thought, given how quickly you ran to Platinum's side," Dane groused.

Since Nickel had involuntarily collapsed into sleep about ten minutes later, he just growled at Dane instead of answering. Hearing Platinum scream like that had literally made his heart skip a beat. It hadn't mattered how weak his legs were, Nickel had to get to Platinum's side to assure himself his mate he was okay.

It still felt strange to feel so strongly about someone. He barely knew Platinum. They had only been able to have two real conversations, one of which occurred while Platinum was so upset thunder was rumbling overhead. Yet the simple fact was that Nickel would do almost anything to learn more and to find out if their instant attraction really would lead to them being together forever.

It didn't have to, Nickel knew. One of them could leave and never look back, and sometime in the future they might find someone else who called to them as strongly. At the same time, Nickel didn't want to go anywhere. The warmth of Platinum in his arms was far too comforting to want to ever give it up. They would have to be really incompatible in other ways for Nickel to even entertain the thought of leaving, and so far, Nickel hadn't seen anything about Platinum that he didn't like.

"Stockton was definitely interested in the fact the leader was either paraplegic or had some sort of impediment in their legs. He said he'll narrow his search parameters," Dane explained when Nickel still hadn't replied to his previous comment. "He's doing the search himself since he doesn't know who to trust just yet."

"There has to be thousands, if not millions, of people in the world with bad legs." Nickel groaned. "I'm not sure that's the best avenue to focus on."

Dane was shaking his head before Nickel finished speaking. "Stockton's looking for some very specific things. Possible paraplegic, computer experience—since he was able to create a fake chat room to lure you in without the SupFeds knowing—and we have a timeline thanks to Platinum. For example, we know he was living in Chicago from the time we ousted the air dragon lab in Maryland up until Jessica failed in her mission."

That was a lot more than Nickel had thought. Still, it was going to take a while. "If it's just Stockton doing the search, by the time he finds who the culprit is, he'll be hiding again."

"But if we find out who it is, Stockton can freeze his assets and put out an alert. No bank account, no flights or trains. Maybe we'll be able to track properties he owns and see if anyone is hiding there or being kept captive. We want him on the run with only the clothes on his back to his name and no safe place to hide."

Nickel couldn't help grinning at that image.

"Unfortunately, that's going to take time. Stockton doesn't want to spook the guy into hiding before we at least get a chance to capture him. Be patient, Nickel, and take the time, while we're searching, to recuperate."

Nickel couldn't disagree with that statement. He wanted the lead scientist magicless and behind bars yesterday, but he also wanted the strength to be able to take a bath without help. Neither was possible at the moment.

Patience wasn't something Nickel had ever tried to embrace, but as one day turned into one week, which quickly drifted into two weeks of almost total inactivity, Nickel was ready to tear his hair out and drown patience violently. For the first week he had to be helped everywhere and with everything, but now he could feel himself getting stronger every day, and it was a pleasure to finally be able to kick Mercury out of the bathroom while he bathed. Nickel admittedly hadn't quite healed enough to shower by himself, but he could maneuver a bar of soap perfectly fine. That was amazing progress.

What really grated his nerves was how out of the loop Nickel was feeling. A normal day for him consisted of almost constantly searching for any whisper of enemy activity, around which he would fit in his work at Dane's consulting firm. They wouldn't even let him have a computer for an hour. Nickel was totally cut off from anything work related, and that was driving him nuts.

Platinum, on the other hand, barely had a moment to himself. Nickel was absolutely amazed at everything Platinum fit into his day. Platinum spent the morning doing Nickel's job at Dane's firm. Someone had to do it, so Nickel couldn't begrudge Platinum for it. Before Platinum and Dane came home for lunch, they worked together to help Platinum get control over his magic so he would stop calling thunderstorms whenever he got upset.

After lunch Dr. Krantz came over to work with Platinum. They had progressed to Platinum very slowly and painfully opening his wings himself with Dr. Krantz providing some stability support. It was amazing progress even if Platinum was still wiping tears away when he was finished. Zinc had started helping Dr. Krantz every day and had gone up to Dane one evening and declared her intentions to go to nursing school. She was going to finish the high school curriculum and graduate only a year late. Copper, not to be outdone, had also taken more interest in his studies. He didn't know what he wanted to do after high school, but he wasn't about to let Zinc graduate and move on without him.

Platinum had surprised everyone with his schooling over the last two weeks. He had gone from barely being able to sound out words to a fourth-grade reading level. According to Dane, the tutor all the kits used, and Platinum saw in the afternoons, thought he was working with a genius. In his excitement, he had gone from figuring out a way to survive the hours he had to teach the kits to coming up with really engaging lessons for Platinum. He almost—almost—had Lumie interested in learning math.

When Nickel woke from the afternoon nap he was still annoyed he had to take, he always found Platinum in the chair at his bedside, working on his homework. Nickel admired how much effort Platinum was putting into gaining everything he had missed out on thanks to the evil scientists.

At night, they talked for hours. Nickel had nothing to complain about there. They would curl up in bed together and say whatever was on their minds. Platinum knew all about Nickel's frustration with being kept in the dark about how the search for the enemy was going, while Nickel knew how difficult Platinum was finding it to fit in with the rest of the crazy kits.

About two and a half weeks after coming out of the coma, Nickel woke one morning desperately needing to pee. It was near six o'clock, and Platinum was snuffling quietly into the pillow they shared. Half awake and without much thought, Nickel carefully untangled his body from Platinum's, got out of bed, walked to the bathroom, returned to bed when he was done, and curled up around Platinum again. It took him about five minutes of trying to go back to sleep before he realized just how effortless the entire sequence of actions had been. He hadn't needed to use any walls for support or to sit on the toilet for the brief moments he was in the bathroom. His legs didn't hurt or feel shaky; in fact, they felt strong—like he could have gone to the bathroom downstairs and not had any trouble navigating the staircase.

Nickel knew it was time to get up when Lumie and Alloy started running up and down the hallway, squealing about something to do with their cats. Platinum rumbled unhappily and pulled the covers over his ears, but Nickel couldn't stay in bed any longer. He had been lying in bed for far too many weeks, and he wanted to test the idea that he could make it downstairs and back without trouble.

Climbing out of bed without waking Platinum was easy enough. Platinum had decided to braid his hair before bed, so it wasn't a tangled mess around them. Nickel kept his hair short so it couldn't be used against him in a fight; Platinum's hair tied back in braids had the same effect, but Nickel still didn't want to grow his hair out. He loved the way it looked on Platinum. It just wasn't something he ever wanted to try for himself.

Nickel tucked the covers back over Platinum as he stood at the bedside. He didn't want the air-conditioning blowing overhead to give Platinum a chill; plus, Nickel wanted to take a moment to double-check that his legs were sturdy.

Lumie and Alloy had moved on from the hallway. It was suspiciously quiet after their making so much noise just a few minutes earlier, but it also wasn't Nickel's business what they might be up to. As long as they didn't try to set the place on fire and kill him or Platinum, Nickel really didn't care.

He made it down the hallway without needing to lean on anything for support. The hallway opened up into a windowed sitting area that split the two wings of the house. As sunlight rose over the house, it made patterns on the floor. Nickel didn't pause to rest on one of the couches; his legs still felt strong enough to continue.

The staircase beckoned. Nickel did put one hand on the banister as he started going down, just in case. The last thing he wanted to do was take a header down the stairs and end up on bed rest for another two and a half weeks. He took it one stair at a time, testing his feet and knees with each downward step.

Nickel was about halfway down when his legs started to shake with fatigue. Before the coma, Nickel had jogged up and down the stairs without thought. He honestly had a hard time believing that getting injured, a week in a coma, and two and a half weeks of limited movement meant that now he couldn't even crawl down. Yet, it was blatantly true. Nickel carefully let his body slide downward so he could sit on the step he was navigating and rest.

"You're supposed to be grounded," Dane said from above Nickel's head. Nickel jumped in surprise and craned his neck backward to see Dane frowning at him from over the banister. "In fact, I don't think you're supposed to even be out of bed yet."

"I've been in bed for too long," Nickel said in a growl, while knowing that his sitting helplessly on the steps wasn't exactly helping his argument.

Dane looked thoughtful for a long moment, which was more than Nickel hoped. Nickel half expected Dane to come down the stairs to pick Nickel up and drag Nickel back to bed.

"Finish getting yourself down to the kitchen for breakfast, then," Dane replied finally. "Mercury and I will find something for you to do while we're at work."

Nickel hoped they meant to have him in Dane's study with the laptop to do research, but he was honestly just as glad to avoid heading back to bed for the rest of the day. Dane walked off in the direction of the bedroom he shared with Mercury, and Nickel returned to looking at the last half of the staircase he needed to navigate.

He waited a few more minutes to rest his legs, then used the banister to lever himself back to his feet. Nickel knew he was lucky the banister was so sturdy as it held the majority of his weight while gravity did most of the work of getting him all the way down. He rested again at the foot of the stairs. It was easier to walk from there to the kitchen, but his legs were still shaking and weak. Lumie and Alloy zoomed past him three times, the last time followed by Mercury who was wearing one of the button-up shirts he wore to work.

Platinum ambled into the kitchen, yawing widely, just as Nickel was letting his body drop onto a stool at the counter. His theory that he could have used the downstairs bathroom and then been able to make it back upstairs to Platinum last night was bogus. Nickel clearly needed more recovery time, yet he was proud he had made it to the kitchen entirely under his own power. No one had to carry him or spot him. That was amazing progress. Staying in bed wasn't an option any longer. He needed to work his muscles in order to get back into fighting shape.

Once Platinum finished one last yawn, he caught sight of Nickel slumped exhaustedly on the stool.

"I thought you were still upstairs, in the bathroom or something," he said as he hurried to the stool next to Nickel. Platinum took a seat and turned to look Nickel up and down as if looking for injuries. "How did you get down here?"

"I walked," Nickel said grumpily, which made Platinum crack a smile.

"Are you going to be able to walk back?" Platinum's grin gained a cheeky edge.

Nickel growled playfully, but answered truthfully. "Not sure. Guess I'll find out after breakfast."

Mercury popped a stack of plastic bowls onto the counter in front of them, and quickly added three boxes of cereal and a carton of milk. He took his own stool farther down the island and helped Lumie and Alloy fill their bowls with their favorite cinnamon cereal. Nickel reached out to snag the much less sugary cereal he preferred, filled a bowl, added milk, and dug in. Platinum did the same at Nickel's side.

Breakfast was quiet except for the sounds of their crunching. Dane joined them a few minutes later, took a seat next to Mercury, and poured himself a bowl too.

It never took them long to eat breakfast. Lumie and Alloy were finished first, and they both dumped their dirty dishes in the sink and ran off. Mercury added his bowl to the pile in the sink, kissed Dane quickly, and headed off to work. Nickel felt the surge of power in the air as Mercury called on his magic to transport himself away.

Dane walked over to where Nickel and Platinum were sitting and took the stool next to Nickel.

"I put the vacuum in your room," he said to Nickel. "Don't strain yourself, but I need you to vacuum the entire upstairs. Make sure you get every bedroom, the schoolroom, and the hallways. The guest bedrooms too."

Nickel nodded with a sigh. Vacuuming wasn't fun, but he was grounded, so he should've expected this.

"Anything else?" Nickel asked. He somehow managed to keep his voice from sounding begrudging or sarcastic. It was his own damn fault he felt so weak and was being given menial chores as punishment.

"Just the vacuuming," Dane replied easily. "It's fine if you can't get it all finished today. It's more important that you rest. Do whatever you can; you can pick it back up tomorrow. Daisy knows to check on you if you need anything." He turned to look past Nickel to Platinum. "Ready?"

Platinum nodded. He stood and walked around Nickel to Dane's side so he could place one hand on Dane's shoulder. A stab of envy hit Nickel. If he weren't still feeling yucky, he would be standing with Platinum to head to the office for work. It sucked a lot that he had to remain behind. Platinum gave Nickel another smile as if to reassure him that soon enough Nickel would be leaving with them; then Nickel felt magic swell through the kitchen. Dane and Platinum vanished.

Nickel stayed slumped on his stool for a few more minutes. His body felt heavy. Part of it was because he shouldn't have tackled the stairs, and he was having a hard time mustering the energy to go back up. The rest of it was caused by the many difficult emotions swelling and swirling inside him. His stomach was a mixture of nausea and heavy lead, and Nickel was regretting eating a full bowl of cereal. He couldn't stay focused on one thought, his brain jumping around as he tried to find a way to fix his problems.

He fought an internal battle as he grumbled to himself about how unfair it was to be left behind and tried not to be envious of Platinum. He could have easily gone into the office and sat at his chair in front of his too-small desk for the entire day. Working on his laptop would not have been stressful in any way. He could have continued the search for the enemy while helping Dane with his caseload. That would have been nice, actually, which was why disappointment was quickly replacing envy. Instead of helping to save the dragons, Nickel was stuck vacuuming.

Anger was the next emotion to flare. It wasn't fair that he had to be left behind. Grounded or not, he was one of the best Dane had in the fight. They needed Nickel with them, not sidelined. Nickel had proven how much better he was feeling by coming down to the kitchen under his own power. He could keep up now, but he had still been left behind in the empty kitchen.

But he couldn't deny the fact that he was still sitting on the kitchen stool, trying to find the energy to get back upstairs. He wasn't better yet, not really. That admission was depressing, but true. They were right to leave him behind. Should something happen, he would be a liability. Never before in his life had Nickel felt so damned impotent. He had always found a way to fight back, from his first kill to find a way to freedom from the scientists' lab, to fighting for the dragons. Nickel had always had a claw in the action, but not this time.

Nickel growled and levered himself to his feet. He couldn't continue sitting in the kitchen feeling sorry for himself. Nickel might not be able to go to the office, but Dane had left him something to do. All Nickel had to do was vacuum and hopefully prove to Dane and Mercury that he was able to return to the fight.

He gathered the bowls left on the counter, rinsed all the dirty dishes and placed them in the dishwasher, then resolutely turned toward the kitchen door. First, he needed to get back upstairs.

The walk back to the staircase was easy enough. Nickel locked both hands around the banister, put his foot on the bottom step, and levered himself upward. He only made it four steps before he had to let his body rest. Nickel sat on the steps and waited impatiently for his arms and legs to finish shaking. When they did, he clambered back to his feet, got his grip on the banister, and started climbing again. Three steps later, and his foot missed a step. Nickel slipped and crashed down onto the stairs with a thud. He lay there for a few long seconds, trying not to cry. He swallowed a few times and kept his eyes open wide to let the air dry the tears before they could fall.

This sucked. He couldn't even climb the stairs. Instead of trying to stand again, Nickel crawled his way to the top of the stairs. He reached the long couch in the sitting area, heaved himself onto the cushions, and flopped down face-first.

Nickel couldn't stop the tears this time. He cried into the couch cushions, wishing desperately that he were strong enough to get back on his feet. There were chores to do. He had to vacuum the upstairs to prove to himself and to Dane that he was ready to return to work. Only he wasn't ready, and Nickel was starting to doubt he ever would be.

Sleep came suddenly as exhaustion from doing too much pulled him under.

Chapter Six

Platinum grunted as his arm hit the doorjamb, and readjusted his grip on the heavy desk before he sent his end crashing down. The desk was brand-new, just off the delivery truck, and Dane and Platinum were trying to maneuver it through the messy office and into one of the side rooms. The movers were dealing with the long conference table Dane had also ordered.

"You all right?" Dane asked. He had paused to let Platinum get a better grip, but was quick to keep walking when Platinum nodded.

"It's just heavy," Platinum grumbled. He was still trying to put on muscle. His wing muscles might be the most messed-up part of his body, but the rest of him was only in marginally better shape. Platinum did have to admit he was improving; he wouldn't have been able to lift his half of the desk two months ago.

Dane laughed. "I might have gone a little overboard with the new furniture, but I want the office to look nice. Let's set it down here and see what you think."

The new office was easily triple the size of the old one that Platinum had destroyed. He had created a massive thunderstorm inside that building, killing one of the attackers he was fighting against and incapacitating the other. He had also drenched the place, damaging the walls, floor, furniture, and just about everything else. Dane had a private office within the space that had survived the worst of the storm, but everything on and around the desks belonging to his secretary, Becky, and Nickel was utterly drowned.

Dane hadn't been upset in the least, which had surprised Platinum. It turned out that Dane had already purchased and begun renovating the new office just down the street. Platinum had destroyed computers and paper files that Dane would have liked to keep, but the rest of the office furniture and supplies would have gone to charity.

"What do you think?" Dane asked as he stepped back from the desk they had placed. Platinum joined him, looking at the very large oak desk that filled most of the room. It was nice—a very formal and official-looking piece of furniture—and Platinum thought it was in a good spot in the space.

"There's enough room behind it for a bookshelf and his chair," Platinum replied.

"And enough room on the side for the hutch," Dane agreed. "Let's get the bookshelf next?"

Platinum nodded and led the way out of the room. The new office was going to be much nicer than the old one. Dane had purchased two adjacent storefronts, knocked down the wall between them, closed off the extra outside door, and had the space split into four separate rooms. The central space had three desks in it. Off to the right, perpendicular to the door, was Becky's new desk. It was the first thing visitors would encounter upon walking into the room. She had positioned her bank of filing cabinets against the front wall behind her. At the end of the row of filing cabinets, Dane had put the small desk that Nickel had used in the old office. It had survived the deluge and fit into the new space pressed against the wall just between the filing cabinets and the side of the room.

The door to Dane's private office was along that side wall. At the moment, the door was closed, but once the movers were done with the conference room, they would be bringing in Dane's furniture. Along the same wall was a set of French doors with white-frosted-glass panes. The movers were just setting down the long conference table inside. It would sit ten comfortably, but there was enough room to squeeze a few more chairs in if Dane ever needed to.

The back wall was blank for the time being. Platinum didn't know what, if anything, Dane was planning to put there. The left-hand wall was the shortest of the walls in the room thanks to the way the shopping complex had been built, and it had the door to the office they had just put the desk in. Outside of that door and to the left, so it didn't block the entry, was another new desk. It was smaller than Becky's and the one in the office behind it, but it still looked stately enough. It was Platinum's new workspace for when he began his job as Nickel's secretary. A little thrill of happiness shot through him every time he looked at his new desk. It was a statement that he had a place here in Dane's office and in Nickel's life, which meant a lot to Platinum.

It wasn't difficult to cart the bookshelf into Nickel's space, but the hutch had drawers that kept popping open if they tilted it the wrong way. By the time Dane and Platinum had Nickel's room set up, the movers had finished with the conference room and Dane's office.

Becky was standing outside talking with one of the movers while the rest packed up the now-empty truck. She came to join them a moment later and, while the truck drove away, she took another look around the new space, and nodded with a satisfied smile.

"I'll start getting the printers and decorations set up if you two want to go practice now," Becky said happily. She squatted down next to three large, unopened cardboard boxes adjacent to her desk.

"You sure you won't need another set of hands?" Dane asked.

Becky pulled a box cutter out from one of the drawers in her new desk before making shooing motions toward the door. "If I need help, I'll save it for when you get back this afternoon. Go have fun."

Platinum knew it was as fun for Dane as it was taxing for Platinum. They left the office and headed down the street to a nearby park. It was summer, so there was always someone there to watch what they were doing, but it seemed to amuse the voyeurs more than frighten them.

"Today I want you to focus exclusively on the wind," Dane instructed once they had found a wide area clear of people or trees. "Take a small breeze and swirl it into a whirlwind, please."

Platinum obeyed. A breeze came to his call easily enough, and he turned his finger through it for emphasis as it quickly solidified in a head-high whirlwind.

"Make it small enough to fit in the palm of your hand," Dane continued.

That was more difficult. Compressed air had a nasty habit of turning into a cloud and starting to rain or even snow. He had to keep the air spinning and turn the water accumulation into a tornado-style twister instead. It was hard to make it small, but it didn't take long before a palm-sized dust devil was churning in the grass at Platinum's feet. He had done this particular exercise before, although this time he had managed it much quicker. It was all about carefully managing the output of power he released.

Admittedly, most dragon kits didn't have to worry about their power output. One of the cruel experiments the scientists had conducted had apparently succeeded, and Platinum was far more powerful than a regular dragon. Only a precious dragon like Mercury could compete with him. And Nickel could, too, Platinum had been told, because Nickel had worked unbelievably hard to become as strong as he was.

"Good. Now split it into two equal-sized ones," Dane said. Dane was Platinum's fail-safe in case Platinum lost control and the magic got away. It was obvious that Dane knew what he was talking about; every lesson helped Platinum increase his skill with the magic that had been forced on him.

It was difficult to take one force moving in a circular motion and split it in half without losing its form. The miniature cyclone wavered in the air as Platinum fought to hold on to control. It was far easier to take all of his power and send out a massive hurricane-strength gale. Finesse was tough, yet each lesson gave Platinum a deeper understanding and far more control over his magic. His nightmares that woke Nickel up now were only accompanied by a few unhappy rumbles of thunder. Before his training, they would have caused hail, wind, and a nasty, booming storm. The goal was to eliminate the storms entirely by making him aware of the powers he was unconsciously using and subduing the magic to his will.

The cyclone split, and Platinum grit his teeth as he focused on both halves to ensure neither lost their spin as he stabilized them. It took a few minutes before he was sure they wouldn't collapse and dissipate the second he looked back up at Dane. Once Platinum was certain of himself, he turned his attention to Dane's next instructions.

"Make the one on your left head-high," Dane said obligingly.

Now Platinum had to keep one small and compressed while letting the other one grow, but he had to keep it from getting so big it started to yank on the nearby plant life and Dane had to step in. The smaller one immediately started to waver in place and lose form when Platinum focused on getting the other one to grow. He had to pause to steady it, and while his attention was diverted, the larger one started drifting away from him. Platinum had to reel it back in, but the loss of attention to the smaller one had it curving drunkenly.

Platinum let out a growl and focused. He forced the big cyclone to stay in one place with a surge of magic and got the smaller one to reform and hold steady. Sweat dripped down his neck, making the collar of his shirt feel itchy. The brief distraction had both cyclones wavering again, and Platinum had to use more power to keep them steady.

Once Platinum had held both cyclones in place without any issues for at least a full minute, Dane nodded. He looked pleased with Platinum's progress. The big cyclone hadn't escaped his control and run off toward the rest of the people enjoying the park—something which Dane had had to prevent three times so far—and the smaller one hadn't dissipated while Platinum's attention was split.

"Bring them both to waist height, please," Dane said, once he was apparently satisfied Platinum wasn't going to lose control this time.

The best part of this training was the fact the sky hadn't begun darkening with ominous storm clouds that he had accidentally called because he was using so much of his power. The summer sun was beautiful in the bright-blue sky overhead.

Getting the two cyclones back to the same size was easy for him now. It hadn't been on day one of his training, and Platinum had to suppress his excitement at his realization of how far he had come in such a short time.

"Now merge them into one without it growing larger."

Platinum frowned at that. This was new; Dane had never before required that he merge two cyclones and regulate the size of the finished one. Either he would have to force the air to stay compressed without turning it into a cloud, or he could find a way to safely let the excess air drift away. Since Platinum had already played with compressed air when making the smaller cyclone, he decided to go with the second option.

Little breezes drifted away from him as he carefully brought both cyclones together. Dane's shoulder-length hair blew into his face when one breeze that Platinum let go was a little too strong. Platinum had made certain his braids were tight to his head before they started and had warned Dane to tie his own hair back, so Platinum had to hide a smile when Dane's fingers got stuck in a knot of hair while trying to brush it out of his eyes.

It didn't take long before his two cyclones became one. Dane nodded again.

"Good job, Platinum. That's enough for today's lesson, but I want you to start thinking about what we'll be doing next time. Can you move the cyclone without losing its form or letting it loose? Next time we'll take a walk around the park while you control your whirlwind like a leashed dog at your side. From there, we'll progress to walking with two whirlwinds, and then two of different sizes. By the time we're done, you'll be able to move around at will while changing the sizes of those whirlwinds with ease."

"All of that tomorrow?" Platinum asked incredulously.

Dane laughed. "No, but I believe you'll reach it by the end of the month. You're doing really well."

Platinum's stomach let out a growl, which made Dane laugh again.

"Put that away and let's go find lunch."

Platinum obliged, safely dispersing the cyclone, and placed his hand on Dane's shoulder. Dane's magic pulled them away from the park, taking them home to where lunch and Nickel were waiting.

Chapter Seven

Nickel woke tucked into bed with no memory of how he had gotten there. Someone had moved him from the couch in the sitting area to his bed without him waking. It was another blow to his confidence.

The answer as to who had moved him appeared as Daisy pushed open his bedroom door and bustled inside. She was wearing a bright-purple dress that clashed horribly with her green skin, but she had helped raise Nickel, so he couldn't be mad at her for moving him, and he didn't dare say he didn't like her dress.

"Well, yer finally awake," she said with a smile. "Good on ya." She put a tray on his bedside table and then helped him sit up all the way before moving the tray to his lap. A large turkey sandwich overstuffed with veggies greeted him. "I know ya don't mind lettuce," Daisy scolded, correctly interpreting the unhappy twist of his lips he involuntarily let loose at the sight of the thinly sliced carrots, tomato, onion, and cucumber mixed in with the slices of turkey. "The rest have lots of vitamins and nutrients that will help ya get better faster. I put on extra turkey to try to help mask it." At least the glass of lemonade she had included on the tray was palatable.

Nickel sighed, but reached out to pick up the sandwich and started to choke it down with frequent sips of lemonade. Daisy left him to it, apparently trusting that he wouldn't hide the vegetables under his bed, which Chrome had actually done the one time he had been sick.

Once his tray was empty, Nickel rolled over to place it on the bedside table. He sat for a few more moments, trying to work up his courage. Nickel definitely still felt weak; he had a light ache in his muscles as if he had just finished a good, healthy workout. At the same time, he didn't feel broken. Only inside his head, where he was still wailing about his inability to even climb one flight of stairs, did he still seem damaged. And, of course, the damned vacuum was right at the end of his bed, taunting him.

The vacuum's continued presence finally forced Nickel to throw back the covers and swing his feet off the bed. He was slow getting to his feet, unsure whether his legs would be able to hold his weight after their morning's punishment, but they did hold.

Nickel was getting stronger; he couldn't deny that fact, but it was so slow. Well, if Dane wanted Nickel to vacuum, then he would vacuum, and hopefully he would prove to himself and to Dane that he was capable of returning to work.

The vacuum turned on with a loud rumbling hum after Nickel plugged it in and hit the switch. The slow back and forth movements all while juggling the power cord to keep from running over it was far more difficult than Nickel remembered and no different from climbing the stairs. He was panting for breath after only finishing half of his bedroom, but he resolutely continued anyway. Only once the entire carpet had been cleaned did Nickel turn the vacuum off and collapse onto the bed.

"I did it," Nickel forced out through his heavy breaths. Now all he had left to do was the rest of the upstairs, but that would have to wait until tomorrow. There was no way Nickel was going to be able to do anything more today.

"Well done," Daisy said happily as she bustled into the room to collect his empty tray. She smiled brightly at him while collecting his empty tray of food. "Dr. Krantz is here to work with Platinum. Did you want me to send Dane upstairs to carry you outside?"

"Yes." The answer rankled, but it was sadly true.

Daisy left, and Dane hurried inside a few minutes later. He bent to unplug the vacuum before coming over to where Nickel was sitting.

"Probably better if I just carry you," Dane explained. He slid one hand under Nickel's knees and let Nickel wrap his arms around Dane's shoulders as he lifted.

Dane didn't waste time getting Nickel downstairs. The sun was hot on Nickel's face, helping to conceal the sweat caused by his efforts with the vacuum behind sweat from the heat. Platinum was already in dragon form, and Nickel couldn't help marveling yet again how beautiful he was. Dane set Nickel in one of the deck chairs.

Lumie and Alloy ran past them, giggling happily about something, and Nickel could see the downed tree moving in the yard, making him suspicious about what the rest of the kits were up to.

"The tutor called in sick today," Dane explained when he saw where Nickel was looking. "I wanted to watch Dr. Krantz work, and Daisy is still cleaning up from lunch with Copper and 'Ron, so they get a few extra minutes to play before I have to force them into the schoolroom to work on the assignments the tutor sent over." He sounded resigned to having a long and difficult afternoon.

Dr. Krantz finished with Platinum after about ten more minutes. He looked very satisfied with Platinum's progress, which made Nickel smile. It was nice to see Platinum getting better, and it was also heartening to know that if Platinum could—slowly—recover from a lifetime of torture and pain, Nickel could definitely recover from one lost battle.

Yet there was one thing Nickel didn't think Platinum would ever be able to get used to. Lumie and Alloy zoomed around the house again, circling Platinum's large form twice as he was shifting back into human form. Nickel wasn't referring to how long Platinum took to change forms because even that was improving every day. It was the way Platinum immediately shrank back from Lumie and Alloy as if totally unsure of how to handle them, and it was instantly clear by the slight frown on his face that he wasn't happy being bombarded by all the noise and exuberance.

"Dane," Nickel said softly, still carefully watching Platinum sitting on the grass while exchanging a few final words with Dr. Krantz. "Do I have enough money saved up to buy a house?"

Dane looked down at Nickel thoughtfully, no doubt not missing the way Nickel was watching Platinum.

"You've been working for me for ten years and haven't spent any of your paychecks," Dane replied. Nickel tore his eyes away from Platinum to look at Dane and saw a smile flit across his face briefly. "What sort of house were you thinking about buying?"

"Is there a small cabin off of Mountain Road that I could afford?"

This time Dane's smile lasted much longer. "I'll have Becky take a look. Do you want Platinum to walk through any cabins she finds to make sure they're okay?"

Nickel looked back at Platinum, who was slowly getting to his feet. "I want to surprise him with it," Nickel explained. "I want to give him a safe place to escape to if he ever needs it." Nickel wanted it to be a gift, but he also hoped that Platinum might want to move into the cabin with Nickel. At the same time though, Platinum had enough on his plate at the moment. The last thing Nickel wanted to do was put pressure on Platinum to decide right now whether he wanted to move out of Dane's house and into a cabin with Nickel.

"I'll bring you blueprints to look through in your downtime between your vacuuming," Dane said in apparent agreement.

Platinum staggered up the deck stairs and collapsed onto the chair next to Nickel.

"All I'm doing is moving a few muscles, and not even that fast," Platinum whined, but he was smiling good-naturedly.

"Are you getting better?" Nickel asked.

"Yes," Platinum admitted, "but it's probably the hardest thing I've ever done."

"You've made admirable progress," Dr. Krantz called as he walked up onto the deck. He nodded politely to Dane and smiled at Platinum and Nickel, before walking into the house so he could gather his things and head back to work.

Platinum's preening was interrupted by a wide yawn. "Nap time," he murmured, leaning against Nickel without an ounce of shame. Nickel curled his body sideways so Platinum could rest comfortably on his shoulder. Another nap after just waking up from one not long ago seemed silly, yet with Platinum's comforting weight combined with the warm sun against him, Nickel soon found himself nodding off as well.

*

Nickel's improvement was slow and draining to the point where he still needed to rest far more often than he would have liked, but, as the days passed, he could tell he was making a lot of progress. Nickel had taken two naps that day: one in the early afternoon curled with Platinum on the back deck after Platinum's session with Dr. Krantz, and a second one after he had accomplished a little more vacuuming and been exhausted afterward. It was now somewhere in the nebulous hours of the night when the house was silent and the sky black with no hint of the approaching sun. Nickel was wide awake and unable to sleep even a smidge longer. He didn't want to just lie there—three a.m. was the perfect time to sneak into Dane's office and do some clandestine searching on Dane's computer—yet he didn't want to move either.

Platinum, the reason Nickel didn't want to move, let out a heavy sigh in his sleep. Since he was usually a quiet sleeper, any noise Platinum made was generally the first sign that he was heading into nightmare territory. The last thing Nickel wanted was to be sneaking around in the other side of the house when Platinum might need him.

Platinum's nightmares were what had gotten them this close in the first place. Since the first night Nickel had woken because of Platinum's nightmares, Platinum had ended up crawling into bed with Nickel two more times. Dane had gotten tired of hearing Chrome whining about not being allowed to jump on his bed when Nickel and Platinum clearly were, and one day, Nickel had returned to his room to find the twin beds gone, replaced with one queen-sized bed.

At first, Nickel had found it strange that Platinum hadn't commented on the difference. Their first night together, Platinum had simply climbed under the covers and turned to wait for Nickel, who had taken a few extra seconds to pull himself together before following. All the implications were in Nickel's head—a shared bed meant a shared life, and he had just started figuring out the mate thing—but those implications had only spurred him on. Spending every night with Platinum so close, being able to feel the bed shift with Platinum's body movements even when they weren't touching was kind of... Nickel couldn't think of the right word, but he could feel his cheeks heating at the thought.

Platinum let out a little growly rumble and rolled over, almost rolling right on top of Nickel. His gray eyes slowly slid open, and he blinked sleepily a few times before they focused.

"Why're you awake?" Platinum said, his voice deep and scratchy from sleep.

"I napped too much."

Platinum snorted, and his lips tilted upward in a soft grin. "You're not going to be able to stay awake at all tomorrow, and then you're going to spend all night up again. Dane and Mercury are going to start worrying," he added cheerily, his grin turning playful. "Although, whether Dane notices given what the rest of his kits are up to..." He paused and then smiled again.

"He'll notice," Nickel replied grumpily, which made Platinum laugh.

"He really does notice everything, doesn't he? He's definitely noticed how much stronger you're getting." Platinum shifted until his body wasn't twisted around, which in turn pushed the covers back to reveal the fact that Platinum hadn't gone to bed wearing a shirt. He was still very thin; Nickel could see every rib highlighted under pale skin, yet there was definitely muscle there too.

"You're getting better too," Nickel tried to say, but his voice came out as more of a whisper than actual words. He lifted one of his hands, but then reality returned and he put it back down before he could touch. Except, Platinum's hand met his before Nickel could tuck it safely away beneath the blankets. Their fingers tangled together.

Nickel looked up from their clasped hands to Platinum's face, but Platinum wasn't looking at him. His cheeks were as red as Nickel's felt, and there was a small smile still lifting his lips. He was adorable. Nickel's chest tightened just from looking at that beautiful blush. The feel of Platinum's fingers intertwined with his brought up those same feelings Nickel still didn't have words for. Love, maybe. Certainly a bit of lust. There was also want, but Nickel had been feeling that from the first moment he had set eyes on Platinum.

They were mates, he reminded himself, so he should be feeling these things, yet he hadn't expected such a simple act to set him off so heavily. With Platinum, though, it felt right and easy. Nickel wouldn't have to fight for this to exist, which was a novel idea. He had been fighting his entire life for everything he had ever wanted. Freedom from the scientists, the right to continue fighting them at Dane and Mercury's side, and even now, he was fighting to get his strength back. Platinum understood that better than anyone Nickel had ever met. He had fought to escape the scientists just as Nickel had and was still fighting them with all his heart. What Platinum brought that Nickel had never previously understood was a moment to stop fighting and just revel in being alive. Nickel had never wanted to simply lie in bed holding hands with someone before. Being awake had always meant finding something to do to better himself for the fight ahead. He still wanted that, of course—his determination hadn't waned in the least—but at the same time his priorities were shifting.

It was an amazing feeling.

"Don't worry about anything tonight," Platinum finally said after they were both silent for a long, awkward—yet still comfortable—moment. "Don't think about everything that's new or different. Just enjoy the fact that you have it. That's what I'm trying to do."

Nickel couldn't help squeezing Platinum's hand tightly in his, but he didn't have any words of comfort to add. Platinum used his free hand to pull the covers back over them. He let out a soft breath, not quite a sigh, but close, and closed his eyes. He didn't fall asleep right away, but Nickel could feel his relaxation spreading through the room. Nickel closed his eyes too. He didn't expect to fall asleep, but under the influence of Platinum's calming presence, it wasn't long before he drifted off.

*

The next week passed by far too slowly for Nickel. He was falling into a routine of sorts. Nickel would wake, thanks to one or more of his siblings being loud in the hallways; he would struggle his way downstairs for breakfast and back upstairs for a nap; and after lunch he would carefully wheel the vacuum into another room.

Each successive room was farther from his own, which required he be strong enough to walk the distance there and back with the damned vacuum, and be able to actually vacuum the room. Even in the mornings, he found that he didn't have to rest nearly as often on the stairs and he could make it all the way back to his bed on his own instead of collapsing onto a couch in the sitting area.

The best part of his recovery was the fact that his magic was also starting to return. He could feel the strength of it tingling through his fingers as what had been reduced to a mere pond grew into a small lake, and then a large river, and slowly became the ocean he was used to.

Nickel finished the long climb down the stairs and grinned to himself. This was the second time that day he had managed the stairs. First for breakfast, and now he had made it downstairs in time for lunch as well. There would be no more bouts of helpless tears, not from *this* dragon, Nickel told himself firmly as he strode down the hallway toward the kitchen. He was anything but helpless; he just needed a few more days to finish recovering.

He had barely settled onto a stool when magic flared and then dissipated as Dane and Platinum appeared.

"Nickel!" Platinum called, a wide smile immediately stretching his face the second he caught sight of Nickel. "Are you still downstairs?" he added cheekily.

"Ha, ha. Very funny," Nickel grumbled good-naturedly. "I'm *back* downstairs. I managed the stairs a second time today!" He couldn't help how excited he sounded, but this was the first real, tangible proof of his recovery.

Platinum completely understood. He rushed over to give Nickel a hug, which Nickel happily returned. They were both getting a little stronger every day.

"I'm starving," Chrome whined as he walked into the kitchen. "What's for grub?" He was covered head to toe in brown mud and looking very pleased with himself.

"Wash yer hands!" Daisy gasped when she saw him. She pointed toward the kitchen sink with her spatula. "Grilled cheese."

Chrome grumbled, but Nickel had seen him try to fight this battle before and lose, and he wasn't surprised when Chrome obediently went over to the sink.

"With soap," Dane added sternly. "What have you been doing?"

Chrome looked shifty-eyed, unwilling to look up at Dane to answer, which told Nickel all he needed to know about what Chrome was doing. Nickel stifled his laughter on Platinum's shoulder.

"I'm building a tree fort," Chrome finally answered. He shut the water off and turned to look at Dane. Chrome's chin was set, and he had his stubborn face on.

"Tree forts are usually high in the branches of a tree," Dane said slowly, no doubt working through what Chrome wasn't telling him, "yet instead, you knocked a tree down onto my lawn."

"Earth dragons don't make forts in the air. I'm not Zinc," Chrome said with a low growl.

"Are you tunneling under my lawn?" Dane gasped, looking shocked. "Chrome, that's really dangerous!"

"It's my fort, and I don't have to share it!" Chrome declared just as 'Ron walked into the kitchen.

"Our fort," 'Ron replied firmly. She went to the sink to wash her hands, but she was only marginally cleaner than Chrome.

Chrome growled at her words, but didn't disagree. Dane was muttering under his breath, something about idiots and mining regulations, but the rest of the kits streamed into the kitchen before he could say anything else.

Between Daisy and Dane, everyone was soon happily munching on grilled cheese. Lunch was always one of the quicker meals during the week. The kits didn't have to clean up as it wasn't part of their chores; plus, they only had a few minutes between the end of lunch and the arrival of the tutor. Nickel watched as Chrome and 'Ron scarfed down their sandwiches, placed their plates in the sink, and hurried back outside. Lumie and Alloy weren't far behind.

Daisy grumbled under her breath. "They need to change before their tutor gets here." She hurried off after Chrome and 'Ron, yelling about washing off all the mud.

Dane's cell phone rang. He pulled it out of his pocket and checked the caller ID before answering.

"Director," Dane said sharply. Both Nickel and Platinum sat up and turned toward Dane, eager to hear what Director Stockton had to say. "You found him," Dane stated, clearly repeating what Stockton had just said.

Nickel let out a heavy breath. Stockton wouldn't have called about finding just anybody. He had found the lead scientist. Finally! Nickel couldn't believe it. After so very many years searching desperately to find him and stop him hurting any more dragons, they had a result.

Now Nickel had to find a way to convince Dane to let him help even though he was grounded.

Dane listened to Stockton for a few more minutes before hanging up. He turned to where Nickel, Platinum, and Zinc were sitting at the kitchen island and grinned at them.

"We've got him. Stockton was able to figure out who it is between Nickel and Platinum's descriptions. He did a little digging into the guy's history and found quite a few red flags that confirmed it. A guy Stockton trusts is going to be following those red flags to see who else they might lead to. We don't want to spook anyone too soon, so he wants to wait a week before we spring the trap."

"Who is he?" Platinum spoke slowly, as if he didn't quite want to know but had to ask anyway. Nickel couldn't help reaching out to take his hand, and was glad when Platinum clutched Nickel tightly in return.

"His name is Brice Carnegy, not that his name will mean anything to you," Dane answered. "He was born in Sweden, but his parents moved around the world almost constantly. He contracted polio while in Africa when he was seven and lost the use of his legs, which is when his family moved to the US permanently where there was good healthcare to help him.

"He had US citizenship by the time he was thirty and now works for the SupFeds as a low-level IT guy. That's all Stockton had time to tell me," Dane concluded, "but I'll start digging on my end and see what else I can find."

"What can I do?" Nickel asked. He had been part of this fight for so long. They couldn't shut him out now, grounded or not. That fact didn't stop Dane from giving Nickel a sharp look. "I'll finish the vacuuming," Nickel promised, "but I know I'll be back to full strength by next week, and I need to be part of this fight. I need to."

"I know, Nickel," Dane said after a few seconds of looking hard at him. Nickel couldn't help the immediate shot of relief that went through his body at the admission. "I'll need your strength at my back in this fight."

"I'm coming too," Platinum said quietly, but firmly. He squeezed Nickel's hand as if he needed the physical support to make his demand heard. Nickel squeezed back, trying to send Platinum all the strength he could.

Dane looked at Platinum for a while, but his face was blank so Nickel couldn't guess at his thoughts. Nickel did see Dane's eyes flicker down to their clasped hands for a brief second, and that was apparently all the reassurance he needed, because he nodded a moment later.

"What about me?" Zinc asked softly.

Dane had an answer ready immediately. "Mercury has to be with me, so we're going to need you and Copper to keep watch over the house and the rest of the kits, just in case."

Zinc nodded. It wasn't the first time she had been left behind, although it was usually with Mercury. She preferred guarding to fighting, Nickel knew, and should something happen, she and Copper were strong enough to keep everyone safe until help arrived.

"I'll go tell Copper," she said before swiftly leaving the kitchen.

"Finish your vacuuming," Dane told Nickel sternly. "We're still in the planning stages right now, and you need to take time to heal. We'll bring you up to speed once we have a plan."

Dane might have said more, but the sound of the front door opening echoed back to the kitchen. It was one o'clock, so Nickel wasn't the least bit surprised to see Dr. Krantz walk through the kitchen doorway a moment later.

"There you are, my boy," Dr. Krantz said jovially to all three of them. "Good to see Nickel up and about. Ready for your physical therapy, Platinum?"

"No." Platinum sighed heavily, but he got up and followed Dr. Krantz out of the kitchen toward the back door obediently.

"Don't leave me out of this, Dane," Nickel said sharply as he carefully climbed off his stool.

"I won't, I promise," Dane replied solemnly. "This is more your battle than mine, really. Just remember everything you learned from your last fight," he added with a pointed lift of his eyebrows.

"I've learned my lesson," Nickel promised. "Now it's really time to win this war."

He shared a cold smile with Dane before leaving him alone in the kitchen. Nickel followed Platinum outside as quickly as he could, hoping that Dane wouldn't notice that Nickel had left him with all the washing up until after Nickel was safely ensconced in a deck chair.

Chapter Eight

Platinum would be the first to admit he didn't know anything about preparing for a battle. He could barely read and write his own name, so everything he had seen over the last week was completely and totally strange to him. He didn't like feeling so ignorant. That was one of the reasons why he had been studying so hard—he could spell his own name now and much more besides that—and was glad that Dane let him tag along. Platinum was learning, but it wasn't enough. He needed to know more about the spells Dane and Mercury were talking about using to keep Carnegy's powerful shield from having an impact on the battle. He wanted to learn more about the wards and other defenses Copper and Zinc were going over every time he chanced upon them.

Even Nickel had gotten in on the excitement, using terms that were going right over Platinum's head. He willingly explained every question Platinum had in bed at night, but between trying to rush through the last of his recovery by getting enough sleep and ensuring he was personally prepared, Nickel tended to fall asleep before all of Platinum's questions were answered.

The change in Nickel was amazing to see. Platinum couldn't help the smile that lifted his lips at the thought. Nickel had been battling depression over his injuries and how long it was taking for him to heal. Platinum knew what depression felt like, although growing apathy to the terrible situation he had been living in while held captive by the enemy scientists had caused his. Platinum couldn't really commiserate, but luckily he didn't have to find a way to help Nickel now.

Nickel's entire being had lightened. He practically vibrated with eager energy. It wasn't that he was excited to go into battle; it was that he had a purpose again. That, Platinum could understand completely.

Platinum snuggled closer to Nickel. He wished his whirling thoughts would quiet so he could go to sleep, but he had too much on his mind. Nickel mumbled incoherently in his sleep and threw one arm around Platinum's waist to hold him tight.

It was impossible for Platinum to pinpoint the exact moment when being this close to Nickel had become so natural. Certainly all those nights he had spent in the chair pulled up to Nickel's bedside, shaking his way out of a nightmare and comforted by the peacefulness in Nickel's even breaths, hadn't caused this. Platinum hadn't crawled into bed with Nickel once during that long week.

The most likely time was the moment Nickel had finally opened his blue eyes. Platinum had looked into them and had immediately been captivated. The growth in their relationship as they became closer had been gradual, of course. First Nickel inviting Platinum closer for a hug, then Platinum finding the courage to ask for one. Pretty soon Platinum had only used his own bed as a place to dump his schoolbooks at the end of the day, and now they were sharing a giant queen-sized bed. They weren't jumping on the bed, or any other euphemism Dane might come up with, but that was perfectly okay with Platinum. Right now, the comfort and security he felt with Nickel's arm around him was worth so much more.

Platinum loved Nickel. He had zero doubts about that. Nickel liked to call them mates, which was apparently the dragon term for the connection between them, but Platinum hadn't been raised with the correct terminology. All Platinum knew was that in the coming fight he would make sure Nickel made it home safely no matter the cost to himself.

What Platinum really needed was to be asleep. His worries over what to expect in the morning, especially considering how little he understood the preparations, needed to stop keeping him awake. He would be a liability if he yawned his way through the fight, and that wasn't acceptable.

Platinum focused on the warmth of Nickel's arm around him and the comforting sound of Nickel's breaths in his ear. He tried to clear his mind of every worry and kept his eyes closed so nothing new could distract him. Sleep came slowly, but it did eventually come. Platinum drifted off in Nickel's arms, hoping that tomorrow would go well and he and Nickel could fall asleep like this again tomorrow night.

*

The plan was simple. Director Stockton was going to invite Carnegy to a meeting in the SupFeds building claiming to need an IT professional to support the case Mercury and his work partner, Valerie, were spearheading. Stockton would claim to have brought in

Dane, Nickel, and Platinum as part of the team from Dane's Supernatural Consulting Firm, something which the SupFeds did regularly in cases that were too difficult for their mostly human—and nonmagic—agents. Stockton had slowly been trying to hire more employees with a background in magic, which Platinum guessed was why he had hired Mercury, but he still relied on Dane heavily.

When Carnegy arrived, Dane would place a magical tether on him. Stockton had balked at that idea, thinking it might violate a law or five, but Dane's explanation had made him eventually agree.

"If we fight here," Dane had said, "we'll destroy much if not all of this building. I'm sure the SupFeds and any other government agencies that use this building don't want to be forced to relocate... Plus, I'm hoping if we spook Carnegy, he'll run back to his rabbit hole where he'll have computers and paperwork outlining his crimes. You'll have an open-and-shut case, and I'll have all the information on any remaining dragons he has confined."

Stockton had still gotten the appropriate warrants from a judge he trusted, just in case: one for putting the tether on and another for searching Carnegy's rabbit hole.

The plan was to follow Carnegy via the tether and confront him in a safer location, where if Platinum called up a thunderstorm inside a building again no one would get ticked off at him.

Platinum tried not to squirm in his chair. He was present as part of Dane's firm; it wouldn't be right to act like he was impatient and restless. Nickel was completely still and watchful in his chair next to Platinum, so Platinum tried to emulate that. Dane was on Nickel's other side. He looked bored, but then being called in to consult on a case was a regular occurrence for him so he likely adapted a bored expression to cover his own excitement. His face was so still, however, that Platinum couldn't tell whether he was nervous at all. On Dane's other side was Mercury who had his head pressed together with a woman whose brown hair was loosely pulled into a tail at the nape of her neck. She had been introduced as Valerie Robertson, and they were discussing something in low voices, their faces hidden behind the paperwork in the manila folder Valerie was holding.

The door popped open a moment later, before Platinum could squirm in his seat again, and Director Stockton strode into the room. Stockton was a big guy, large in the shoulders and intimidating. His skin was deep brown, as were his eyes, which swept the room with a calculating gaze as he stepped forward. He courteously held the door open for another man in a wheelchair, who rolled into view.

A low gasp of recognition escaped Platinum before he firmly clamped his lips shut. Platinum hadn't thought seeing the lead scientist again would hit him so hard, but his gut had tightened from the first glimpse, which had forced out that gasp. Dane, Mercury, Valerie, and Stockton didn't miss it; Platinum could tell from the way all their eyes cut to him for a brief moment. Luckily, Carnegy was busy muttering disparaging comments under his breath as he forced the chair to roll over the bump that separated the hallway from this conference room. Nickel's hands had also tensed on his chair's arms, a much more controlled reaction, but one that said he also recognized the man.

Carnegy was difficult not to recognize. His balding, pasty head, the crooked mouth, and the broad shoulders were exactly what Platinum saw in his nightmares over and over again. The only difference was that Carnegy was in his awkward chair instead of looming ominously over a prone Platinum right before they knocked him out for another experiment.

"Good, everyone's here," Stockton said sharply as he took a seat across the table from Dane.

Carnegy rolled to a stop at the very end of the table, closest to Valerie, and placed his hands on the table in front of him. His eyes cut to Nickel and Platinum, and Platinum could see a flash of worry there that he quickly suppressed.

"We think we've finally figured out how to capture the man who has been kidnapping dragons," Stockton continued. "He's on the web, talking to his subordinates that way, which we discovered last time. Carnegy, I have authorized you to work with this team. Your skills with a computer will help them find the real chat room that is being used."

Dane was doing something with his magic. Platinum felt it swelling with power while Stockton spoke, and then suddenly it shot forward. Platinum could barely see a gentle loop of magic fall around Carnegy before abruptly tightening. Dane's magic cut off, and he lifted one hand to casually brush through his hair. It was the signal to Stockton—who couldn't feel magic—that the spell was done. It was a gamble whether Carnegy could feel magic, too, but he didn't seem to have noticed.

"But you already knew that," Stockton said in an abrupt turn. "Since you manufactured the last chat room that sent Nickel straight into a trap. It was very clever to hide right under my nose, especially since it allowed you to keep an ear out for what the SupFeds were doing. That's how you were able to clear out of the facility in Chicago before my agents arrived." Stockton stood and advanced toward Carnegy. "You are under arrest for murder, unlawful incarceration, and for cruel experimentation and manipulation of minors. Agent Robertson will read you the full list of your crimes when she has you down in interrogation." Valerie rose when her name was called, already pulling out a pair of handcuffs.

"I knew this day would come," Carnegy said calmly, but with bitterness turning every word sour and cruel. "When you would side with the animals over your fellow humans. Well, Director," he spat, making the title sound like the worst of insults, "I'll leave you to your menagerie."

With the last word spoken, a sudden swell of all-too-familiar tainted magic filled the room, and Carnegy vanished with a faint pop, leaving only his chair behind as evidence that he had ever been present.

"You've got him?" Stockton turned to look at Dane to double-check.

Dane nodded and grinned, much to Platinum's relief. "He's moving northwest of here, heading toward the Adirondacks. Actually, he's stopped just south of Plattsburg."

"I'll contact Border Patrol to make certain he doesn't drive into Canada, and I'll have the Albany office on standby. They're the closest we have to that location."

"It'll take them hours to drive that far north," Dane said. "Have them start driving now with evidence vans. We'll have a firm address for them before they arrive. Plattsburg isn't somewhere we've tracked him before, so I have a feeling we might have finally found the center of operations."

"Will do. Be safe," Stockton said as he stepped back from them and pulled his phone out of his pocket.

Everyone else in the room stood and crowded around Dane. Magic flared, and Platinum felt the tug as the conference room faded away.

Valerie drew her gun the second the magic dissipated. She held it carefully pointed to the ground and ran to the nearest tree. They were in a forest with trees towering overhead. When he craned his neck, Platinum could just make out a small cabin tucked among the trees ahead. A light shining inside the building showed an outline of a man scrambling from window to window as he gathered things into a bag. Valerie was hiding behind a tree close to the house. She studied the house and the man inside quickly before hurrying back to where everyone else was still safely hidden.

"I need you to keep him from running again," she told Dane. "Stop any transportation spells he might use, and make sure that magic-sucking shield of his is down. Mercury and I will circle to the front with the warrant. Dane, Nickel, and Platinum, take the back door. Don't let him escape."

Everyone split up. Dane turned to focus on the house and the man they could just barely see through the trees and the windows. Platinum stuck close to Nickel, who resolutely headed through the trees, carefully sneaking from tree trunk to tree trunk to minimize the amount of time he could be seen from the windows. Platinum did his best to emulate Nickel. They managed to get within sight of the back door without raising any alarms.

Nickel couldn't be fully healed yet, Platinum knew, but he didn't wobble or appear to be weak in the least bit. He was all business, a place where Platinum knew Nickel didn't allow weakness to intrude. Platinum wouldn't have to worry about Nickel staying safe in this fight, so he ought to focus on keeping his own head attached instead. That didn't stop him from worrying, of course, but he would let Nickel take point and do what he could to support him.

"He comes out the back door, we nab him," Nickel whispered over his shoulder to Platinum, his eyes not moving from the door as he spoke.

Platinum understood this part of the plan. Mercury and Valerie were going to knock on the front door to confront Carnegy, who would either answer and Mercury and Valerie would grab him, or he would try to run out the back, and it was Nickel, Platinum, and Dane's job to stop him.

He was nervous, Platinum realized as he stared at the back of Nickel's blue hair. This was another new aspect to his new life that he didn't know how to navigate just yet. He was done running—that was for certain—but he wasn't a fighter. Not yet.

He was just learning how to do algebra. What the heck was he doing in the woods of northern New York about to confront the evilest person in the world? Okay, he was exaggerating a bit, but it still felt that way in his admittedly limited worldly experiences. Nickel was so steady in front of him. His hands weren't shaking where they were pressed against the tree he was hiding behind, and his knees didn't look weak in the least. Platinum couldn't say the same about himself. He took strength from Nickel's strength and stood tall, firming his knees and calling on the magic he was just starting to learn to completely control. It fizzled along his fingertips like little lightning bolts.

Platinum wanted to be part of this aspect of Nickel's life just as much as the rest of it. Nickel needed someone to watch his back like Dane and Mercury did for each other, and Platinum was going to be that person. He was pretty sure Nickel wanted him to be that person too.

But this wasn't the place to be thinking about everything he wanted to be for and with Nickel. There would be time to figure that all out later, along with the rest of his crazy life.

The knock on the front door of the house was loud and authoritative. Platinum could hear it all the way at the back of the house. Valerie must have pounded on the wood with something heavier than her fist.

"This is the Federal Bureau of Supernatural Investigations. We have a warrant to search the premises." Valerie's voice was just as authoritative as the knock.

Platinum couldn't see the windows from where he was standing to know what Carnegy was doing, but the silence after Valerie's words faded away was telling. It wouldn't be long before Carnegy tried to get away. Platinum called more magic to his fingers to prepare himself. It took him a few seconds to realize that the tingling, almost scratchy feeling he was getting under his skin wasn't more lightning. There was magic building in the air—dark, horrible magic.

"He's doing something," Platinum hissed in warning, as if Nickel didn't also feel the magic in the air.

"He can't get past Dane's shields," Nickel replied firmly. "He'll expend all his magic fighting Dane in a few seconds and—"

The rest of what Nickel was going to say was lost as the small house exploded with a thump that made Platinum's ears ring and his heart skip a beat in surprise. Heat flooded his face, probably singeing off his eyebrows, as he flinched back behind the tree he had been hiding behind. The flicker of fire lit up the forest, adding light under the trees where the sun overhead struggled to penetrate.

Nickel growled low in his throat, and a second later, a cooling mist drifted across Platinum's scorched face, soothing the burnt spots until the pain faded away.

"He won't have stayed inside the explosion," Nickel said, his voice sharp in warning. His eyes were roving the forest around them, searching for Carnegy before he could get away again. Platinum turned to put his back to Nickel's so they could search more of the forest.

Mercury and Valerie had been too close to the building, Platinum's inner worried voice reminded him. He fought to keep that thought from distracting him from his search and reassured himself that Mercury was a precious dragon with the power to shield both himself and Valerie from whatever Carnegy did.

"There!" Nickel growled out. Platinum spun around just in time to fall into step with Nickel as he dashed off through the trees.

It took half a second to find what Nickel had seen. Carnegy was awkwardly shuffling through the trees. His legs didn't quite want to bend properly, and he was using a long stick for a crutch as he wove between the wide trunks. Platinum's best guess was that the stolen dragon magic hadn't quite had time to finish healing Carnegy's legs to the extent that he could walk properly, and whenever he went without magic for a while, his old injuries resurfaced and he had to heal all over again. He therefore couldn't move quickly and had to be extra careful of tripping over sticks or sliding along the mossy ground.

Platinum called even more magic to his fingers, slowly letting it flow outward to manifest in a small cyclone. He knew how to move his magic with him now, so it was barely a moment of thought to grow the cyclone even as he was keeping up with Nickel's fast pace.

It took more magic than Platinum could handle while running to simultaneously condense the cyclone and make rain to add to the whipping wind. The cyclone towered over them, ripping the leaves from the trees overhead as they hurried past.

"Give me water," Platinum instructed as they drew within a hundred yards of Carnegy. "Turn my twister into a proper hurricane."

A cyclone was scary and dangerous, but it was just wind. There was no telling what powers Carnegy had injected into himself, and thanks to his practice with Dane, Platinum knew it was harder for an opponent to combat a single storm. Platinum wanted to double the magic in his storm to make it as difficult as possible for Carnegy to escape.

Nickel obliged without asking any questions. Water made the cyclone heavier, and low clouds began to drift through the forest in a deepening fog as the water and wind together made the trees creak and sway dangerously. The funnel vanished into the clouds, spreading its force over a larger area so it increased the scope of the violence into a full hurricane.

The hurricane was a massive, twisting thing, roiling overhead with lightning and hail. Platinum directed it ahead of them, and Carnegy whipped around to direct his own magic in defense.

Carnegy had the wind blow away from him, probably using powers he had stolen from Platinum, and the hurricane stalled and then started to move backward. Platinum let out a low growl. He stopped running forward and instead dug his feet into the ground softening under the heavy rain that had begun to fall. He gritted his teeth and added even more magic to the hurricane, pushing his own winds against Carnegy's.

"You can't win, idiot dragons," Platinum heard Carnegy yell over the howling wind and creaking trees. "I created you both and have bettered myself with that knowledge. You can't beat me!"

Platinum ignored Carnegy's words. The cruelty and disdain in them were familiar and hated. They evoked memories of his apathy as experiment after experiment had been conducted on him. Platinum would never let himself become so helpless ever again. He poured even more magic into the hurricane in response and felt it triple in size. Slowly it began to inch forward. He was growling and shaking with exertion as he dug as deep as he had ever dared to put all his magical reserves into play.

This wasn't anything like the simple rainstorm he had drowned the kitnappers with in Dane's office not long ago. He had grown in power level, ability, and control since then. All of his training with Dane was clearly paying off.

Nickel added his own magic along with Platinum's, making the rain lash against his face and his shoes sink into the mud as the forest began to flood. The feel of their magic twined together was almost as thrilling as when their legs were tangled together under the blankets at home. It sent a wonderful shiver up Platinum's spine and gave him a jolt that only increased his power.

They needed more to beat Carnegy, who, despite Nickel and Platinum's tandem storm, was still standing on his broken legs with his hands outstretched toward Platinum and Nickel to direct his magic. The hurricane alone wasn't enough to win, but thanks to the scientists,

Platinum was more than just an air dragon. Lightning came to his call, rumbling through the hurricane briefly before shooting downward directly at Carnegy. It didn't touch him, arcing away to destroy a nearby tree with a crack of thunder that shook the ground. The tree fell to the earth with a wet splash as splinters and large shards of wood were whipped up into the storm. It still wasn't enough to win.

"We need more!" Platinum called to Nickel desperately, hoping Nickel had another trick up his sleeve.

"Keep going," Dane disagreed sharply as he hurried up to them from behind. "He's got more magic than any other scientist we've encountered, but it's still a finite source. Keep battering at him steadily; don't waste all your magic for one blow. I'll see if I can't get that defensive shield of his down, and maybe another lightning bolt will end this fight."

Platinum obeyed automatically, now used to listening to Dane as a teacher and mentor. Nickel didn't question him either, and together they slowly and carefully fed the hurricane to keep pushing it at Carnegy. Platinum also called on the lightning, cautiously charging the clouds so they rumbled ominously, but didn't discharge. Despite being soaked, the hairs on Platinum's arms began to lift into the air from the static charge.

"Any time now, Dane," Nickel called. There was a note of desperation in his voice that forced Platinum to look over at him. Nickel had his feet planted wide and his knees were locked, as if that were the only thing keeping him upright. His teeth were bared on a grimace of pain. He wasn't 100 percent healed, Platinum knew, and apparently that was starting to take its toll.

He didn't dare call out to Nickel to reassure him. The last thing Platinum wanted to do was let Carnegy know Nickel was struggling. Nickel wouldn't appreciate coddling anyway. Instead, Platinum had to trust that Nickel would stay strong until the fight was over.

Platinum sent another jet of magic into his storm. The eye was between Platinum and Carnegy, where the storm had stalled, but the heavy bands of powerful wind and rain were focused over Carnegy's head. He ought to be blown over and drowned by now. How much stolen power did he have?

The ground shivered in front of Platinum, which was odd because he wasn't doing anything to the waterlogged earth. Roots shot out of the ground, pointed and deadly as they headed toward Platinum like rockets. Platinum dodged them with a desperate shout, falling to the side with a splash. One of his shoes had gotten stuck in the mud and slipped off when he threw his body to the side, and it hung, impaled from the large root sticking up from the ground where Platinum had stood.

He glanced desperately over at Nickel, who hadn't made a sound, and saw that Nickel was lying flat on his back. The rain was falling too quickly, washing away any blood and keeping Platinum from seeing how seriously Nickel had been hit. Platinum didn't dare hurry over to Nickel's side, no matter how desperately he needed to check that Nickel was okay. The storm was unraveling because of his inattention, the eye losing form as the bands of wind and rain lessened and began to dissipate. Platinum sent more magic into the storm, forcing the various elements back into formation. He could feel Dane's familiar magic nipping at the edges of the storm to keep it from getting away and hitting any nearby civilization where it would cause devastation before it finished disintegrating.

"I've got it," Platinum called to Dane. "Get that shield down!"

Dane didn't say anything in reply, but his magic abruptly pulled away from the storm and Platinum had to grit his teeth and focus.

Nickel let out a low groan and rolled onto all fours. He didn't get up, but he lifted his head toward Carnegy, and his eyes glowed blue with power. Suddenly, the storm had more rain in it than wind, and the water levels flooding Platinum's feet began to climb up his ankles. Platinum answered in kind, adding more wind to the storm until a funnel cloud opened up and dropped a tornado down into the middle of his hurricane. It continued to inch ever closer to Carnegy. The clouds were filled with so much charge it was impossible to tell the difference between the roaring of the wind and the roaring of thunder. Platinum's braids were trying to lift into the air despite how sodden and firmly pinned down they were.

He wouldn't be able to hold the storm much longer. It was taking most of his magic just to keep it together and heading toward Carnegy. His magic stores were quickly depleting. He would either have to dismantle the storm to keep it from getting loose or let it go and hope that Dane and Mercury would be able to contain it. He only had mere moments to make that decision.

"Got it!" Dane crowed, sounding furiously elated.

Platinum didn't wait for further direction. All of that lightning was anticipating a target, and Carnegy was perfect. The flash and roar as lightning came down from the hurricane was blinding and deafening. Platinum had to throw a hand in front of his face to shield his eyes, and his ears were ringing. Thunder boomed and the ground shook. Trees fell, their roots unmoored because of the water and their branches thrown by the impact of the lightning. Platinum blinked lightning-spots out of his eyes and saw that Carnegy was lying prone on the ground, his face hidden in the flooded water.

"Shut it down," Dane yelled. He inched past Platinum, and Platinum saw that he was glowing. He didn't look the least bit damp and the wind wasn't blowing his hair, but he couldn't simply walk through Platinum and Nickel's combined powers with ease.

Platinum obeyed, letting the winds harmlessly flit away. Lightning discharged a few more times with much smaller bolts that hit trees until the storm was neutral again. Platinum could feel Nickel reeling in the water magic making it rain, and he was directing the flood downhill, most likely toward a nearby lake or river. The tornado vanished first as that was just twisting wind that could easily be separated and dispersed.

It took longer for the hurricane to be dismantled. It stopped raining first, and the winds keeping the hurricane in its circular shape went away as easily as the tornado. Soon enough, bright-blue sky began to peek through the clouds.

Dane was kneeling at Carnegy's side, and when Platinum was satisfied that the storm was gone, he looked around to find Nickel. He saw that Nickel was still on all fours and was panting desperately for breath.

Platinum hurried over to him. "Are you okay?" he asked as he fell to his knees with a splash at Nickel's side.

Nickel smiled, and it was such a bright and happy smile that all of Platinum's worries immediately faded away.

"It's just a—it's just a scratch," Nickel forced out through his panting. "Help me up so I can see."

Platinum wrapped his arm around Nickel's chest so Nickel could carefully roll into a sitting position. He leaned against Platinum for stability with Platinum's arm thrown over his shoulder and Nickel's arm warm against Platinum's back. The front of Nickel's shirt was ripped where the root had clipped him and there was some blood, but it looked no worse than a skinned knee from what Platinum could tell.

"I can't believe we finally got him," Nickel crowed, his grin even brighter as he looked over at Carnegy.

Platinum looked, too, and saw that Mercury and Valerie had joined Dane. Valerie was putting handcuffs on Carnegy's prone form, so despite all the immense power Platinum had put into that storm, Carnegy had somehow managed to survive. That was fine with Platinum.

"See how he likes a lifetime of solitary confinement," Platinum said with a satisfied growl.

It was strange to know he was safe now. He wouldn't have to look over his shoulder every moment for Carnegy trying to recapture him. Platinum knew there were still a few scientists hidden away, but without their leader they would be fairly ineffective. Hopefully, the cabin hadn't been completely destroyed, and the SupFeds would find the information to capture them too.

He leaned against Nickel's side, feeling buoyant and happy, and enjoyed Nickel's warmth even more than usual because he knew that nothing would tear them apart.

Dane walked over to them, leaving Mercury and Valerie with Carnegy.

"That was some storm," he said as he kneeled down at Nickel's side to check on him. "I don't think I could have come up with anything more effective at pinning Carnegy in place and draining his magic."

Platinum hadn't exactly been planning that far ahead. His magic was in storms, so he had called a storm to fight. It had lacked finesse, now that he thought about it. Nickel probably would have put up walls or trenches of water that would trap Carnegy and force him to use magic to get free. Platinum could have used the wind to trap Carnegy inside the eye of a storm.

"It was really cool, wasn't it?" Nickel replied in complete agreement. Platinum looked at Nickel in surprise, unsure if he believed him. There were so many other useful things Platinum could have done. "I've never been part of a spell that complex," Nickel continued. "We should do it again sometime."

Nickel's smile was full of mischief, and Platinum couldn't help returning it. He was right, of course. The storm had been a ton of fun, and all of the little things his magic had needed to do to keep the storm strong, yet completely controlled, were finesse. Nickel's smile was insisting that he should be proud of the accomplishment, so Platinum let his concerns go. Instead, he did something he had wanted to try for what felt like forever. He leaned the last two inches closer and saw Nickel lift his chin to accommodate him, and then their lips were pressed together.

It was like he was caught in the storm again, lightning-charged air running through his body with bolt after bolt of electric shock. Platinum's lips were dry from the breeze blowing and his hair was dripping into his eyes, but none of that mattered against the feel of Nickel's equally chapped lips pressed against his and the warmth of Nickel's body where he was leaning against Platinum.

The kiss was brief, Platinum pulling away after a wonderful eternity that in reality was only a few seconds, but it changed everything. A new dimension in their relationship had been irrevocably opened, yet Platinum was in no way upset. It mostly just meant that sharing a bed was probably going to become a little more interesting in the future, a thought that had Platinum smirking. Nickel's answering smirk told Platinum his brain was heading down the same dirty, albeit definitely thrilling path, and he didn't mind the idea in the least.

"I sincerely hope neither of you ever have cause to call that much magic ever again," Dane said very sincerely, apparently choosing not to notice the fact that they had just kissed in front of him. "That was a lot of power you two were able to combine. I would have been hard-pressed to stop the storm if you had lost control of it."

"Is that what took you so long to get that shield down?" Nickel asked, echoing Platinum's own question. Platinum wanted to know what had taken Dane so long too.

Dane's grimace was at himself. "That man might be evil, but he had a fine touch with magic. The shield he was using to stop magical attacks was probably the most advanced spell I've ever seen. Don't tell my mother I said that," he added to Nickel, which caused Nickel to laugh. "He was powering it with a rejuvenating cycle. Every time you attacked with magic, it absorbed the magic to power itself, which we knew about already. I got that part of the spell down quickly. It was the part where Carnegy's own magic usage was being siphoned into powering the shield that took me a while to dismantle.

"I had to get underneath the shield itself first before I could begin unraveling that power matrix. That's what took so long, but I knew the two of you would keep him contained until I figured it out, and you did. We can talk about more particulars back home. Dr. Krantz needs to have a look at that scratch, and you both need warm baths before you freeze."

"What about them?" Platinum asked with a wave toward Carnegy, Mercury, and Valerie.

"They're fine," Dane insisted, and Platinum let out a relieved breath. Valerie and Mercury looked unharmed from where he was standing—which meant Mercury had shielded them in time from the explosion—but it was still good to hear Dane's confirmation. "I made certain Carnegy had no more magic. Valerie's figuring out the best place to transport him. They'll get Carnegy in a jail cell and his cabin cordoned off, and the SupFeds will handle the rest. Our job is done, so let's go home and rest."

Dane placed one hand on each of their shoulders, and Platinum felt the pull as magic transported them away.

Epilogue

Nickel had to wait two days after the battle before he was allowed to return to work. He spent much of the time vacuuming. He had finished the upstairs, so Dane had sent him to work on the downstairs as well, which was totally unfair. He had shown strength in defeating the enemy—why was he relegated back to mundane chores?

Because he was still grounded, Mercury had insisted when Nickel had gone to him to whine. Whatever. They couldn't keep him confined in the house forever.

Nickel finished lugging the heavy vacuum back upstairs and rolled it into the storage closet, then hurried back downstairs and out the back door. Platinum had already changed shape, and Dr. Krantz and Zinc had begun his physical therapy. Nickel walked across the deck, almost tripping over Chrome, who was lying in a sunny spot reading a book on mining, of all things—Nickel didn't even know Chrome could read at a high enough level for a book that thick, and did the topic have something to do with the massive hole Dane was still ticked about in the yard?—but he managed to get down the steps and onto the grass where he could be with Platinum while he was poked and prodded.

Platinum grinned at Nickel when he caught sight of him, but that grin quickly turned into a grimace when Dr. Kranz pulled at Platinum's wing sharply.

"Very slowly...draw your wings in," Dr. Krantz said.

Platinum obeyed, pulling first one wing tight against his body and then the other. It was a slow process, far slower than Nickel had hoped to see after Platinum had so much therapy, but he managed it without screaming in pain. Nickel was proud of how much Platinum had progressed.

"And slowly...back out."

Dane hopped down the deck steps, deftly avoiding Chrome as well, and sat in the grass next to Nickel.

"Your bid was accepted," Dane said softly, keeping his voice low so Platinum wouldn't hear it over Dr. Krantz's instructions. Nickel's heart jumped in glee at the news. "You need to do a final inspection this afternoon, and then we'll meet with the lawyers to sign the paperwork."

"You mean you're going to let me out of the house?" Nickel asked, only half joking.

"Your grounding is over," Dane agreed. "Keep up the good behavior, and you'll even get candy after dinner again." Nickel laughed. Dane got back to his feet. "I'll go set up a meeting with Gregory for you."

"Thanks," Nickel said before Dane walked away.

"You're my kit," Dane replied with a shrug. He walked back into the house without waiting for Nickel to come up with a response.

Nickel refocused on watching Platinum, but he couldn't help feeling elated. He was about to buy a house for himself and, hopefully, for Platinum. Nickel couldn't be grounded anymore if he didn't live under Dane and

Mercury's roof, but he also wanted to give Platinum a quiet place where he could escape the kits and the constant noise. It was the best present Nickel could think of, and he couldn't help hoping that it conveyed his feelings to Platinum as well.

Nickel had absolutely zero doubts that he loved Platinum and that he wanted to try being mates and see where the relationship would take them. The house was the first step in that direction, and Nickel wanted to yell in excitement that he had done it, but he didn't want to ruin the surprise either.

He liked the idea of having a future with Platinum, although that returned his thoughts to what he would be doing with his life from now on. He had devoted himself to saving the dragons for so long, and now that the dragons were saved, he had no idea what his life focus should be. He had Platinum, which was an amazing something, but Nickel wanted to use his hard-won abilities.

Of course, he knew that his position with Dane's Supernatural Consulting Firm was secure, but helping little old ladies get their magically spelled kittens out of trees wasn't nearly the same as trying to save his race. He wanted something more to fill the space defeating Carnegy had opened up. The problem was, Nickel had no idea what that might be.

It felt like everyone else around him was starting to get their lives together. Zinc was already researching colleges with strong nursing programs. Copper was trying to catch up on his schooling so he could go with her—although he admittedly had no idea what he was going to do aside from something with fire. Chrome had gotten engrossed in his book about mining a day ago and was still reading, which was huge for Chrome who avoided reading whenever possible. 'Ron liked the pretty things that came out of the ground thanks to mining and had been badgering Mercury for a book on diamonds and gold just that morning.

And yet Nickel was sitting on the grass, clueless. What did he want to do now that his life's goal was accomplished? He didn't have an answer to that question.

He was forced out of his spiraling thoughts when Platinum dropped to the ground at his side. Platinum sighed happily and slid downward until he could rest his head on Nickel's shoulder.

"Dr. Krantz says after another week of stretching, I should be able to start flapping and building up flight muscles."

"That's amazing, Platinum," Nickel replied immediately, honestly excited. "I was ungrounded today."

"So you're coming to work this afternoon? Dane said I could do my schoolwork there today, since it's Friday." That was probably just the excuse Dane had come up with to get Platinum to the house Nickel had picked out, and Nickel appreciated Dane's help.

"Yup. I'm hoping to get back to helping Dane with his cases."

Platinum just grinned at him in response, so Nickel settled in to rest with Platinum until Dane was ready to take them to the office.

*

They appeared outside, which Nickel hadn't expected. Every other time Dane had transported them to his office, Dane had them appear inside. Nickel looked up at Dane curiously, but Dane's face was very blank before looking at the building he was standing in front of.

The sign on the front door read Supernatural Consulting Firm, which was odd because Nickel could see the firm's front door just down the sidewalk to the left.

"I, um, accidentally destroyed the old office," Platinum explained awkwardly. "But with me now working here, Dane said he needed to expand anyway, so we moved."

Moved? That made sense to Nickel. He hadn't thought how he, Dane, Platinum, Becky, and whichever other kits decided to stop by would all fit inside the old office.

"Go in," Dane urged, but he waited for Nickel to pluck up the courage to reach forward and pull the door handle. Nickel stepped inside and immediately felt his jaw drop. The outer office was easily double the size of the entire old office. It was a nice change, one Nickel thought he could get used to. The entire back wall was filled with a stylized dragon in flight done in a silver-colored metal. It was absolutely gorgeous.

"You got mail," Becky said from Nickel's right. He looked away from the wall to find Becky at her desk, sitting sentinel right next to the front door. She was holding out a sealed envelope, which he took. Behind her desk he could see his own small one directly adjacent to a door with a nameplate that read: Private Investigator Dane Fitzken. To the left of that door was a set of frosted double doors with a plate that read Conference Room on it. They had a conference room now? As far as Nickel was concerned, that was awesome.

"What does the letter say?" Platinum asked, peering over Nickel's shoulder curiously. His chest was pressed against Nickel's back, a warm and comforting weight that Nickel very much needed the second he saw the official state seal on the letter. His hands were shaking as he ripped open the envelope, and he almost couldn't hold the letter inside steady enough to read.

"I passed," he whispered, reading the letter inside. "I have a license!" He was officially a private investigator just like Dane! Platinum squeezed Nickel tightly in a hug and then abruptly spun Nickel around so he was facing the other direction.

There was a door in the short wall there with an empty nameplate on the wall next to it. Dane was holding out a plate for Nickel to see and on it read: Private Investigator Nickel Chicago.

"My firm is rapidly expanding. I would like to hire you as an investigator if you're interested."

Nickel gaped at the nameplate and had to swallow hard to keep the tears he could feel building in his eyes at bay.

"Is there really enough work for two?" he had to ask.

Dane grinned. "I use this office as a private detective, yes, but I am also a territory leader, Nickel. This is my headquarters to keep an eye on any problems cropping up in my territory and to investigate and stop them before they escalate. I definitely need someone else on my team there as well as to handle the cases brought to the firm."

"Then, yes. I would like to work here," Nickel replied with a smile. All of his worry about what to do with his life was over. He had been preparing for a position like this from the first day he and Dane had met. It was only natural that he'd move forward as a full investigator for the firm and for the territory. He really liked the idea of being Dane's second hand in his territory.

"Let's go look at your office!" Platinum said happily. He pulled away from Nickel, but only far enough that they could walk across the room hand in hand. They passed another desk set in front of Nickel's office. "This is mine," Platinum explained with a smile. He pushed the office door open. "And this is yours."

Platinum gently pushed Nickel ahead of him so Nickel walked into the room first. He had his own private office. He was speechless. He had his own, full-sized desk. A hutch, a bookshelf... He knuckled his eyes to prevent any tears from falling before stepping forward so he could run his fingers over the dark wood of his beautiful desk. Then he caught sight of the papers spread across his desk, and his tears turned into a grin.

"I have a surprise for you too, Platinum," Nickel said. They were still holding hands, so it was easy to draw Platinum up to the desk and position him in front of the papers. "I bought something, and I was wondering if you would be interested in sharing it with me."

"What did you buy?" Platinum asked, but his gaze was already darting over the paper in front of him. He was smart enough to figure it out for himself, so Nickel stayed quiet and took a few moments to study his beautiful new office. He couldn't believe Dane had gone to this much effort, and he had no idea how he was going to thank him for it. This was beyond anything Nickel could have hoped. All he had wanted was a desk where he didn't bump his knees. This was... He was fighting back tears again just from thinking about it.

"You bought a house?" Platinum breathed out as if he couldn't get in enough air to even speak.

"It's just up the mountain from here. An easy walk except when it gets really snowy. And I wasn't planning on inviting Lumie, Alloy, or any of the kits to stay over. A quiet home just for you and me."

Platinum turned around and threw his arms around Nickel, tucking his head under Nickel's chin so all Nickel could see were his carefully pinned braids. Platinum didn't say anything, but Nickel heard him anyway thanks to the tightness of his grip and the way he was trembling slightly in Nickel's arms.

Nickel still had to ask. He needed to hear Platinum say it.

"Will you move in with me?" he said softly to the top of Platinum's head.

Platinum pulled back so their arms were still around each other, but Nickel could look Platinum in the eye.

"Yes," Platinum said as he smiled widely, and his happy grin was the most beautiful thing Nickel had ever seen.

Dragon

Adventures

Part One

Dragon Adventures

Chapter One

"Ugh."

"Blarg."

"Pbtth."

"Frrpth."

"That's enough, boys." Uncle Willy's frown of displeasure was pronounced. Rios shut his mouth on another fart noise and Aqua did the same at his side. The long table was quiet, Rios realized, and they were all staring at him and at Aqua. Uncle Dane, with his shiny blond hair, was easily recognizable sitting farther down. He was hiding a smile, but the rest of the people didn't look happy at all.

"Really, William. This is an important meeting. Send the children away," Ming said sharply. She was the tiny Asian woman who controlled everything west of the Sierra Nevada and Cascade Mountains. The entire table was full of territory leaders, and Uncle Willy had explained who each one was and the territory they controlled before they'd arrived for the North American Territory Leaders Conference that occurred every ten years. The last conference had been in Mexico, and the next two or three were going to be in the US before it went back to Mexico.

Uncle Willy controlled Canada, and he always hosted the conference after Mexico.

Uncle Willy had been very stern with the boys about the conference. He had been teaching them all about his duties as territory leader and wanted them to sit quietly so they could listen and learn. But that was boring!

Rios opened his mouth to explain how bored he was, but Uncle Willy's frown grew even sterner, so he shut his mouth again. Uncle Willy was his and Aqua's caretaker. He had found them making a mess in a river and had ended up adopting them instead of punishing them. Living with Uncle Willy was fun. He played games with them and taught them magic. Even though they had to do chores, it was much better than living in the wild. Uncle Willy had even lost a lot of weight over the years so he could go swimming with them; he wasn't skinny, of course, but he could keep up now, at least. But then he had said that being fifteen years old signified that they could now take on some responsibility. Well, if responsibility meant sitting in boring meetings while people did a lot of useless talking, then responsibility was awful.

Both Aqua and Rios hated being bored, and Uncle Willy knew that. Rios hoped his answering pout at Uncle Willy explained his reasoning.

"Go on, then," Uncle Willy finally said with a sigh. Rios refrained from cheering happily as he jumped down from his seat and scampered out of the room after Aqua.

It took them ten minutes to realize there was nothing to do outside of the meeting either.

"Nickel should have come," Aqua grumbled into the pillow that he used for a face-plant. His blue hair was spread around his head like a wave.

He should have. Rios couldn't agree more. Nickel was awesome. He was an older water dragon, about twenty-two, and Aqua and Rios had been playing with him for ten years. He had taught them so much about their shared magic and was happy to see them whenever they could convince Uncle Willy that they should go visit. Except, the last four years of their friendship hadn't been nearly as fun. Nickel had a new playmate: an air dragon named Platinum. Instead of coming to the territory leaders' meeting with Dane like Nickel should have, he was home playing with his new best friend. It wasn't fair.

Aqua rolled onto his side so his face wasn't being smushed by the pillow. He growled under his breath and then let out a heavy sigh. They were both brothers, and the fact that they had definitely hatched from the same clutch was obvious in their shared brow line and rounded chins. Aqua's nose was a little longer than Rios's, his eyes a smidge wider, and he was about four inches taller, but they were clearly brothers. They hadn't been entirely certain of that fact when they were younger and had been confused for twins more times than Rios could count. When they had been kits covered in identical blue dragon scales with identically colored hair, no one could tell them apart. Only as they grew had their differences become apparent, but as far as the issue of being bored and being abandoned by Nickel, they were of the same mind.

"We should go tell Nickel how sad we are that he couldn't come," Rios whined, knowing he was speaking what Aqua was also thinking.

"Not on the phone," Aqua grumbled in reply immediately. The phone number for Nickel's new house that he was sharing with Platinum was written in a little book kept next to the phone in the kitchen, but a phone call wouldn't convey just how upset they were with Nickel. It had to be done in person.

"Uncle Willy won't take us there when he's still in the middle of a meeting," Rios mused aloud, "and Uncle Dane isn't going back home until the meeting is over, so we can't tag along with him."

"So we'll have to travel on our own," Aqua said insistently.

That made sense to Rios. They weren't too far away from Dane's territory, or at least Rios didn't think so. Uncle Willy owned big houses all over Canada. He didn't want to use his main house—where they lived most of the time—for the meeting, so he had brought them all to his house in Ontario instead.

"Wasn't there a map on the wall of Uncle Willy's office?" Rios asked. They didn't spend too much time in Ontario, but they had made sure to thoroughly explore the house.

They ran out of the living room eagerly, up the stairs, and down the hall to the office. Since Uncle Willy was downstairs in the meeting, they didn't knock. Aqua threw the door open and they piled inside.

It wasn't hard to find the map on the wall. It was only about five feet by five feet long, and Rios could easily grip the wooden frame and take it off the hook. Some of the lines were a bit different than Rios thought he remembered, but it was definitely a map of North America. Although, only the right half of the US portion of the map had the lines that denoted the States. The rest of the map was mostly blank. It definitely looked weird, but they could still pinpoint where Uncle Willy's house was in Canada and Uncle Dane's house was in Massachusetts.

"There is a river, see!" Aqua ran his finger down the big lake that Rios knew was called after a big bird. Lake

Seagull didn't sound right—maybe it started with an H, but it wasn't Hawk. The big lake connected to another slightly smaller lake via a river, which then connected to a third lake that was close to where Dane lived.

It looked like it would be faster and much more direct to walk on land, but they were water dragons and could traverse through the lakes and rivers at much greater speed. Once they got to the last big lake, they could find smaller rivers to get to Nickel's house.

Aqua held his finger over the distance from the third lake to Massachusetts and grinned at Rios. "It's only a few inches long. With our water magic, we can get there in a few hours."

Something didn't seem quite right—weren't they supposed to measure with a ruler or something a little more accurate?—but it sounded like too much fun not to go anyway. Rios glanced at the clock, which read eleven in the morning.

"We had better pack lunch," he said with his own grin.

*

Twenty minutes later found them out in the backyard of Uncle Willy's house. It was lakefront property, right along the first big lake Rios had seen on the map. Uncle Willy had a boathouse there, and between Rios and Aqua, they were able to lever a heavy rowboat down into the water. They didn't bother with oars, since they wouldn't need them, and dropped the large backpack with their lunch into the bottom before they climbed in.

Aqua called on his waterpower first. Rios had lost at rock, paper, scissors, so had to wait until Aqua got tired and decided to swap with him. The rowboat pulled away from the dock swiftly, and Aqua directed it into the current.

The water smelled fishy, with a tinge of gasoline as a nasty overlay. There were other boats on the water of all different types and sizes. Some had big sails while others revved by with their large motors, rumbling extremely loudly and causing waves that Aqua had to carefully steady their boat through. There were other boats heading in the same direction they were going—downriver with the current—and once Aqua had them safely situated among the rest of the boats, Rios let himself relax and enjoy the ride.

It was nice being on the water. Much nicer than being stuck in a stuffy boardroom with Uncle Willy frowning at him every time he shifted unhappily in his seat. The boat rocked side to side in the wake of all the other boats around them, and it was soothing, especially with the fresh air blowing across his face. Rios brushed wayward strands of blue hair out of his eyes and enjoyed watching the people on the other boats and the houses along the coast.

This was a great idea: one he should have thought of sooner. Rios let out a happy sigh, and the first smile he had felt like giving in days spread his cheeks.

Chapter Two

"It would appear my kits have decided to run away," William said as he approached Dane, who was relaxing at William's kitchen table after a long and rather pointless meeting.

The meetings were a necessary evil as far as Dane was concerned. The one relief from the very long day had been the brief interlude when William's kits had finally succumbed to boredom and acted out. The only kit Dane had ever met who didn't have issues sitting patiently was Nickel. Every other kit usually managed at most ten minutes before acting out. That William's kits had lasted most of the morning was impressive and spoke of a lot of hard work on William's part to teach them manners and good behavior.

Nickel was a special case. He had a particularly difficult childhood: one that had taught him patience and that hard work could be very effective. That was a lesson most kits never had to learn, but Nickel had embraced it. Which didn't explain why William's kits had hared off.

"You're certain?" he had to ask.

William let out a sigh. "Pretty certain." He dropped a piece of lined paper onto the table in front of Dane.

Went 2 se Nikle. B hom soon.

"That had to be Aqua," William said with a sigh. "He isn't interested in mastering writing or reading, but if I put a math problem in front of him, he finishes it so quickly that he's bored of math now too. Rios has his head on a little better, but not enough to dissuade Aqua from deciding to run away."

"Any idea of where they went?" Dane asked. He looked up from the letter—once again glad that between Mercury and himself, they had gotten all of their kits to high-school-level reading and writing—just in time to see William place a framed picture onto the table next to the letter.

The picture was actually a map that was particularly dusty. It was of North America and looked like it was from the very early 1800s, as only the Eastern Seaboard states and territories had defined borders while the rest was mostly blank. The dust was disturbed by what looked like fingerprints directly over the Great Lakes, tracing from approximately where William's house was located all the way down to where the map read Massachusetts, which as far as Dane could tell was all William's kits knew about Nickel's home address. The prints followed the water route the entire way.

"Why are they on the water? Wouldn't it be easier to fly?" Dane asked curiously.

William snorted. "Those two idiots always prefer to be on the water, even if it would be much more logical to fly. The only water dragon I've met who thinks differently is your Nickel."

"Nickel is a bit of an odd duck, but he's happy in his little mountain retreat with Platinum. He's also not about to get in a ton of trouble. Isn't Niagara Falls along that route?" Dane had to ask, tracing his own finger just above the disturbed dust line.

"Along with locks and other impediments that won't let two kids sail through without proper documentation," William added with a heavy sigh. "There was no forethought to this adventure of theirs. I thought I had taught them better than this."

"They're being kits. Did I ever tell you about the time Chrome and 'Ron knocked a tree down in my yard?" They were the two earth kits Dane had been taking care of with his partner, Mercury, for years. Chrome had always been a messy kit, prone to the same lack of forethought as William's kits. Admittedly, 'Ron was just as wild, but she had her lucid moments much more often than Chrome. "Chrome was building his first mine in my backyard about four years ago. He was probably going to get himself buried alive, but luckily I caught him before it escalated that far. He's going to be starting an apprenticeship with some dwarves this spring, once he's finished with high school, so that mistake turned out fairly well for him. That's how dragon kits figure out the world."

"I know that," William agreed. "I have tracking magic on them, of course, so I know they're still in Lake Huron, just north of the St. Clair River, and heading south. You think I should let them have their adventure and not go after them."

That wasn't a question, so Dane didn't bother answering. Kits only learned by making messes and experiencing the results, which William already knew. Aqua and Rios were due for a real shake-up anyway; hopefully, one that would lead them toward the rest of their lives, just like Chrome's had.

"I'm going to be keeping an eye on them, anyway. I would appreciate your backup if I need to mount a rescue."

"You have it," Dane replied easily, knowing William would agree to the same if it had been Dane in this situation. "I'll give Nickel a call to be ready, just in case your kits actually end up in Massachusetts instead of lost on the Hudson River or if they end up somewhere in the Atlantic."

"I'll most likely have to collect them before they get that far, but having Nickel prepared on the other end would be good. Thanks," William said sincerely.

Dane honestly never thought he would make friends with a rival territory leader, particularly one with William's reputation. To be able to control all of Canada like William did required a level of ruthlessness and power that ordinarily didn't mesh well with a rival like Dane. Their kits had given them something in common aside from their territories, and over the years, Dane had spent a great deal of time on the phone with William to gripe about the latest crazy scheme their kits had gotten up to much more often than about something to do with their territories.

It took a moment to dig his phone out of his pocket. William smiled at him before leaving the room to give Dane some privacy. Since Dane was planning on calling Mercury, too, to catch up because they hadn't seen each other all day, he appreciated the gesture, but first he had to warn Nickel that two of the most rambunctious kits he had ever met were heading in Nickel's direction.

Chapter Three

They had switched off around four o'clock when Aqua needed a break, so Rios was the one piloting the boat as dusk began to cast long shadows across the water. Luckily, some of the boats around them were heading in the same direction and had showed Rios where the river was that led farther south to the next big lake.

It was quickly getting too dark to see. A lot of the boats that had been in the water with their little rowboat had turned back to return home for the night, while most of the others had gone ahead, thanks to their electric lights. Rios passed a few more that had dropped anchor for the night.

"Why aren't we there yet?" Aqua whined, squinting through the long shadows cast by the trees around them, as if Nickel's home was just up ahead. Rios tried to picture the map in his mind and place them on it, which—if he had their positioning correct—said that they had just left the first big lake, the Bird Lake, and needed to still traverse the entirety of the Ghost Lake before they would finally reach the river that would take them across New York State and into Massachusetts.

A trip that had looked like it would only take a few hours on paper would probably take a few days in actuality. They needed a proper boat with lights, so they could continue sailing after dark, and it needed to be stuffed to the brim with food and blankets. The lunch they had packed had been yummy, but now they didn't have any food for dinner or breakfast, nor did they have any comfy beds to sleep in.

It had been years since Aqua and Rios had lived in the wild, and they had gotten comfortable with having a house with their own bedrooms and food available whenever they were hungry. Rios hadn't forgotten how to hunt for fish, but he also wasn't interested in getting wet at the moment. With the sun setting, it would be very cold to sit in the boat with damp clothes all night, and Rios didn't want to get sick on top of everything else.

"I don't think we're close yet," Rios told Aqua, trying to be gentle about it.

"But we've been sailing all day!" Aqua whined. "We have to be almost there. I'm hungry, and I'll bet Nickel has dinner waiting for us."

It was getting to be too hard to see as the sun dipped even lower in the sky. Without lights on the prow, it would be far too easy for another ship to hit them without realizing, so their safety was quickly becoming an issue.

"It's too dark to keep going tonight," Rios disagreed sharply. He turned the boat toward shore, where they could tie it to a low-hanging branch for the night and sleep in the bottom.

"Hopefully Nickel will have breakfast ready then," Aqua grumbled, luckily deciding not to argue with Rios. He helped Rios get the boat to shore and found a tree to tie the mooring rope around. There wasn't a lot of room in the bottom of the boat, but they managed to curl up. Rios watched the stars until exhaustion from a long day of using a lot of magic finally caught up with him, and he fell asleep.

Chapter Four

It was actually a pleasant night. It wasn't too cool in late summer, and the gentle rocking of their little craft was soothing. The hard wood of the boat itself wasn't exactly a pleasant surface to sleep on, but Rios wasn't using a rock or tree branch for a pillow like he had when they had still lived in the wild, so he couldn't really complain.

Rios drifted in and out of sleep, unable to stay asleep for more than an hour at a time. Aqua was sniffling softly, deep asleep and completely unaware of Rios's difficulties. Worrying wasn't something that had ever kept Aqua awake at night.

They had chosen a secluded space with no other boats nearby, so it was very quiet, except for the gentle lapping of the waves against the riverbanks. It took Rios a moment before he realized that rivers didn't lap unless they were being disturbed. It was the middle of the night, and Rios couldn't imagine who would be out on the water this late, especially since he didn't see any lights to indicate a boat. He was about to sit up to investigate when a dripping, wet hand latched onto the side of the rowboat next to the oarlock. It was quickly followed by a second hand, and then those hands levered the body they were attached to up and over the side of the boat. A young man about Rios's age fell to the bottom with a wet-sounding splat, right next to where Rios was curled up.

Rios quickly moved closer, and the boy looked up at him in surprise. His eyes were a shade of green so vibrant they almost seemed to glow in the dark, and they immediately mesmerized Rios, but they weren't entrancing enough that Rios missed the way the boy's long fish tail split in two and the scales receded into a pair of legs.

"What—" Rios began but instantly shut his mouth when the boy held one finger to his lips and his surprised look turned frantically worried. The boy rolled over so he could carefully peek over the side of the boat. Rios joined him a second later, lifting himself high enough that just his eyes were above the rim of wood.

There was a small motorboat in the middle of the river. It had its lights and motor off, and Rios thought he could see paddles awkwardly hanging from the side of the boat. Rios had no idea why someone with a perfectly good motorboat had instead decided to use paddles that weren't made to fit a boat like that. They weren't paddling now though. Rather, one man was standing tall in the middle of the boat, looking around like he was searching for something, while two other men heaved bundles over the side of the boat and gently let them down into the water with soft splashes. After about five minutes of watching, the men finished, and the two who were dumping things quickly moved to the oars. The boat slowly moved upstream, and only once it was a good hundred yards away did the motor rumble to life. In seconds, the boat was out of sight.

The boy looked both ways briefly before abruptly standing and jumping over the side of the boat. Rios wasn't about to let him go without explaining the mystery, so he kicked off his shoes and carefully climbed after him into the water.

His night vision wasn't great, but the day's silt and muck had settled most of the night and the dropped boxes hadn't stirred up too much, so he was able to make out the boy's tail heading deeper into the water where the men had dumped their cargo.

Rios wasn't going to catch up in his human form. It took a moment of thought to shift forms, and then he dove deep as a dragon with four paws and a strong tail to propel him at a much faster pace. He caught up with the boy in moments, who looked over at Rios with surprise in his eyes. He didn't jump or run away, although Rios thought that might only be because he was on a mission.

All of the dropped bundles had settled on the base of the river in the dirt and rocks. They looked like square boxes that had been carefully wrapped in plastic to keep them watertight. A long length of string that waved lazily in the water connected them all. Sitting on the surface was a clear water bottle, filled only with air and carefully sealed with the string knotted around the neck. It wasn't doing anything to keep the bundles in place since the string was so long, but it probably served as a good signaling buoy for whoever had to collect them. There was no indication of what the bundles actually were, but that didn't stop the boy from gripping the string and pulling them toward shore.

The boy wasn't going to get very far with only his tail for leverage, Rios could see. He swam forward and wrapped one curled paw around the rope just above where the boy was gripping and added his strength. The bundles moved quickly after that. It wasn't long before they had all of it pushed up onto the bank of the river. The boy clambered out, and Rios watched again as his tail split down the middle and his legs emerged. That probably had to be the coolest thing Rios had ever seen.

His body as a dragon was far too large, so Rios returned to human form and climbed out of the river after the boy. Together, they lifted all the bundles out of the water and pulled them up the bank until they were hidden by the trees.

"What's going on?" Rios whispered as he and the boy together carried the last and heaviest bundle.

"Drug smugglers," the boy hissed. "One group comes from Canada and drops off the drugs. Another comes from the US to pick them up. They're fouling the river and scaring off all the fish." He spat in disgust, but his eyes were bright with purpose and reflected his happiness at thwarting tonight's attempt to smuggle drugs. He looked so focused.

Rios couldn't remember a time in his life when he had any sense of purpose. He spent his days playing with Aqua, except when Uncle Willy made them study or do chores. Even their little jaunt to Nickel's house had been done without much forethought. Rios had only wanted to escape the boredom of Uncle Willy's meeting—he hadn't thought any further beyond that point. That was why he and Aqua were stuck on the riverbank for the night: hungry, tired, and most likely very lost.

On the other hand, the boy was the exact opposite. He had made a solid plan, executed it, and he looked unbelievably pleased with himself. Rios was jealous. He couldn't think of a time when he had ever wanted to execute a carefully laid plan, but now Rios found himself regretting that lack. He wanted to feel what this other boy felt. Rios also wanted to know what the other boy was.

"Are you a mermaid?"

The boy lifted one eyebrow as if to say "Are you an idiot?" and Rios felt his face flush in embarrassment.

"Those salt-water-addled jerks wouldn't be caught dead in a freshwater lake," the boy replied scathingly. "Besides, I'm a man, not a maid."

"Then what are you?" Rios asked, unwilling to allow himself to be put off by the boy's harsh tone.

"I'm a nix; a water shape-shifter," the boy replied, his voice slightly mocking as if Rios should have already known that. Yet, Rios thought he caught a slight defensiveness in the way his shoulders were stiffened around his ears—ears that Rios was now noticing had two points, like the fins of a fish.

"Do you have a name?" Rios continued kindly, hoping he would stop frightening the boy. "My name is Rios. It's not my birth name, but I couldn't remember that when Uncle Willy found my brother and me, so Uncle Willy named me Rios and my brother Aqua."

"Never had anyone to give me a name," the boy said gruffly.

They dropped the last bundle with the others and then stood side by side for a few moments as they shook out sore arms. The boy's green eyes were lowered, as if he couldn't make himself look at Rios after admitting that. It was too dark to see much else, aside from the fact that the boy was naked and his body was very pretty.

"Well, I'm going to call you Nixie, because I think it's cute, and you're cute to match," Rios said finally. He opened his mouth to say more, but Nixie suddenly held out a hand to stop his words. His head was tilted slightly toward the river, and after a moment of listening, Rios also heard the light splashing of oars in the water. It must be the people from the US side of the border coming to collect the goods.

Nixie crouched down among the trees, and Rios quickly followed suit. From his vantage, Rios couldn't see the boat or whoever was on it, but he could hear the curses.

"Bottle must have come loose," Rios heard a man say. "We'll have to come back in daylight to find it before the cops do."

"Let's get out of here, then," a second man said. The engine roared to life a second later, and the boat sped off.

Nixie stayed crouched for a few more moments before standing and starting to walk back toward the river. Rios hurried to follow.

"They're going to be back, and they're going to realize you moved the drugs," Rios said sharply as he fell into step next to Nixie.

"I know that," Nixie said with a sigh, "but I'm going to keep taking their drugs from the river until they give up and move on. It's the only option I have."

"But, Nixie," Rios began. He wasn't certain what he wanted to say, only that he felt like something wasn't quite right with that statement, but Nixie spun on him suddenly and poked him in the chest with one long finger.

"I am a nix, not 'Nixie.' You can't just make up a name like that!"

"Aqua and I are Aquarius," Rios replied with a shrug. "Uncle Willy said it fit us, since we were accidentally trying to destroy a dam when he found us. I think Nixie works perfectly for you."

"Are all dragons idiots?" Nixie asked sharply. His green eyes were blazing in the night like two lightbulbs set in his beautiful face.

Rios had to nod an affirmative answer. "Nickel's not an idiot, but I think I am and Aqua probably is too. We ran away from home because we were bored, and now we're stuck in a silly rowboat for the night. But I liked helping you fight the bad guys," Rios went on quickly when Nixie scoffed at him. "Can I keep helping you? We can come up with a better plan than just hiding the drugs."

"Go home to Mommy before you get hurt," Nixie said, his voice scathing. He turned away from Rios as if that dismissal would be enough to get Rios to go away. Clearly, he didn't know anything about dragons.

"I haven't got a mommy. It's just Uncle Willy, me, and Aqua. You could come home with us though. If you wanted. Uncle Willy has lots of rooms in his house, and I'm sure he wouldn't mind you staying."

"I'm a nix, Rios," Nixie cut in. "No one wants a creature known for drowning people and bewitching them with song to live with them!"

Rios shrugged. "Uncle Willy won't care about that."

Nixie's disbelieving snort told Rios what he thought about that. Rios tried to come up with another argument. He had no idea why he was so desperate to stay with Nixie, but he really, really wanted to. Even more than he wanted to stay with Aqua and Uncle Willy. Something about Nixie just seemed so intriguing, and Rios wanted to learn more about him so very badly.

In that brief moment of silence, Rios heard a soft *putt-putt* noise that had him grabbing for Nixie and pulling them both to the ground. They were exposed at the river's edge, but hopefully in the dark, the oncoming boat wouldn't see them.

Nixie gripped Rios's arm with strong fingers, holding tight as if Rios was a lifeline that would keep him safe from harm. Rios liked that feeling, and he couldn't help carefully wrapping his arm over Nixie's shoulder to hold him close while they waited for the boat to go by.

Rios could just barely make it out at this point. It was larger than the smugglers' motorboats, but it made far less noise. The boat was also running without lights, so Rios knew it wasn't up to anything good. He and Nixie stayed as still as they could as the boat slowly drifted past, heading upstream.

To Rios's horror, he heard a soft rustling noise from the nearby rowboat. Aqua, who could sleep through just about anything, was waking up. Rios mentally willed him to stay down and stay quiet, but Aqua had zero sense of place. Aqua sat up in the boat, rubbing his eyes as he looked around.

"What's going on?" In the quiet of the night, his voice seemed to echo.

Lights immediately turned on, so bright they were blinding. A spotlight focused on Aqua right away, and after a moment of men shouting to each other, a second light settled directly on Rios and Nixie.

"Put your hands up!" a voice called over the loudspeaker. Two smaller boats deployed from the big one. One headed over to Aqua, and the other ran aground right next to Nixie and Rios. Men hopped out of the boat and surrounded them.

"Hi?" Rios tried calling out.

"Put your hands up! Hands in the air!"

They were holding guns and looked unbelievably scary in black flack vests and uniforms. It was the uniforms that had Rios looking at them more closely, which was when he saw the little Canadian flag sewn in a patch on one sleeve.

"Rios? Rios?" Aqua called desperately, tears audible in his voice.

"I'm here, Aqua," Rios called as he slowly lifted his hands into the air. "Just do what they say."

"In the boat," one of the men surrounding them insisted sharply. "On your feet. Get into the boat."

Rios obeyed, carefully standing and walking toward the boat. Nixie had no choice but to follow him. The faces of the men and women went from stern and focused to consternated the second they realized Nixie was naked.

Rios climbed into the boat first, aided by a man who gripped his arm and helped him get up and over the side. Nixie was forced to wait in line, and Rios watched as Nixie faked a stumble and fell to his knees in the lake. It took half a second for his tail to reemerge, and with one powerful flip, he dove deep into the water. Rios clambered into the boat and hurried to the other side, but Nixie was nowhere to be seen.

"I'll come back, Nixie!" Rios called, hoping Nixie would be able to hear him beneath the water. "Just stay safe until then!"

The small boats headed back to the larger one, and Rios was helped aboard and led to a seat. A man stood over him with his gun in hand, so Rios stayed quiet. A few minutes later, the boat sped off.

It didn't take long to reach their destination: a long dock cut into the shoreline with a half-dozen mooring posts. The boat pulled up to one and was safely tied off, and then Rios was escorted onto the dock and into a squat building a few feet away.

Rios couldn't see Aqua, since Rios was in front, but he heard Aqua's miserable sniffles behind him. There wasn't time to comfort Aqua; they reached the building too fast, and once inside, Rios was shuttled to the left and Aqua to the right. They put Rios in a holding room. It had a small table, two chairs, and a long mirror, just like the interrogation rooms he had seen on TV. He was alone for the moment, but he had no idea who might be watching him through the mirror.

Instead of bothering to ask questions or complain, he sank into a chair and let out a yawn. Rios very much wanted to whine at the top of his lungs, since being stuck in a holding room while wearing wet clothes, and while knowing Nixie was all alone in the river with the drugs they had stolen wasn't fun. An entire night with no sleep was starting to take its toll, but he also knew he had to get back to the river and to Nixie's side. The drug smugglers had said they would be back, once it got light, to search the river again, and Nixie was still in harm's way. The only way to get out of the room quickly was to convince the people who had taken him that they needed to let him go, and Rios only knew of one person with the power to do that.

He only had to wait a few minutes before two women entered the room. One was wearing a suit and looked slightly rumpled, as if she had been pulled abruptly out of bed for this. The other was wearing a uniform that read "Canadian Coast Guard" on a patch across her chest.

"We are required by law to provide council for minors," the woman in the uniform explained. "I'm Officer Moore, and this is Ms. Jan. Can you tell us why you were on the river last night?"

"I need to call my uncle," Rios replied firmly. Uncle Willy would get him out of the interrogation room and back to Nixie much faster than telling these women about his night.

The women shared a look at his words, and then the officer pulled a cell phone out of her pocket with a sigh. "Go ahead and give him a call. Then we want you to answer our questions."

Rios took the phone without replying and swiftly typed in Uncle Willy's cell phone number. It rang three times before it picked up.

"Hi," Rios said when the line connected.

"Do you know how much trouble you're in?" Uncle Willy asked, his voice sharp with disapproval. He didn't sound at all groggy like he had been woken up by Rios's call, so he had apparently had a sleepless night too. That sent a strange pang of shame through Rios, an emotion he had never actually acknowledged before.

"Probably a lot," Rios admitted. "We've been picked up by the Canadian Coast Guard. Can you come take us home?"

Uncle Willy let out a heavy sigh. "At least you're not calling to say you accidentally destroyed Detroit," he grumbled. "All right, where are you?"

"Um..." Rios pulled the phone away from his ear to talk to the women. "Can you give Uncle Willy the address?"

Officer Moore took the phone from Rios and held it to her ear. She rattled off an address, listened briefly, and then hung up. She opened her mouth, no doubt to keep asking him questions, but the sound of running feet outside the door and then a knock had her closing her mouth again. She stood to go answer the door.

A man was standing on the other side looking frantic. "A man is here, claiming to be their guardian. You're going to want to see him right now."

"Why?" Officer Moore asked tersely.

"Because it's William Armistead," the man gasped out.

Officer Moore glanced briefly at Rios in surprise before nodding and hurrying out the door. She was only gone for five minutes, during which time Rios sat silently with Ms. Jan, and when Officer Moore returned, she had Uncle Willy with her.

"We believe he was entranced by a siren, sir," she said deferentially to Uncle Willy.

"Well, Rios?" Uncle Willy asked him sharply. "You're in enough trouble as it is. Answer the officer's questions."

Rios sighed, but obeyed. "I was entranced, Uncle Willy. Nixie's so pretty. But he's also in lots of trouble. He's been stealing the drugs the bad men are leaving in the river and hiding them, but the bad men are coming back to look for them today, and they're going to find Nixie and hurt him!"

Uncle Willy studied Rios for a long moment, no doubt taking in Rios's damp clothes and the earnest expression on his face. Then a small smile lifted the corner of his mouth, and Rios relaxed in relief.

"Would you please show me on a map where on the St. Clair River you picked them up? I believe we might have a rescue mission to organize."

"Thank you, Uncle Willy!" Rios gasped out. He jumped up from his chair to give Uncle Willy a hug, which Uncle Willy returned.

"You're still in a lot of trouble. No candy for two weeks, and you and Aqua will be getting extra chores every day. Plus, I'm getting you a better tutor, one who won't allow either of you to ever leave me a note with so many misspellings on it."

Rios deflated a little under Uncle Willy's admonition, but it also gave him an idea. "Do you think the tutor would be able to get me into a school for the coast guard?" he asked. "Nixie's been working hard to protect the river, and I really liked that. The coast guard protects the river too, right? So maybe I could do that?"

"Maybe you could. We'll have to research the requirements and see what you need to accomplish to be eligible, but first let's collect Aqua and see about finding a map so you can go find your Nixie."

Chapter Five

The coast guard owned a nondescript boat and had men and women out of uniform to pilot it. One look from Uncle Willy had Officer Moore promising him the full resources of the coast guard to go find Nixie, which was really nice of her. Also, Uncle Willy could be that scary, but Rios was firmly hoping to avoid having Uncle Willy be scary. They just needed to get back to the river where Nixie was hiding before the bad men came back for their drugs.

Apparently the boat was usually used for camouflage. It had three fishing poles hanging over the back end and was called *Flower of the Deep*, according to the bright and flowery writing along the side.

The sun was rising already by the time Rios was allowed to walk out of the building where he and Aqua were being held. The boat was ready and waiting, stocked to look like it was going on an early morning fishing trip, and Rios eagerly scrambled on board.

Officer Moore had taken a few moments to change out of her uniform. She climbed onto the boat after Rios and took a seat next to him.

"Your uncle isn't joining us?" she asked curiously.

Rios shook his head. "Aqua needed a bath and to get to bed, so Uncle Willy took him home. He said between the coast guard and me, we'll be able to save Nixie."

Uncle Willy was putting a lot of trust on Rios, and in some ways, it weighed him down. Yet, at the same time, Rios had never felt freer. With the weight of responsibility keeping him grounded, he felt like he might be able to fly even higher. He had never thought about it that way before, and even now, his brain tried to automatically shy away from the idea. What if—and it wasn't fun to think about it this way—but what if all the chores and homework Uncle Willy had forced them to do over the years were more about teaching Rios responsibility than about punishing him? It was a radical thought, one he knew Aqua wouldn't share and he was struggling just to acknowledge, but one he thought Nickel might heartily agree with.

"We will certainly try our best," Officer Moore replied firmly. "The coast guard is very interested in catching the drug smugglers and doing whatever we can to keep your friend safe."

The boat rumbled to life a moment later, the engine loud enough that they couldn't continue talking. Rios shifted around so he was facing forward and carefully watched the shoreline as they headed downriver.

It was still really early in the morning, so they didn't pass any other boats as they went. Birds were just starting to chirp their morning songs, although they all fell silent as the fishing boat sped past. It hadn't taken long to reach the base last night, so Rios wasn't surprised when he saw the disturbed mud along the bank where the coast guard had landed their boat to grab him after only ten minutes of travel. Nixie was nowhere in sight.

The boat slowed to a stop, and Officer Moore and another man went to the fishing lines to pretend to check them and then drop the lines into the water. Rios crept to the side of the boat where he could look down into the water to try to catch a glimpse of Nixie.

"Nixie," he called, hoping Nixie would hear him. "Nixie, are you there?" No one answered.

The coast guard let the boat idle, drifting along with the current while Rios continued to call out Nixie's name. The sun was rising higher in the sky, and pretty soon other boaters would be out on the water. The smugglers had said they would be back today, but they couldn't wait too long or there would be people around to see them.

A half hour went by, but it felt like hours and hours to Rios, who just wanted to find Nixie before it was too late. The sun rose quickly, and with it, the opportunity for the smugglers to return in secret faded. When Rios heard the engine of the first of what would be dozens of day boats coming closer from down the river, Rios realized the smugglers weren't coming and Nixie was safely hiding. It was too late in the day to catch any smugglers. Officer Moore apparently thought the same thing, because she walked over to Rios and put a gentle hand on his shoulder.

"It's too late to find him today," she said softly. "My men and I need to secure the stash of drugs you and Nixie hid yesterday. We can come back here tomorrow morning if you would like to search some more. I'll have patrols doubled on this stretch of the river for the next few nights as well."

Rios nodded sadly. He had been so certain Nixie would be waiting for him. As aloof as Nixie had appeared, he had also seemed to be really lonely. Having Rios with him to hide the drugs had been fun, Rios knew, and he had to give Nixie a chance to lower his protective shields and let Rios in. At least, Rios hoped he might be given that chance.

"I'll come back tomorrow, Nixie," Rios whispered to the water before stepping back from the edge so they could get the boat ready to move again.

The other boat he had been hearing drew close and then sped up. It was a small, flat-bottomed motorboat—the same as last night. In the back of the boat, covered by heavy rope netting, was something very green—a very familiar shade of green.

"Nixie?" Rios yelled.

"Rios!" Nixie replied immediately and then gasped in pain when one of the men on board the ship kicked him.

"Nixie!" Rios screamed. His friend was in trouble! He kicked off his shoes, which had been recovered from the abandoned rowboat by the coast guard, and leaped up onto the edge of the fishing boat. He threw his body into the air and called on the magic that allowed him to change forms. He could swim fast, but not as fast as that boat. He could fly that quickly though, so he kept to the air as he chased after Nixie, flapping his wings furiously. The coast guard fishing boat's engine roared to life behind him, but the ship was too large to be able to keep up.

The men on the small boat caught sight of him almost instantly. They swore, and the boat suddenly started swerving back and forth across the lake, turning sharply to evade him and making Rios have to dive after it. One of the men pointed his gun in Rios's direction, and Rios dodged, plunging down to skim the water with his claws before throwing his body upward again. He was gaining on the boat slowly but surely, and he could see Nixie's frightened green eyes peeking out from between the heavy rope netting keeping him captive. The sight of Nixie bound and afraid only made Rios beat his wings even harder.

Finally, he got close enough. With one last powerful pump of his wings, Rios positioned himself over the boat. He dropped down fast before anyone could bring their guns around and landed hard on the aft of the motorboat with a thud, crouching protectively over Nixie as the boat shuddered and sank with the addition of his weight.

The men were swearing and they turned their guns toward him, but Rios had magic and was ready for them. He called on the water in the river, and it answered him swiftly. A wave grew to one side of the boat, frothing and thundering with his power. He directed it to splash down with a bruising impact that cracked across the boat. Men were thrown into the river, and the boat began to list as it took on water. The remaining foam washed harmlessly over Rios and Nixie. Rios carefully got his front claws around Nixie, and the ropes holding Nixie captive, and pumped his wings until they were airborne and well away from the men and their guns.

A glance downward showed the coast guard's fishing boat was busy pulling the men out of the water. Officer Moore was handcuffing one of the men while also keeping an eye on Rios. She looked grimly satisfied and nodded at him when she saw he was all right.

Rios headed toward the riverbank that he and Nixie had huddled on the night before. He gently placed Nixie down onto the soft ground, then landed and swiftly shifted forms so he had hands to help pull the netting off Nixie. The second Nixie fought free, he threw his arms around Rios and let out a gasping sob.

"I'm sorry it took me so long to find you," Rios said, his arms circling Nixie in a comforting hug as Nixie started crying into his shoulder. "I had to explain everything to Uncle Willy first, and then he had to convince the coast guard to bring me back here. How did they catch you?"

"I was trying to move the drugs somewhere better, but they must have heard me," Nixie explained into Rios's shoulder, where his face was pressed. "Next thing I know, they have a net over me and are yanking me onto their boat, yelling about retribution and all sorts of nasty things. I'm so glad you came back."

"Of course I did," Rios replied softly, tightening his hug and running one of his hands down Nixie's very green hair. It was the same shade of green as his eyes, a vibrant emerald color that Rios wanted to bury his hands in forever.

"You kids want a ride?" Officer Moore called. Rios pulled away from Nixie slowly, but didn't release his arms, so Nixie was kept safe with him.

"Do you want to come with me, or do you want to stay here?" Rios asked, hoping there wasn't too much pleading in his voice. He really, really wanted Nixie to come home with him, but he couldn't demand or force him. The weight of responsibility he was just learning to bear said so.

"Will your uncle really be okay with me?" Nixie asked, sounding hesitant and unsure of his welcome. Rios immediately nodded his head up and down as emphatically as he knew how. "Then, is it okay if I try living with you for a while?"

"Yes!" Rios replied excitedly.

"Let me go get my stuff," Nixie said. He extracted himself from Rios's arms and jumped back into the water. Rios stood on the riverbank and watched the water while Officer Moore waited for an answer.

"I think he's coming home with me," Rios told her, "so we won't need a ride. Thanks for all your help."

"The coast guard is supposed to help, especially when William Armistead asks for a favor. Kid, if you're interested in joining the coast guard, you're going to have to learn a little more about boats. You won't always be able to fly or swim everywhere."

Rios nodded. "Thanks for the advice." He would have to pester Uncle Willy for a boat to practice with. Although, Rios didn't know if he should get one with sails or one with a motor. Maybe both. He'd have to see what Uncle Willy said first.

He caught sight of Nixie's green hair coming up from beneath the shimmering water. A moment later, he emerged carrying a sodden backpack.

"Ready?" Rios asked him.

Nixie smiled and nodded, drawing close and then tentatively reaching out to take Rios's hand. "What am I in for?" Nixie asked as his fingers gently squeezed against Rios's.

That question had Rios grimacing, because he had forgotten to warn Nixie. "Well, there's me and Aqua, of course. We have the run of any of Uncle Willy's houses."

"Houses, as in more than one?" Nixie gaped at Rios, as if he was wondering just what he had gotten himself into.

"Uncle Willy is the territory leader of Canada," Rios admitted. "He has a house in every province."

"The territory leader?" Nixie said with a sudden squeak in his voice. His beautiful eyes were wide in shock, but his hand was still tight in Rios's.

"There's also a maid and whatever tutors Uncle Willy hired," Rios rushed on before Nixie got overwhelmed, except then he had to admit who else was currently at Uncle Willy's house. "Uncle Willy's in the middle of a meeting right now though," he began slowly. "All the territory leaders are currently at the house for a few more days."

"All of them!" Nixie squeaked again.

"Well, you'll have to meet Dane, of course. He's the territory leader of the Northeast in the US, and Aqua and I end up at his house a lot for sleepovers. He's really nice."

"The Genie of the East," Nixie gasped out, giving one of Dane's names that meant Nixie had heard of how powerful he was. "Maybe I'll go back to the river instead."

"It'll be fun, I promise. And if you need to run away, I'll run with you. Okay?"

Nixie was quiet for a long moment, just looking at Rios as if the answers to all his questions and worries were written on Rios's face. Rios honestly hoped that Nixie liked Uncle Willy and Dane and Nickel. He wanted Nixie to feel at home in his home. Rios had never felt this way about anyone or anything before. It was a new sensation coming to him as strongly as his new responsibility. The responsibility he could take or leave. The weight of that was as heavy as it was freeing and letting it go every once in a while would be a lot of fun. By the same token, he never, ever wanted to let Nixie go.

"Okay," Nixie said, apparently coming to a conclusion, because he squeezed Rios's hand again. "I've never had a home before, either, so this should be another fun adventure."

"All right! Let's go home, Nixie. Uncle Willy, we're ready!"

"Hey! Who said I agreed to be called Nixie?"

Magic flared around them, and with a tug, Rios's feet left the ground as the world swirled around him and Uncle

Willy's magic called them home. Nixie's hand was warm and secure in his the entire time until the magic finally released them just inside the front door.

"I think the name Nixie is as cute as you are," Rios insisted for a second time. "Welcome home."

Nixie looked around the large foyer of Uncle Willy's Ontario house, and a small smile lifted his lips. "It's good to have a home."

Epilogue

"I think you win for strangest kit," Dane muttered softly to William as he studied the two kits standing awkwardly by the front door.

He knew Rios already, of course, yet there was something different about him. It was a bit cliché to say he was standing taller with his shoulders back, but it was the best description Dane could come up with. Rios and Aqua had always looked like children rather than the young adults they were growing up to be. That was actually fairly normal for dragons. They were immortal creatures in terms of number of years they could live, but most dragons were killed too young, thanks to the difficult living situations they had to endure. Staying young was a defense mechanism of sorts for them. Being smaller meant they didn't need to find more to eat to sustain them in the wild, and they were less yummy-looking to other predators. They were faster and could live in smaller dens too.

When they reached the age of adulthood, dragons had the capacity to continue growing, but most didn't right away. It took an emotional push to get them to take that step, and Dane thought Rios might have made that decision. He had to applaud Rios for that.

The young man standing next to Rios was a different matter entirely. He was completely naked and very, very pretty for a youth his age. His green hair practically glowed in the sunlight coming in the front windows. Aside from the hair—which conceivably could have been dyed— he looked like an ordinary fifteen-year-old boy. Except he followed Rios farther into the house, and despite the fact that he appeared to be completely dry, he left behind wet footprints as he walked.

"I can see a lot of mopping in my future," William replied with a sigh.

He didn't disagree with Dane's assessment of having an odd kit. None of Dane's kits had gone out on an adventure and brought home a nix. At least, none of them had yet. So far, Nickel had mated with Platinum, a fellow dragon. Dane was pretty certain Copper and Zinc, two of his other kits, were mates as well, although they were still too busy trying to kill each other to have figured that out. Two more of his kits, 'Ron and Chrome, were most likely also mates, but they also weren't ready to take that step. His last two kits, Lumie and Alloy, were still too young for it to be a possibility yet, but he also had some suspicions there. A nix was definitely far outside of anything his kits had ever brought home, and that included Lumie's demon cat, Cinnamon.

The truth of it was that Rios looked happy. A dragon always knew who their mate was, and Dane had zero doubt that Rios had found his.

"I think I'm also going to have to renovate the indoor pool at my main house. Turn it into a freshwater space with some fish and plants for the nix. He's not going to be happy only living in a dry environment, even with Rios." William didn't look particularly upset at the added expense. Dane knew he could afford it, and he was probably just happy to have one of his wild kits settle down, no matter whom it was with. Besides, a water dragon kit with a nix did make some sense in terms of compatibility. And, again, Rios looked happy, which was what was really important to William anyway.

"Shall we go meet this nix, maybe find out his name?" Dane asked.

William took in a slow breath, then let it out. He was nervous to meet the person who Rios had chosen for himself, Dane realized.

"Once he gets over the fact that you're the territory leader, I'm sure he'll like you," Dane insisted, trying to soothe William's nerves. "You'll see."

William nodded in reply before resolutely turning toward the stairs that would lead him toward Rios and his mate. "Let's go welcome them home."

Part Two

Dragon Home

Chapter One

There was a mermaid in the pool. Aqua growled to himself and stomped past the indoor pool toward the kitchen. There wasn't anything he could do about the mermaid, mostly because he had been living in the pool for months now and didn't appear to be the least bit interested in leaving.

Okay, so the mermaid wasn't actually a mermaid. They lived in saltwater oceans and wouldn't have anything to do with a dragon or the confines of an Olympic-sized swimming pool. The creature in the pool was a nix named Nixie, with bright-green hair and a fish tail that split into legs when he was on dry land. He was also mated with Aqua's brother, Rios.

Rios was another problem that made Aqua stomp his feet even harder. It just wasn't fair.

Uncle Willy was sitting at the kitchen table reading the newspaper and eating a bowl of cereal when Aqua stomped into the room. He glanced up at Aqua briefly, then returned to his paper without noticing Aqua's mood. Uncle Willy was a very powerful man. He was the territory leader of all of Canada, a responsibility he took far too seriously in Aqua's opinion. He had the look of a man who had been fat, but had recently lost a lot of weight. His skin was still a little too fleshy, although every day there was some improvement. He was immortal, which meant he would eventually heal even the stretch marks and excess skin that being overweight for so long had caused. His eyes were as hard black as coal, and his hair was also black but with a softer wave to it.

Rios was washing his own bowl at the sink. He had grown two inches over the winter, which meant he and Aqua could no longer share clothing and were also no longer mistaken for twins. Rios looked years older than Aqua now, his face filled out and muscles tightening the fabric of his shirts. Aqua, on the other hand, looked like he was twelve, despite being nearly sixteen years old, and hadn't grown even a centimeter all winter.

Aqua stopped in the middle of the kitchen, and Rios turned and smiled at him, but when Rios spoke, it was to Uncle Willy. "The auxiliaries are training on sailboats today and have invited Nixie and me to come play. We'll need a ride to Lake St. Clair in ten minutes."

Uncle Willy nodded. "Do you know how long you'll be there?"

"At least until lunch, although if they feed us, we may stay until dinner instead." Rios shrugged and grinned, and Aqua had to clench his teeth. That was the grin he remembered, one that Rios used to only use when they were up to some sort of mischief together. It wasn't right that Rios was so excited about the coast guard and some silly boats. He hadn't been so excited before he'd found Nixie, which meant that Nixie was the problem. Yet the way Rios looked at Nixie, the way they held hands and smiled at each other, meant that if Aqua did something to separate them, Rios might hate him forever. He really didn't want Rios to keep abandoning him like this. Yet getting rid of the problem might only make it all even worse.

Aqua hated feeling so left behind.

"Don't forget you have that essay due," Uncle Willy added pointedly.

Rios grinned again. "I don't know what you're talking about," he replied slyly. "See you tonight!"

He hurried off without saying goodbye to Aqua, no doubt going to find his precious Nixie and then get Uncle Willy to transport them magically to the training facility. Which meant Aqua would be spending the day alone again, except for the endless lines of tutors Uncle Willy had hired to get him up to speed on his schoolwork.

"It's not fair," Aqua grumbled, only realizing he had said that aloud when Uncle Willy dipped one corner of his newspaper to look at Aqua. "Well, it's not. He's off having fun with his friends, and I'm stuck here with the tutors."

Uncle Willy put down his paper so he could look at Aqua properly. "Aqua, if you want friends, you need to go out and find them. They're not going to come to you."

"But when Rios was here, we had each other. Why did he have to leave?" Aqua was whining, but he couldn't help it. The feeling of being abandoned tightened his chest until he couldn't breathe, and made his stomach hurt so that he didn't feel like eating.

"Maybe it's your time to leave as well. Pack some clothes, food, and money and see where the wind takes you. Go find friends of your own, and maybe you won't feel quite so alone any longer."

Maybe Uncle Willy was right. He should just go. On their last adventure together, Rios had found Nixie and his love of boats. Maybe now it was Aqua's turn to have an adventure and find a nix of his own. He spun around and hurried out of the kitchen, heading upstairs to his bedroom to pack a bag.

It only took a few moments to stuff some shirts, pants, and underwear into a backpack. Aqua hurried back downstairs, meeting Uncle Willy at the foot. In one hand he held out a wad of cash. Aqua could see both American and Canadian money in the stack.

"For emergencies," Uncle Willy instructed as he passed over the money. "Don't lose it or spend it on something silly." He held out a small brown paper bag for Aqua to also take. "This is some lunch. Eat it on your way." He reached behind him for a paper-towel-wrapped bagel to give to Aqua too. "And eat your breakfast."

"Thanks, Uncle Willy," Aqua said as he took the bagel. He stuffed the money deep into his bag and tucked his lunch carefully on top.

"Be safe, Aqua," Uncle Willy said firmly. "If you leave Canada, I can't physically come for you if you get in trouble, but I can sneak a transportation spell into most territories. Dane can, too, if you have better luck getting in contact with him. Stay out of Texas though. That territory leader won't welcome you."

Uncle Willy wasn't the hugging type, but he did pat Aqua on the shoulder and give him an encouraging smile. Aqua grinned in return before hoisting his bag onto his back and heading out the front door.

It was absolutely freezing outside, with an icy wind blowing around the feet-high drifts of snow that covered every surface. It was early spring, but the temperatures wouldn't rise much in this part of Canada for at least another month. He shifted forms smoothly, the transition from human to dragon as effortless as breathing. It was considerably warmer with his scales covering him. Aqua gripped his bag in one paw and tossed the bagel in his now much larger mouth with the other. He chewed and swallowed before jumping into the air. A few pumps of his massive wings had him soaring upward.

Where could he go to find friends anyway? North was way too cold; even his scales would freeze off if he went any farther in that direction. He had also spent plenty of time gamboling around at Uncle Willy's houses to the east and west. It had to be south, but where in the south? Aqua had absolutely no idea.

He flew even higher, until the ice in the clouds began to coat his wings. He kept going until the clouds were just below him and he could see absolutely forever in every single direction. The winds this high up were intense, blowing in every direction to varying strengths. He found one heading south, spread his wings in the current, and let the wind sweep him away wherever it happened to blow.

Chapter Two

Aqua's stomach rumbling broke him out of his reverie. He had gone into a sort of trance as he flew, one where he didn't have to think and his body knew what to do to keep him aloft without him actually paying attention. He didn't know how many hours he had been flying, but it was long enough that the bagel was gone. Now was as good a time as any to stop for lunch, so Aqua angled his flight slowly downward.

There weren't any clouds below or above him, just blue sky as far as the eye could see and tan, sandy ground far beneath him. He took his time drifting down. The air was very warm, and there were nice thermals lifting his wings. He could have flown for miles without flapping his wings once, but another rumble in his stomach said he ought to take a break.

He must be in a desert somewhere, although he couldn't say where exactly. It was rocky, with low scrub that was more brown than green. Aqua couldn't sense any water anywhere nearby. He found a flat place to land and shifted forms.

The sun was hot on his exposed skin. It was such a contrast to the very snowy environment he had just left.

Aqua couldn't say it was a nice change, but he liked having something different to look at. He unhooked the backpack from around his arm, set it down, and then sat next to it so he could pull out the paper bag Uncle Willy had given him. There were three sandwiches inside and three water bottles. Aqua took out one of each and stuck the paper bag back in his backpack before unwrapping the sandwich and digging in.

Uncle Willy had made him a turkey sandwich thick with mayo and light on the veggies. It tasted like home, and suddenly Aqua knew that no matter where this adventure might lead, he would return home. Uncle Willy, Rios, and even Nixie would be waiting for him.

He finished his sandwich and water, stuffed his trash in an outside pocket of his backpack, and stood. Aqua stretched his arms above his head, staring through his fingers at the very blue sky overhead. The desert really was beautiful, but without any water to play with, it wasn't somewhere he wanted to stay. The air was dry as he sighed out a heavy breath and far too hot for the nap he felt like taking with his full stomach weighing him down. He would keep flying for a few more hours, Aqua decided, and find a good place to sleep for the night.

Aqua reached for the magic that allowed him to change forms, felt a sharp pain at the back of his head, and knew no more. His human body fell back on the hard ground, unconscious.

Chapter Three

"I've done it again," William breathed desperately into the phone. Dane pulled his phone away from his ear to check the caller ID, saw that it was the William he was friends with, and put the phone back to his ear. "I made Aqua run away. What if he hates me for it?"

Had William kicked Aqua out of the house? Dane was missing some important information.

"Start at the beginning, William," he said gently, aware of the touch of panic in William's voice and not wanting to antagonize him further.

"Ever since we finally got Nixie settled, he and Rios have been running off just about every day. The coast guard auxiliary allows sixteen-year-olds to train with them as long as they have a parent's consent, and Rios and Nixie were close enough to that age so when I asked, the auxiliary couldn't say no. It's been a struggle to get them to stay home long enough for the tutor to teach them anything, but even that has changed. Nixie came to me completely ignorant. He couldn't read, write, or do basic math, but in a few months, he's already learned more than Aqua and Rios knew after ten years. And Rios suddenly started applying himself too. He might actually graduate on time! Can you believe that?"

Given how quickly Dane's kit Platinum was learning, he could believe it. Platinum was an air dragon they had rescued from some scientists doing terrible experiments on him, and he had mated to Nickel, another of Dane's dragon kits. He would probably test as a genius if he were interested in actually finding out, but he was happy working with Nickel at Dane's consulting firm. Of course, Nickel and Platinum's success had grated on the other kits—he had six more—but at least the other kits had each other. With Rios gone, that left Aqua all alone.

"How badly did Aqua mope?" Dane asked, carefully cutting in on William's ranting.

William let out a heavy sigh. "Badly enough that I started worrying he might drain Nixie's pool out of spite. He was complaining that he didn't have any friends, so I told him to pack a bag and go find himself some."

That was... Dane had to pause to think about that for a long moment. It wasn't a tactic that would have worked on any of his kits; that was for certain. Aqua was a completely different person.

"Did he leave?" Dane asked.

"Went and packed a bag right away. I had to remind him to have breakfast, he was so eager to go. Dane, what if he never comes back? What if I've lost him?"

"Aqua loves you," Dane replied, his voice firm since he was absolutely certain his words were true. "All kits have to leave the nest some time, but they always remember their home. Nickel and Platinum spend almost as much time with me as they do in their own house. They're going to eat me out of house and home at the rate they're growing."

"That's the same with Rios and Nixie. Rios has grown two inches since you last saw him. Can you believe it?"

"Trust me, I can believe it. Nickel and Platinum were already my two tallest kits, and they've each grown an inch this year. Zinc has grown two inches, so she's almost as tall as Platinum now, and Copper just had another growth spurt too. If it's not the cost of food that cripples me, it will be the cost of keeping them clothed."

"At least your kits stay out of the pool or the river. All the swimming Rios has been doing is starting to fray the seams of his clothes. I can't get him to remember to change into swim trunks before he goes diving with Nixie."

"William, I have an experimental mine in my backyard. There are more holes in the elbows and knees of my kits' clothes than I have ever seen before."

They both laughed for a few moments, commiserating with each other, before they sobered again.

"He'll come home, William. I wouldn't worry about that. I would worry about who or what he'll bring with him, though," Dane couldn't help adding cheekily.

"Because retrofitting my indoor pool to give Nixie a comfortable home wasn't difficult enough," William grumbled without any heat. He sighed. "Should I cash in a major investment now so I can afford it?"

"Wait until you see how bad it's going to be," Dane replied in disagreement. "You might need to cash in more than one."

William let out another heavy sigh. "Why did I ever have to have kits anyway?"

Dane laughed, but didn't bother replying. It was because they had fallen in love with the silly kits, of course, and sometimes kits needed to fly free. Aqua would return, and hopefully he would grow up a bit in the process.

Chapter Four

Aqua blinked for a few long seconds before he realized the reason he couldn't see anything was because there was a dark cloth over his eyes. His head hurt with a sharp pain just above the back of his neck. Had he fallen and hit his head? The last thing he remembered was calling on his magic to change shape so he could continue flying off on his journey to nowhere. Which didn't explain why he was blindfolded and...apparently tied to the chair he was sitting on, since an attempt to lift his hands to his face proved to be impossible.

"So, spy, now that you're caught, what should we do with you?"

Aqua had no idea who was speaking. It was a guy, but not a voice he recognized.

"Hi?" he asked curiously. "Who are you?"

"The real question is: Who are you? Dragons aren't welcome in this part of the Nevada desert. Seeing that you're here anyway, you must be spying for the enemy."

"I made it all the way to Nevada?" Aqua gasped. "No way!"

"Where did you think you were?" the man asked, his voice full of skepticism.

"Saskatchewan," Aqua replied easily. "I caught an air current out this morning. I'm running away from home. Uncle Willy said I should." He couldn't help grinning at that admission, although he quickly wiped it away when he realized his captors wouldn't get the joke.

"He's obviously just as idiotic as those other dragons," another man said with a sigh.

Aqua had heard that before. "My tutor says that all the time," he explained. "I think it's 'cause I have trouble reading still, but then my brother figured it all out. He's training for the coast guard."

"Do you ever stop talking?" the first man asked, his voice sharp and cold with suspicion.

Aqua frowned at that. He didn't think he was talking more than usual, and Uncle Willy had never complained. Although, the only thing Uncle Willy had ever really complained about was the three or four times he and Rios had flooded one of Uncle Willy's houses. Purely accidentally, of course.

"Who are you anyway?" he asked again, instead of answering.

The man sighed, sounding exasperated. A second later, Aqua felt fingers fumbling with his blindfold. It slipped away from his eyes, and he blinked at the sudden light. Once his eyes cleared, he looked around the room he was in.

Aqua was inside what appeared to be a one-room wooden house. It looked sturdy, but weathered. There weren't any holes in the walls, but they were a funny shade of gray. The windows were wide open and didn't have any screens in them.

Three people were looking at him. They all appeared the same at first glance, but a second glance told him they were probably siblings: two guys and one girl. Their skin was darkly tanned, and they had high cheekbones and dark-brown eyes. Their hair varied from shades of red to orange. One of the guys had his sleeves pushed up, and Aqua could see tattoos on his skin in the shape of deep yellow-red stars and lines. All of them were tall, probably the tallest people he had ever seen.

"What are you guys?" Aqua asked. They weren't human—he could tell that much—but his experience with strange creatures was limited to the few that wandered through Uncle Willy's domain, mostly ones that dealt with snow and cold. He had no idea what other types of creatures existed in the world.

The man closest to him sniffed, his lip rolled in disgust. He no doubt thought Aqua was an idiot, and maybe he was, but at least this time it was only ignorance.

"Let him stew for a few hours," he said with a glare for Aqua. "Maybe then he'll have softened up enough to talk." All three of them sneered at him before stalking out the front door.

Well, that was fun. He had no idea where he was, who had captured him, or why. Best thing to do was get himself free and get away. He looked down at his wrists and saw they were bound to the chair arms with simple rope and knots. He wiggled his right wrist and only felt the rope dig in. He tried the same on the left, and again there was no room to get free. He didn't want to shift and accidentally break their house with his bigger size, since that would be mean, so he saved that idea as a last resort.

"The best way to get those ropes off is with fire," a new voice said softly from behind him. "They're expecting you to give yourself away by burning your way free, and then they think they'll have a leg up on the fire dragons they're fighting the desert for. But you're different from those dragons. You taste like water."

Aqua craned his neck around to try to see who was speaking, but it was darker in the back of the room. It wasn't until the speaker took a few steps forward that Aqua could see him.

He shared the same basic features as the others—high cheekbones and he was very tall—but he didn't have the same coloring. His hair was pale gold, almost white, and his skin was even paler than Aqua's. But his eyes mesmerized Aqua the most. They were red, much like the others' hair had been, and piercing.

Never before had Aqua felt so bare, as if those eyes had torn his body open and dissected everything Aqua was in one quick glance. It was a strange feeling, but it wasn't an unwelcome one. Aqua thought it should have been, but there was something else in those eyes, a sort of emptiness that spoke of what being so different had meant in his life so far. He looked lonely.

"You're different too," Aqua whispered, unable to make his voice any louder under that red-eyed scrutiny. "You're like them, but not quite. Sort of like how I'm similar to a fire dragon, except I'm a water dragon."

"I wish it was like that," he replied, and his eyes finally closed. Aqua didn't know whether to feel sad or relieved that those eyes were no longer focused on him. "I'm broken, not different."

"You don't look broken to me," Aqua replied truthfully. He had a different coloring to the others, but that was it.

"I'm a fire salamander who lives in the desert, and I can't go outside into direct sunlight!" he snapped with a pained snarl. "I can't call on any fire like my siblings, and when it gets too hot, I faint. I'm weak and broken."

"Why don't you leave? Move somewhere that isn't as hot or sunny?" Aqua asked.

The salamander let out a hard laugh. "Where would I go? There's no one to take me in even if I could get out of this desert without burning to death. Besides, those damned fire dragons have us boxed in. We couldn't get out even if we wanted to."

"That's kind of mean," Aqua said grumpily. "Has anyone ever tried talking to them about it?"

The salamander let out another laugh, but this one just sounded tired. "It's a long story," he said.

Aqua shrugged. "I'm not going anywhere. Oh, what's your name? I'm Aqua."

"Ash, because I'm what happens when the fire goes out," Ash explained stoically. All of a sudden, Aqua wanted to strangle whoever had given Ash that name. "The story starts about three months ago. Safara—that's my older sister—was dating one of the fire dragons. I don't know all of it, but Phyre—that's our oldest brother—went to meet the dragon Safara was dating, and then he dragged Safara home, saying they had broken up and she wasn't to see the dragon any longer. She was sad, but Phyre talked some sense into her. The feud started shortly afterward. I think the dragons are demanding we hand Safara over to them, but Phyre isn't about to let her suffer."

Suffer? No, something wasn't quite right with Ash's story.

"Ash, does your family know anything about dragons?" Aqua asked gently. He didn't wait for an answer, pushing on quickly. "Dragons don't date."

"So they really were cheating Safara," Ash cut in.

"No. Dragons mate. They find the one person in the world who is right for them, and that's it. A dragon always knows. Safara leaving probably broke her dragon's heart, and the fire dragons want her back because that will help. I wonder what happened that made Phyre drag Safara back?"

"That can't be what this fight is about," Ash disagreed. "Phyre was so mad."

"There's only one way to find out," Aqua decided. "If Phyre and Safara won't tell you what went wrong, then we should go ask the dragons."

"We can't do that!" Ash gasped. "I can't go outside, and you're a prisoner until Phyre says otherwise."

Aqua grinned. "So we'll go at night when you can go outside."

"They all sleep here at night," Ash disagreed. "You're not going to be able to get away, even if you could get out of the ropes holding you captive."

"You're going to let me out of the ropes," Aqua insisted with a grin. "I'll take care of the rest of them."

"I'm not going to do that!" Ash said, sounding incredulous again.

The door was flung open before Aqua could tell Ash more of his plan, but that was okay. All three of the other salamanders strode back into the room. The one in front was holding two dead jackrabbits by the ears. He thrust them at the girl, who had to be Safara.

"Dinner. Make it good this time," he told her. He must be Phyre.

Safara took the rabbits obediently, but she didn't look particularly happy to be forced to clean and cook them. Was she stuck in that role because she was a woman? That was really silly in Aqua's opinion.

"Well, dragon," Phyre asked sharply, "anything you want to tell us now?"

"Nothing's changed," Aqua replied, even though so much already had. He was very careful not to glance over to where Ash had found a spot to sit along one wall. "I'm still from Canada and have no idea why you've tied me up like this. How about you let me go?"

Phyre laughed. "Not a chance, spy." He turned away, going to sit on the other side of the room from Aqua.

Aqua watched the rest of the room, since he didn't have anything better to do. The sun was setting outside, casting long shadows through the open windows. The heat from the day was beginning to cool, which was a nice change as well. Safara was busy with the rabbits, carefully cleaning and skinning them, while the salamander whose name Aqua didn't know started a fire in the fireplace. It took a while before the fire had burned down enough so they could cook on it. Full dark had fallen, and Ash had been sent to close the windows to keep the chill of the night out of the room.

The smell of the rabbits cooking made Aqua's stomach rumble. It was meaty and fatty, and he wanted some, but he knew better than to ask. He would only get one chance to ask for something tonight, he guessed, and he needed to be very careful with it.

Safara took her time with the cooking, and when the rabbits were done, Phyre split the rabbits in half with a large knife so all four of them had an even portion. Aqua got to watch them eat, which, despite his rumbling tummy, was actually very interesting.

Ash got a full portion of food to eat, but no one spoke to him the entire time. He sat slightly apart from his siblings, and Aqua didn't miss the guilty look he shot Aqua one or two times, as if he didn't think he should be eating when Aqua was going without. Safara picked at her food as if she knew she had to eat to keep up appearances, but didn't have the stomach for it. Her plate was full of pulled-apart scraps by the end of the meal, which made it look like she had eaten without much of it going into her mouth.

The other two ate gustily, ripping chunks of meat off the bone with their teeth. Even though Aqua had seen Phyre cut through both rabbits exactly in the center, for some reason, his portion looked larger than the others'. They both licked their plates clean and then passed them over to Safara when they were done.

"I'll go wash up," she said softly, taking all four plates outside. Since Aqua didn't see a sink in the room, he guessed they must have some sort of water system outside. It was too far away for the range of his magic, so he couldn't say where for certain.

Phyre looked content. He was leaning back in his chair with his hands on his stomach, as if he was ready to take a nap. This was probably the most amenable he would be, so Aqua decided to take his chance.

"Um, I'm thirsty," Aqua said quickly, just loud enough to be heard over the crackle of the fire. Phyre glowered at him for daring to interrupt his good mood. "You don't have to go out for it or anything. I have a bottle in my backpack," Aqua added before Phyre could immediately say no.

"I'll get it," Ash said. Aqua didn't know if that was because Ash was still feeling guilty about eating dinner accompanied to the sounds of Aqua's stomach growling, if Ash wanted to stop Phyre from getting into a fight, or if he just wanted to help Aqua because Ash liked him. Aqua couldn't help hoping it was the latter.

Ash scrambled behind Aqua, going into the more shadowed portion of the room. Aqua heard his bag unzip and then a rustling as Ash dug through Aqua's things until he found a water bottle. The sealed plastic cap popped when Ash turned it, and for the first time in hours, Aqua could sense water. He called it to him, feeling it erupt from the bottle and head in his direction.

Phyre let out a shout just before a ball of water coalesced around his head. Aqua sent a second ball to choke the other brother, then waited with his fingers crossed. He watched them both turn red, then blue, and hoped they wouldn't be stupid and breathe in the water. Aqua just wanted them to keep holding their breaths.

"What are you doing?" Ash gasped, reaching forward to grip Aqua's arm as if that could stop him.

"Knocking them out."

Phyre's eyes rolled back first, his body sagging bonelessly in his chair. Aqua immediately recalled the water so Phyre could breathe again. Hopefully he would stay unconscious long enough for Aqua to escape. The other brother dropped a few seconds later. Aqua directed the water back into the bottle Ash was still holding.

"Untie me, quickly," Aqua told Ash. "It's time to make a run for it."

"You hurt my family!" Ash gasped out furiously. "I should leave you where you are for when they wake up!"

"Safara isn't happy anymore, is she?" Aqua said softly, trying to convince Ash to cut the ropes holding him captive. "Not since Phyre dragged her away from the dragons and started the feud. We need to know what happened so we can fix it, and the only way we can do that is by talking to the dragons. You have to let me go, Ash."

"Phyre's going to be so mad," Ash whispered, but his eyes were on the door where Safara had vanished a while ago, more than long enough to have washed four plates.

She was avoiding having to come back to the room and Phyre's overbearing presence.

"He's going to be mad no matter what, I think," Aqua replied. "Let me out, Ash."

Ash stepped up to the fire, where he carefully picked up the large butcher's knife Phyre had left there after splitting the rabbits. He hurried over to Aqua and carefully slipped the knife under the ropes. Once Aqua's arms were free, he stood and stretched, glad to be off his numb butt. He walked toward the back of the room to find his bag and found it pressed against the wall next to a small pallet of blankets. There was only one bed in the entire room.

"Where does everyone sleep?" Aqua asked curiously. He popped open his bag to grab one of Uncle Willy's sandwiches and stuffed a bite into his mouth even as he zipped the bag back up and hurried toward the door.

"In the fire. They're fire salamanders, remember? I'm the one who's different. The fire burns me." Ash spoke like that was a guilty admission, his voice heavy with shame.

"The fire burns me too," Aqua said.

He pulled the door open and stepped outside. It was dark out, with every star visible in the sky overhead, and it was cold. Not as cold as at Uncle Willy's home, but chilly enough that Aqua wanted to hurry and shift forms. He finished stuffing the sandwich in his mouth as he moved far enough away from the house to change without breaking anything. He stretched his wings wide once he was a dragon again before turning to look at Ash, where he was hovering in the doorway.

"You should come with me," he told Ash. Aqua didn't want to leave Ash behind. It wasn't just that he was afraid of what Phyre might do to him when Phyre woke up. Aqua genuinely didn't want to be parted from Ash. He wanted to know what Ash looked like when he smiled, and he wanted to be the one to put that smile on Ash's face. He wanted Ash to be the friend he was on this journey to find. "Please come with me to see the other dragons, Ash," Aqua pleaded.

"Go with him," a woman's voice added. Safara stepped into the light cast through the open door and looked hard at Aqua before gentling her gaze to look at Ash. "You don't belong here, but you might find somewhere happier with that idiot. Don't let Phyre ruin your chance like he did mine."

"Safara..." Ash began, but he trailed off as if he didn't know what to say.

"You can come with us too," Aqua said recklessly.

Safara let out a harsh laugh. "There won't be a warm welcome for me there, I assure you. Go, and tell them I am sorry, even though I know an apology from me won't mean much." She gently pushed Ash out of the doorway, stepped around him, and shut the door behind her.

Aqua didn't have time to go after her. Instead, he turned to look at Ash imploringly.

"I will beg some more," Aqua insisted.

Ash let out a little snort of laughter. "You are an idiot. Can you carry someone while you're flying?"

"I've never tried, actually," Aqua admitted sheepishly.

Ash let out another little snort, and Aqua was suddenly upset that it was so dark because he couldn't see Ash's facial expression. A second later a small lizard scampered up his front claw to perch on the back of Aqua's paw. Aqua leaned in close to look and saw a pale white salamander with yellow markings on its back and red eyes. He carefully turned his paw until Ash was securely cupped in his palm before spreading his wings and jumping for the sky.

The wonderful thermals were long gone, which meant Aqua had to work for every inch of height as he beat his wings as hard as he could. The little house was in the middle of nowhere and was the only building Aqua could see for miles. He went a little higher and then spread his wings to soar so he could tilt his head downward to look at Ash.

"Where are we going?" he asked. The salamander quivered as if it was laughing, then peeked out from between Aqua's claws to look around them. He pointed toward a tiny speck of light off in the distance before safely withdrawing to the center of Aqua's paw. Aqua turned in the proper direction, angled his flight toward the light, and flew off into the night.

Chapter Five

The light Ash had pointed out turned out to be a large bonfire. It was burning in the middle of the desert with no houses or other signs of civilization around. Six or seven dragons were lazing around it. Aqua didn't get close enough to get a proper count, instead choosing to land well away from the fire and approach in human form. He was less threatening that way.

Ash scampered to the ground and shifted forms, the small salamander exploding upward until he was back to being six feet tall. Aqua followed suit, calling on the magic that triggered his change.

"I shouldn't have come with you," Ash said worriedly. "What if they attack first instead of listening to what we have to say?"

"I wouldn't worry about that," Aqua replied, glancing around the dark desert. He thought he sensed familiar magic surrounding them. He knew fire magic from spending time with his friends Lumie and Alloy, two of Dane's fire kits, and he suspected dragons had already flanked them.

"I don't think we'll listen, but we won't attack right away," a new voice called out from the darkness. "You're that dragon that flew right over our heads a few hours ago. We sent someone to warn you off, but you were so out of it, lost in your thoughts, you didn't even notice him. Why are you back?"

Aqua couldn't see the speaker, but he could tell there was more than just one dragon nearby. He didn't have access to enough water to even try fighting off that many dragons, not that he wanted to fight. His only choice was to answer truthfully.

"I got hungry and stopped for lunch," he explained sheepishly. "The salamanders didn't like that very much."

"No need to ask which family you ran into," the man said with a sigh. "Only one has an albino lizard."

"Not a lizard," Ash said grouchily, but quietly.

"They send you here?" the man continued sharply. "You're not welcome if that's the case."

"I spent the rest of the day tied to a chair," Aqua grumped. "They thought I was spying on them for you, but Ash helped me get away." Aqua reached awkwardly behind himself and bumped his fingers against Ash's arm. He followed the soft curve of Ash's skin until their fingers tangled. Ash didn't pull away, but his fingers didn't tighten either. They stood there with their hands loosely clasped.

"We got ourselves another one, Boron," a woman grunted. "Let the poor things sit by the fire before they freeze."

"Come on then," the man—Boron—said.

Aqua obeyed, gently gripping Ash's hand to pull him forward toward the fire. Aqua counted nine dragons sitting around the fire when he got close enough to see. The dragon standing directly in front of Aqua and Ash shifted forms, turning into a lanky red-haired man. He waved them forward until Aqua could make out individual facial features in the flickering light.

There was something in the fire too, he noticed. Little salamanders were sprawled on or curled up beneath the logs. Some were scampering around, reveling in the heat.

"There's so many!" Ash gasped. He had stopped walking with Aqua when they had gotten close to the fire, and his free hand was gripping Aqua's upper arm as he stared at all the salamanders.

"We've never understood why your family has always insisted on remaining separate from us," Boron said. He was the dragon who had shifted forms. "We work together to survive the desert."

This went against almost everything Aqua knew about dragons. They were territorial, often fighting with any dragon that encroached. As far as Aqua had previously known, Dane was the only person who had ever tried to have more than one adult dragon live near one another. He was building a dragon village, for reasons Aqua had never really bothered to learn, and figuring out how to keep everyone living in harmony was his biggest struggle.

"How?" Aqua asked, and Boron grinned.

"It's all about having a sense of community. We work together, protect each other, and take care of one another. There are things we can get territorial over, like our mates, but if we foster a culture of sharing, we've found that the territorial urge diminishes. The salamander clans are so similar to the fire dragons that it was only natural for us to exist together, especially when we found out dragons could be mates with salamanders. Only one family refuses to join us."

"Safara tried to join," Ash gasped in surprise, as if he was just starting to realize what had gone wrong between his family and these dragons and salamanders. "And Phyre didn't like that, so he dragged her away."

"If only it were that simple," Boron said softly. He looked at them for a few moments, as if he was weighing a heavy decision, before turning sharply and walking around the fire. "Come with me."

They followed, edging around the fire and between the dragons lying around until they were on the opposite side. They walked out into the darkness for a while until they found another dragon who was lying as far from the fire as she could while still being within the reach of its light. Aqua could make out what looked like a dozen trucks parked just beyond that dragon, so that must be how the dragons and salamanders had gotten to the desert in the first place.

"This is Alkaline. She and your Safara are mates, but Phyre refused to allow two women to be together. He said it was unnatural. When he was forcing Safara away, in desperation, Alkaline ran at him. He hit her with a whip of fire and took Safara away. The damage is extensive, and Alkaline hasn't been able to heal it. She can't shift to human form without terrible pain, and with her scales damaged, it hurts to move at all."

"Phyre did this?" Ash asked. He was shaking slightly as he looked at Alkaline, and Aqua thought he might have seen a tear trace down Ash's cheek, but his voice was steady despite that.

The distance from the fire didn't do anything to hide what had happened to Alkaline. There was a line running down the side of her body, broken into her scales in a red and vicious-looking cut with yellow pus leaking out in spots. The pain had to be excruciating. Add on the fact that her mate had been taken from her and she must be in utter agony.

"There's nothing we can do for her anymore," Boron admitted. "Even if we confronted Phyre and took Safara back, Alkaline won't live for much longer. We're shocked she's held on as long as she has, to be honest."

"Can't you get a healer?" Aqua asked.

Boron laughed. "What healer wants to come out into the middle of the desert to heal a dragon? Please don't say such silly things, little waterling."

"I'm Aqua, not a waterling."

"And I'm Boron," their guide replied. "Come away before we wake her."

They walked back to the fire. Ash was unusually quiet. Not that he had ever said much at one time before, but there was a sense of shock around him that led Aqua to believe that Ash didn't know what to say any longer.

"If I could get a healer, would that change things?" Aqua asked Boron hopefully as they returned to the warmth of the fire.

"Persistent, aren't you?" Boron grumbled. "If you can get a healer to save Alkaline, we would be in your debt, Aqua."

Aqua grinned. "Do you get cell service out here?" He pulled his backpack off and bent down so he could dig to the very bottom. He didn't wait for Boron to answer, powering up his cell phone the second he found it and holding it up into the air to see if there were any cell towers nearby. Apparently there were because he had a signal. Aqua keyed in Dane's number and held the phone to his ear.

"Hello?" The voice that picked up sounded half asleep. Aqua guiltily glanced at his phone's clock and realized that if it was ten o'clock Pacific time, it was after one on the East Coast. This was too important to wait for morning though.

"Hi, Dane," Aqua said. "Do you know of any healers who could come out to the Nevada desert?"

"You're in Nevada?" Dane asked, sounding slightly more awake. "What did you do that you need a healer? If it isn't an emergency, I'm not waking anyone up."

"Not me. This other dragon. She's leaking yellow pus from under her scales."

"I'll make some calls," Dane replied immediately. "I assume you don't know which desert in Nevada you're in?" Dane continued without waiting for Aqua to ask Boron for an answer. "I'll give William a call since I'm assuming he can track you properly. You need anything else?"

"Not right now. Thanks, Dane."

"Stay safe out there. I don't think the local territory leader gets out into the deserts too often, so there's no telling who or what has claimed space out there."

Aqua giggled. "I've already found the who or what. I'll tell you about it next time I visit."

"I'm glad you're making friends, Aqua. Let me go make those calls."

He hung up, and Aqua put the phone in his pocket so he could hear it ring if Dane called back.

He was making friends, right? That was the entire purpose of his heading south, but a glance at Ash, who was squeezing his hands together as if he was still nervous and upset, spoke of something completely different than friendship to Aqua. Was this what Rios had felt the moment he understood just what Nixie could be to him? This tugging in his chest and a constant desire to make everything better for Nixie? All Aqua wanted to do was hurry over to Ash and give him a hug and tell him that it was going to be all right, so that was exactly what Aqua did.

Ash was a lot taller than Aqua was, and thinner, but he let out a sigh as Aqua's arms came around him and rested his cheek on top of Aqua's head.

"I didn't have any idea what Phyre had done," he mumbled. "He took care of me as best as he could, but I can't go out in sunlight, and it's too cold to go out at night. He never told me anything like this place could exist. All he said was that he'd protect me because I'm so weak. He thought Safara was weak too."

"He's trying hard to protect you in his own way. I don't doubt that about your brother," Aqua said softly into Ash's shoulder. "But his..." He trailed off, unsure how to say that Phyre's morals weren't up to snuff without insulting Ash's brother.

"Phyre doesn't understand love," Ash finished Aqua's sentence easily. "He used to go to these get-togethers when he was younger to try to find a wife, but he always came back alone, until eventually he stopped trying entirely."

"I remember seeing Phyre at those," Boron said, gently cutting in to their conversation. "His beliefs weren't something a modern woman—particularly a dragon or salamander—could adhere to. Women belong in the kitchen and that sort of nonsense. No one wanted to put up with him. It didn't surprise me in the least to learn that what he didn't like about Safara and Alkaline was the fact that they were both women."

"Our parents were like that, I think," Ash replied. He lifted his head off Aqua's so he could look at Boron, but he didn't loosen his arms. "Mom stayed at home, cooking and taking care of us while Dad went out to work. But I think that's the way Mom preferred it, rather than it being the way Dad decided it had to be. They died when I was really little, so maybe I'm not remembering it right."

"No, you have it right," Boron said with a shrug. "Your mother was definitely in charge of that household, and I could tell from the few times we met that she loved being home to take care of you and your siblings. Losing your parents so suddenly in that sandstorm might have warped Phyre's perceptions. It still doesn't excuse the way he attacked Alkaline though."

"No, it doesn't," Ash agreed. "Although I have no idea what to do to change that."

Boron didn't reply, and before Ash or Aqua could come up with something else to say, the ground lit up fifty feet to their left. Dragons sprang to their feet and salamanders jumped from the fire, assuming human form as they got free of the flames.

"Are we under attack?" someone asked.

"It's a spell circle," Aqua told Boron quickly. "I'll bet this is the healer."

The light faded away a moment later, leaving an elderly looking man, holding a doctor's case, standing where the light had been. His back was still straight despite his gray hair and wrinkled face and his eyes strong as he looked at the assembled dragons and salamanders.

"Aqua, my boy, where is this dragon leaking yellow pus?" Dr. Krantz called through the assembly.

"Over here, Dr. Krantz." Aqua lifted one hand in the air to wave it so Dr. Krantz could see him, then gently untangled himself from Ash so he could show Dr. Krantz the way to Alkaline's side.

"How have you been, my boy?" Dr. Krantz asked as soon as Aqua had reached his side and they were both walking around the fire toward Alkaline. "I haven't seen you since that time you tried to go deep-sea diving in a puddle only three feet deep. Shattered your forearm, if I remember correctly. Took me an hour to magically fit all the pieces back into place to get the healing started right."

"My arm's fine now, and Uncle Willy told me I could only go diving in water that's over twelve feet deep from now on." He couldn't help rubbing at the arm he had broken, in remembered pain.

"Good man, your uncle. How's your brother doing? I heard he found himself a mermaid?"

Aqua laughed, unable to help himself after hearing that from Dr. Krantz, of all people. "Nixie says he's nothing like those saltwater-addled idiots. He's a nix, so he looks like a merman, but he's not and he gets very grumpy if you call him one," Aqua added with his voice full of experience.

"I shall keep that in mind," Dr. Krantz replied jovially. He caught sight of Alkaline a moment later, and the smile fell off his face. "Oh dear," he breathed out and hurried forward. He gently touched Alkaline on the shoulder that wasn't leaking pus. Her body shuddered for a few seconds and then relaxed as she sighed with relief.

Dr. Krantz got to work on her scales, doing things with instruments he pulled from his bag, which Aqua didn't understand in the least, with the occasional flash of magic to start the healing process. He left Dr. Krantz to it, with Boron watching him closely, and returned to the warm fire and Ash.

"Now what do we do?" Ash asked as Aqua took a seat on the ground next to where Ash was sitting near the fire.

"You can always come home with me if you don't want to stay here," Aqua said hopefully.

Ash stared at Aqua in shock for a few moments. "That's...not what I meant, but I appreciate it. I will need somewhere to live after this is over, won't I? I can't go back to Phyre, not after helping you run away, and I can't stay outside in the desert with this community. My skin gets blistered after only an hour in the sun, and I think they only go back to their houses to avoid a bad storm and to replenish their supplies. Is it... Would it really be okay if I lived at your place? Is it really sunny there?"

"It can be, but we have a big house with lots of things to do indoors during the day." Aqua would have said anything to get Ash to agree to come home with him, yet at the same time, he knew he had to be entirely truthful. He wanted Ash to decide to come with him, not be coerced into it.

"I'll think about it," Ash replied after a moment of silence. That was probably the best answer Aqua was going to get at the moment, so he let the subject drop. They sat side by side, enjoying the fire and the stars twinkling overhead. There were gentle murmurs around them as everyone awoken by Dr. Krantz's arrival had to talk about it before going back to bed.

Aqua let out a wide yawn, which Ash echoed a moment later. It was far too easy to rest his head on Ash's shoulder. A short nap while they waited for Dr. Krantz to finish wouldn't hurt. Today had been a very long day. Aqua let out another yawn before closing his eyes and letting sleep take him away.

Chapter Six

It got noisy far too early in the desert. Mostly because a lot of people were waking up and talking to their neighbors and breakfast was sizzling over the fire. It smelled great, Aqua's rumbling stomach happily informed him.

He slowly opened his eyes and saw that it was just barely past dawn. The sun was visible over the endless horizon of tan scrub, but only just. Pink and orange colors streaked across the sky with only the smallest sliver of bright yellow beginning to show. The chill of the night was still heavy across Aqua's skin, making him wish he had a blanket. It would warm up quickly as the sun continued to rise, Aqua knew. The sun would get unbearably hot, and Ash would burn and blister without proper shelter, which these dragons and salamanders lacked entirely.

Aqua carefully rolled away from Ash, untangling their limbs. Luckily Aqua had been using Ash for a pillow so it was easy enough to get free without waking Ash up. Aqua moved far enough away that his larger dragon body wouldn't squish Ash and then shifted forms. He crawled back to Ash and gently spread one wing over where Ash was sleeping. With Ash completely covered in shadow, Aqua relaxed. He tried to go back to sleep, but the smell of cooking food was so strong and so yummy he couldn't manage it.

A plate appeared in front of his face almost as if his rumbling stomach had conjured it. Aqua blinked at it for a moment before noticing the hand gripping the edge.

"I guess I shouldn't have brought you a fork and knife," Boron said with a laugh. "Good idea to keep your friend there safe from the sun. I'm sorry we can't do any better without moving him to the cars all the way on the other side of the camp, but keeping him in the shade should help." He passed Aqua the plate, which he awkwardly took with his claws. It took all of three seconds for Aqua to lick the plate clean, which only made Boron laugh. "Looks like you're hitting a growth spurt," Boron said around a chuckle.

"Finally," Aqua grumbled. "Rios grew two inches over the winter, and I didn't."

"Dragons have to grow mentally first before they start filling out physically," Boron replied with an understanding shrug. "Looks like you'll be catching up to Rios pretty soon."

There was a rustling noise from underneath Aqua's wing, and he felt a smooth palm running gently across the underside. Boron winked at him and strode off.

"It's my wing, Ash," Aqua explained. "To keep the sun off you."

"It's still too bright. I can't open my eyes," Ash said.

"Well, that won't do," Dr. Krantz said jovially.

Aqua jumped in surprise and craned his neck around. Dr. Krantz was standing on Aqua's right side, away from his spread wing. He had a plate of food in one hand and a fork in the other. A woman was standing next to him. Her skin was darkly tanned from the sun, which made her vibrant red hair and scales shine. She was only wearing pants, but her torso was covered, thanks to thick bandages that ran from her armpits all the way down below her waistband.

"I saw your friend's interesting pigmentation in the firelight last night, but Alkaline here took precedence." He carefully speared some food onto his fork and put it in his mouth.

"Thanks for bringing him here," Alkaline added while Dr. Krantz chewed. "I'm not completely healed, but he took care of the worst of it, so my natural healing abilities should be able to handle the rest."

"I'm glad you're better," Aqua said with a smile for her. "Now we just have to help you with the rest of your ouchies."

Alkaline winced at the reminder. "Safara needs to do some growing up of her own too. She has to want to leave her brother, not just want me. That's a difficult decision I'm asking her to make."

"Phyre's very mixed up inside," Ash said softly from underneath Aqua's wing. "He means well, but that's not enough. Is it? Safara helped Aqua and me escape, and she says she's sorry. She didn't think you would want her back after what happened before."

Alkaline shook her head sadly. "If I hadn't been so badly injured, I would have been banging down her door the next day. She's my mate, so I'll want her with me no matter what. But it still has to be her choice. That's the really important part that a lot of people have to understand. Mating doesn't have to mean forever. If she outright rejected me, I would be hurt, but I would get over it and eventually find someone else I wanted just as much. Her being forced away from me against both our wishes is just as bad as forcing her to stay with me would be. I'm hoping, now that I'm healing, I'll be able to find a balance together with her."

Aqua could feel Ash's warmth and the hand Ash hadn't yet taken off his wing, and he couldn't help wondering whether Ash would ever be interested in taking that chance. He was thinking about moving in with Aqua, which was a step in the right direction, but being mates was different and they weren't there yet. They needed to build a connection first, and that would require more than a crazy twenty-four hours together no matter how much Aqua's heart was demanding he keep Ash with him forever and ever.

"Right, my boy," Dr. Krantz said, interrupting Aqua's spiraling thoughts. He placed his now empty plate on top of where Aqua's was sitting on the ground, then crouched next to Aqua's wing. "My energy is restored. If you would allow me underneath, Aqua?"

Aqua waited a second to give Ash some time to react to the doctor's words, and then carefully lifted his wing just high enough so Dr. Krantz could move closer to Ash.

"Albinism is actually fairly common in fire salamanders. I admit, I've never seen it in the magical variety, but it does occur in the nonmagical ones." Dr. Krantz was talking to Ash, but aside from that, Aqua had no idea what was going on below his wing.

"What made it happen to me?" Ash asked curiously.

"Ah, any number of things. I couldn't give an accurate diagnosis, but my best guess, in your case, is you most likely have a gene mutation, possibly a magical one. The good news is I know how to help you."

"You can?" Ash asked, sounding incredulous.

Dr. Krantz grunted. "Not entirely. I can't change your pigmentation; I don't have the magical power to alter someone's base DNA. However, there have been many studies done on the albino squirrel since they alone in the albino family don't have vision difficulties. Their rod and cone configuration is different from other creatures, and I can mimic that in your eyes. You should be able to see better and—while I still recommend eye protection—you should also be able to see in bright sunlight. There haven't been any studies done on what I could do to help your skin, aside from offering sunblock, but I have worked to heal some nasty sunburns in the past, and I think I can offer your skin a touch more protection. I can't promise anything, but I am willing to try if you are."

There was silence for a few minutes as Ash no doubt thought over Dr. Krantz's words.

"There's no side effects?" he finally asked. Dr. Krantz didn't answer with words, so he must have shaken or nodded his head. "Then I'm willing to try too."

"Excellent," Dr. Krantz said. "If you don't mind, I would like to shamelessly use this experience in a paper detailing how we might magically aid albinos and potentially save them from difficult and painful surgeries."

"That's fine," Ash answered. "I'm happy to help other people like me." They were quiet for a long while, which got boring for Aqua really fast.

Boron wandered back over carrying three plates of food. He handed one to Alkaline and a second one to Aqua, who licked it up just as quickly as he had the first one. Boron grinned at him and handed over the last plate.

"I'll go get two more for them," he said while pointing a finger at Aqua's wing. He took all the empty plates with him when he left. Boron returned with two fresh plates well before Dr. Krantz was finished.

Twenty minutes later, Dr. Krantz gently bumped Aqua's wing with his hand. "Lift your wing up, my boy. All the way so we can stand up, please." Aqua complied, gradually standing so he could lift his wing high enough for Dr. Krantz and Ash to stand.

Dr. Krantz had his hands covering Ash's eyes, Aqua saw as soon as his wing was high enough that he could observe the two men. Aqua carefully angled his wing so the rising sun was blocked, giving Ash as much shade as possible. Dr. Krantz waited a moment before withdrawing his hands one finger at a time.

Ash's eyes were still closed, and he very slowly lifted his lids as Dr. Krantz stepped back. He gasped in shock, staring around him like he had never seen the world before.

"I can see!" Ash lifted his own hand and stared at his palm, then looked up at Aqua. He was smiling, but there were also tears in his eyes. "I had no idea how out of focus the world was before, and now I can see even in sunlight. This is... Thank you, Doctor."

"Don't thank me too profusely," Dr. Krantz said sternly, but he was smiling. "This was a purely academic exercise on my part, but I am glad to see it worked. If your vision does start to deteriorate again, give me a call. Aqua knows how to get in touch."

Ash opened his mouth, no doubt to say thanks again, but he didn't get the chance. A red dragon swooped low over the camp.

"A car's coming," she called loudly. "Looks like three salamanders are headed this way, and they don't look happy!" She flew off, probably to do some more reconnaissance.

"Safara!" Alkaline gasped.

"And Phyre," Ash added grimly.

"The road's this way," Boron said, turning and hurrying away.

Aqua put his empty plate on the ground and turned toward Ash. "What do you want to do?"

Ash was scowling at the ground, but at Aqua's words, he looked up at him. "I should be there. Phyre's probably upset thinking you kidnapped me. He can stop thinking he's riding to the rescue if he sees I'm all right."

Aqua nodded in agreement. This was also a good chance for Safara to see Alkaline, so he bumped Alkaline gently with the edge of his wing as he turned to follow. She startled in surprise—and luckily not pain because Aqua had forgotten about the bandages that covered her until his wing had touched her—and fell into step with them.

"I would suggest that you stay out of direct sunlight without proper skin protection," Dr. Krantz told Ash as he walked with them, still beneath Aqua's wing. "You shouldn't blister as easily now, but sunburns and skin cancer are still a concern. If you settle down somewhere, I suggest you make regular appointments with your local healer-witch to ensure your skin remains healthy."

They reached the end of the encampment not far behind Boron, and Dr. Krantz stepped out from underneath Aqua's wing so he could stand behind them all. The road wasn't paved; it was a flat area devoid of scrub. From the air, Aqua would have missed seeing it entirely. A cloud of dust was quickly approaching, and a few seconds later, Aqua could make out a Jeep hurtling down the road at top speed. It screeched to a stop at the end of the road, just in front of where they were all standing. All three salamanders climbed out, and Phyre stomped up to Boron.

"Where is my brother, dragon!" he yelled, glaring at Boron as if his eyes alone could set a person on fire.

"I'm right here, Phyre," Ash called. He waved at Phyre as if he were difficult to see.

"Still being held captive, I see," Phyre said with a sneer at Aqua's wing. "How dare you, spy! Come into my home to kidnap my brother!"

There were so many irrational things wrong with that statement that Aqua didn't know where to start. He opened his mouth to reply, but Ash beat him to it.

"You know that's not true, Phyre," Ash insisted. "You kidnapped him when he was enjoying his lunch. Besides, I left willingly. There's no life to live being trapped inside the sparse four walls of that house."

"Mother and Father had that house built when you were born and they realized you needed the shelter," Phyre replied firmly. "It's your house."

"And it's time for me to try living outside of it," Ash retorted.

Aqua couldn't help seeing the parallels between this conversation and the one he'd had with Uncle Willy yesterday morning. Uncle Willy had been the one telling him to get out, to explore and go find new friends. The simple walls of Uncle Willy's house were too confining for a growing dragon like him. It had been necessary, like a mamma bird tossing her babies out of the nest so they could learn to fly, and it was strange to hear a similar conversation from opposite perspectives. Ash had Uncle Willy's viewpoint, although Aqua couldn't say that Phyre was spouting the same things Aqua had. Aqua had agreed to leave, after all, while Phyre was still firmly entrenched.

"You can't walk in the sun; you don't have any magic. What do you think you can do in the outside world?"

Phyre sneered at Ash cruelly, far more cruelly than any brother Aqua had ever met. Aqua and Rios had fought, but there had never been so much hate or disdain between them as Phyre was dishing out.

"I won't know until I find out," Ash said decisively. His chin was firm and his eyes fiercely glaring at Phyre. "Aqua and I are going to see where the world takes us, no matter how bright and sunny it is."

"Preposterous," Phyre spat. "At least find a nice girl first. You're coming back home until you think this through properly."

"Phyre, stop. Please," Safara pleaded from behind him.

"Saf, Saf, we already tried to talk some sense into him once," Alkaline said softly. "It didn't end well for either of us."

Safara's eyes widened when she caught sight of Alkaline, and her hands lifted into the air in front of her as if she could reach out and touch Alkaline despite Phyre standing between them.

"Alky, you're okay," Safara breathed out, her voice shaking with tears and relief.

"Barely. Finally found a healer, thanks to Aqua, but I'm not really healed. I won't be until we get a chance to talk. You know that."

"She knows nothing. What is with you idiot dragons? Don't you know how the world is supposed to work, how we were made to behave?" Phyre hissed. "Your actions are abnormal, and I won't have any of my siblings fall prey to you."

"Too late." It took Aqua a moment to realize that it was Safara who spoke. He half expected it to be Alkaline or even Ash. "It's too late for that, Phyre. I'm in love with Alky, and there's nothing you can do about it."

"Oh, I think there is," Phyre said darkly. Flames erupted in his hands as he turned on Safara.

Aqua could sense water boiling behind him in a large pot over the fire, most likely for the encampment's morning coffee or tea. It was the only water he could feel in the area—Boron must bring the water in with the rest of the supplies. He called that water to him, swirling it around his body in a boiling loop. He sent it toward Safara, until a sheet of clear moisture separated her from Phyre. She slowly sidestepped Phyre, and Aqua had the water follow her, keeping her safe from Phyre's flames. Phyre tried twice to penetrate the water with jets of flame thrown from his fiery hands, but his actions only resulted in steam. Alkaline screamed each time, which only made Aqua grit his teeth and pour more magic into the water to keep it steady. There was activity on either side of Aqua as Boron tried to do something to help, but Aqua couldn't afford to look away.

Safara was getting closer to them, and that only seemed to inflame Phyre's anger. Aqua could hear him growling and muttering to himself over the sound of the water steaming against his fire.

Phyre turned suddenly and threw his hands forward, toward Aqua and Ash. Another jet of fire streamed toward them, vibrant, dangerous red and orange cracking in its fury. Aqua frantically pulled his water toward himself and Ash, barely deflecting the fire in time. A flash of steam blew across Aqua's face at the impact, burning his skin slightly.

Phyre immediately turned back toward Safara, and another jet of flame arced toward her. Fire lit up her fingers even as Aqua was desperately redirecting his wall of water back toward her. Her fire flashed, hitting Phyre's with a shower of sparks. Both flames vanished just in time for Aqua's water to shield Safara. Phyre sneered and shot more fire at Aqua, and he had to scramble to call the water back.

"That's enough!" Boron snarled. All of a sudden, the entire desert was on fire. There were dragons and salamanders everywhere, and each one of them was channeling fire into a wide ring around Phyre.

It was hot, so unbelievably hot. Aqua couldn't breathe—the fire had taken all the oxygen in the air—and he was sweating so much his clothes were soaked in seconds. Except that sweat dried in the heat only moments later. Ash whimpered next to him and pressed his body against Aqua, right under Aqua's wing. Aqua curled around so his back was to the fire and his arms and wings were wrapped protectively around Ash.

"It's time for you to grow up, Phyre," Boron continued firmly. Somehow his voice was stronger than the crackling and popping of the fire because Aqua could still hear him speak. "You have no right to confine your siblings in that old house. They want a chance to live their own lives, guided by their own choices."

"They're making mistakes. I want to save them before it's too late!" Phyre sounded honest and desperate, yet at the same time, there was a deranged quality in the shrillness of his voice that indicated he had no idea what was coming out of his mouth.

"It's not your job to save them. You're their brother, not a god. It's your job to support them and then help pick up the pieces when they fail so they're strong enough to get up and try again. All you're doing is weakening them." Boron spoke as if he knew exactly what he was talking about, which meant he was either a psychiatrist or he had gone through something similar sometime in his life and was speaking from experience. "Go back home, Phyre, and let your siblings have their chance to live."

Phyre was quiet for a few very long moments. Aqua waited with bated breath, wondering what Phyre was going to choose to do. Then, just barely audible over the crackle and pop of the fire, Aqua heard him mutter: "Fine. But they'll come crawling back soon enough. You'll see I'm right. Now let me out of here."

The bright glare of the flames dimmed, and it wasn't long before Aqua heard the rumble of a car starting and the crunch of tires on dirt as it pulled away.

"Idiot," Boron muttered under his breath.

Aqua's skin felt unnaturally tight, like all the water had been squeezed from beneath his scales, leaving only hard leather behind. A hand touched Aqua's back. It was a gentle touch, but it sent a flare of pain through Aqua that had him shivering and gasping. A cooling sensation radiated from that hand a half second later, spreading wonderful numbness like a balm.

"Luckily, I've gotten lots of practice healing burns lately," Dr. Krantz said from behind him. "Next time, try to get the water dragon safely away before you set the field on fire around him."

"Will he be okay?" Boron asked, his voice contrite.

The cooling sensation slowly began to fade away, and as it did, Aqua could feel his skin and scales again. They felt supple and normal, so he carefully uncurled from his protective crouch and looked around. All the dragons and salamanders that had stepped up to confront Phyre were looking at Aqua with apologetic and worried expressions. Dr. Krantz was frowning at some inward thought, his hand still pressed to Aqua's back as he healed whatever damage had been done. The pain had been numbed so quickly that Aqua had no idea just how badly he had been burned, but Dr. Krantz's swift arrival said that Aqua's back hadn't been pretty.

He kept uncurling his body slowly because he hadn't been the only one unable to handle fire nearby. Ash wasn't in his arms any longer; Aqua realized this before he finished unfurling his wings, and a glance downward revealed a small white salamander carefully tucked into the curl of his elbow where he could safely escape the heat.

Aqua had to cough a few times because his throat felt like he had been swallowing sand. "Ash," he called.

The salamander's red eyes popped open. He saw that the fighting was over, and then he leaped from Aqua's arm. Ash landed on two human feet.

"Are you okay?" he said softly, looking worriedly at Aqua. His hand was on Aqua's arm, squeezing gently, as if he needed to offer comfort. Just how badly was Aqua burned?

"Just give me a few more minutes, and he'll be right as rain," Dr. Krantz insisted. "His goose was a little cooked, but I've healed worse before.

Everyone waited quietly while Dr. Krantz continued to work, as if they didn't want to leave until they knew Aqua would be okay. Most of the salamanders and dragons probably felt guilty for forgetting that Aqua and Ash didn't have protection from fire the way they did, and Aqua had gotten hurt by that carelessness. It was awkward to stand under the scrutiny of so many people, but once they started drifting away, Aqua knew his injuries no longer looked so gruesome. Dr. Krantz finished up not long after that, and he stepped away, letting out heavy gasps of air like he was out of breath.

"Right as rain, my boy," Dr. Krantz said. He took in a few more pants of air. "But perhaps I need to take a break from healing for a few hours." He patted Aqua's shoulder twice before turning toward Boron. "I'm going to make a few calls, see if one or two of the local healer-witches would make this encampment a regular stop on their rounds. I can feel the dozens of toothaches and misaligned broken bones even when I'm this depleted."

Aqua tuned them out, focusing again on Ash. "Are you okay? I tried to shield you—"

"I'm fine. You saved me. I'm glad your scales aren't flaking off like ashes anymore."

Aqua craned his neck so he could see his back, but it looked like normal, healthy blue scales to him.

"I guess I should probably leave the desert soon, before someone else lights it on fire," Aqua joked.

"Maybe you should," Ash replied firmly. He glanced around them, and Aqua followed his gaze.

Safara and Alkaline were standing close to each other, closer than friends or acquaintances would feel comfortable being, but they weren't touching. Aqua hoped they were able to figure out their relationship now that they had the chance to talk. Ash's other brother, the one whose name Aqua hadn't learned, was standing by the road, looking bewildered. Phyre had apparently left him behind. A female salamander cautiously approached him, and he followed her into the encampment a moment later.

Aqua shifted to human form, wanting to be at eye level with Ash. He hoped Ash could withstand the sun, which was still rising, for the few minutes they needed to talk.

"I'm going to go home," Aqua continued. "I need a bath and my own bed." He might sneak a soak in Nixie's pool to get rid of the parched feeling being in the desert was giving his skin. "Do you want to come with me?" Maybe Ash would like the pool too?

Ash looked around the encampment again, then over at the rising sun with a wince.

"Are you sure your family would be okay with me?" he asked softly, almost shyly.

Aqua grinned. "They'll like you, trust me. An albino salamander is not the weirdest thing to ever be in my house. So?"

Ash nodded. "Let me say goodbye to my brother and sister. I'll be back." He scampered off, but paused a few feet away to glance back at Aqua as if to make certain Aqua really was going to wait. Aqua grinned at him, elated that Ash had agreed, before heading into the encampment himself to find his backpack.

"Phyre will be back," Boron said as he approached Aqua while he was chugging down his final water bottle. "He won't give up just because we forced him to leave. I'm thinking about sending Safara and Alkaline to some relatives living in Las Vegas for a few months. Brant wants to stay and try talking to Phyre." Brant must be the other brother. "And Ash says you're taking him home with you. Where is home?"

"I'm from Canada," Aqua explained easily. "My uncle Willy takes care of me and my brother."

"Uncle Willy?" Boron said; then a thought must have occurred to him because his eyes widened in surprise before narrowing again to focus on Aqua. "I had heard that William had taken in two wards and that they were dragons. You tell him if he ever wants to act like a ferocious djinni again, instead of a boring cartoon character genie, he can always come to my desert for a few days. The territory leader holds no sway here."

"I'll tell him," Aqua promised. "And I'm sure Ash will want to come visit, so I'll be back."

Boron nodded, and his intense look melted into a smile. "It was nice to meet you, Aqua." He held out his hand, which Aqua shook.

"You too," Aqua replied with his own smile.

Ash trotted up to them a second later. "I said goodbye to Brant and told Safara where I'm headed. Can we get out of the sun now?"

Aqua's smile turned into a mischievous grin. He picked up his bag, threw one arm over Ash's shoulder, and said into the wind: "Uncle Willy, it's time to head home."

Magic flared around them, and with a tug, Aqua and Ash headed home, Ash safely held in Aqua's arms.

Epilogue

William ended his magic spell when Aqua finished materializing in the living room. It took him an extra second to notice that Aqua wasn't alone, after which he rolled his eyes. What was with his kits bringing home other people? Shouldn't they at least ask first? William rolled his eyes again, at himself this time, for even briefly believing that his crazy, wonderful kits would think to ask for permission before doing something.

The young man with Aqua was a bit odd-looking, and it took William a moment to realize he was albino. He was also not human, but his species wasn't readily apparent, thanks to his coloring.

"Welcome home, Ash," Aqua said happily, waving one arm around to encompass the living room and beyond.

Ash looked around the living room with wide eyes, taking in the couches, TV, and coffee table as if he had never seen furniture like that before. Maybe he hadn't. Dane had called to tell William that Aqua had somehow ended up in Nevada, and there was no telling what creatures he had encountered there or what their living conditions were like.

Then Ash's eyes caught on the French doors, specifically on the snow just outside of them.

"What is that?" he asked slowly, almost tentatively.

"The snow? It's frozen water. I bet you don't get a lot of that out in the desert," Aqua replied happily.

"It's so pretty. Can I touch it?" Ash asked.

"Sure." Aqua walked over to the French doors with Ash trailing eagerly at his heels like a puppy about to get the best treat of his life. Aqua popped the lock on the door without thought to William's heating bill, and it swung inward, letting blisteringly cold air into the house.

Ash reached out a shaking hand to touch the snow, and a blissful smile spread across his face. A second later, a tiny white salamander scampered out into the snow, digging a hole and vanishing beneath it.

"Ash?" Aqua called curiously, and then when Ash didn't reappear, he called "Ash" with more urgency in his voice.

William cast out his magic and found the little salamander just a foot outside the doorway. He hurried to Aqua's side before Aqua trampled out the door and started desperately digging through the endless snow. William reached out and carefully dug out a palm full of snow, then opened his hand to show Aqua the blissed-out salamander happily sprawled out to allow his body to touch as much of the snow as possible.

"Apparently a fire salamander that is born without fire inside has an affinity for ice instead." William passed the snow-covered salamander over to Aqua, who ran a gentle finger down Ash's stomach as if he needed to check whether Ash was okay.

Normal salamanders and even fire salamanders would freeze to death in moments in the cold and the snow, but William could see the life inside Ash actually growing the longer he was out in the snow.

"I'm going to have to tell Boron that white fire salamanders like the snow," Aqua said softly. He ran his finger down Ash's stomach again. Ash wriggled happily at the touch, finally opening his eyes again.

William sighed. Of course, Aqua had run into Boron and his motley band of dragons and salamanders. That explained a lot, actually. William suppressed a smile and stepped back when Ash jumped off Aqua's hand and landed back in human form.

"This is amazing," Ash said. He was grinning ear to ear. "I've never felt like this before. Like I could do magic." He waved his hand, and snow flurried through the air, landing on William's carpet. Ash did it a second time, blinking as if he had never seen anything like it before. Living in the desert, he wouldn't have.

William stepped around them and closed the French doors, then turned to look at them. "I want you both to have a bath and get into some clean clothes—Ash, you can have Rios's hand-me-downs that he doesn't fit into anymore until I can get you new clothes. I'll have breakfast cooked by the time you're done, and then we can discuss your staying here, Ash, and what that would mean in terms of schooling as well as learning about the snow and your new magic."

"Oh, right," Aqua said. "Uncle Willy, this is Ash. Ash, this is my uncle Willy."

"Nice to meet you," Ash said shyly. He twiddled his fingers, and more snow drifted down onto the carpet. William had already outfitted the pool so it would run on fresh water with no chlorine. What would he have to do to snow-proof the house? That was a thought for another time though.

"Welcome to my home," William replied with a smile. Ash's return smile was bright and happy, and William had a feeling that up until now, there hadn't been much that was bright and happy in Ash's life. He reached out to grab Aqua's hand, which Aqua gripped tightly.

"Let me show you my room!" Aqua exclaimed, and then he dragged Ash off into the depths of the house.

William looked at the melting snow all over his living room and shook his head at himself. He had wanted Aqua to go out into the world and grow up a little. He should have known this was what he was really inviting into his life. Yet, what was important here was Aqua's happiness; having Ash with him made Aqua smile. There was much William would put up with to make sure his kits were happy.

He waved away the snow with a quick gust of magic before heading into the kitchen. He would ponder over what to do to welcome a snow salamander into his home properly later, but first he had breakfast to make to welcome his kit and his kit's mate home.

About the Author

When Mell Eight was in high school, she discovered dragons. Beautiful, wondrous creatures that took her on epic adventures both to faraway lands and on journeys of the heart. Mell wanted to create dragons of her own, so she put pen to paper. Mell Eight is now known for her own soaring dragons, as well as for other wonderful characters dancing across the pages of her books. While she mostly writes paranormal or fantasy stories, she has been seen exploring the real world once or twice.

Facebook: www.facebook.com/MellEightFiction

Twitter: @MellEight

Website: www.melleightfiction.weebly.com

Other NineStar books by this author

Ge-Mi, Part One

Ge-Mi, Part Two

Supernatural Consultant Series

Dragon Consultant

Dragon Deception

Dragon Dilemma

Supernatural Consultant, Volume One

Dragon Detective

Dragon Soldier

Dragon Adventures

Dragon Lesson

A Little Fairy Dust

Also Available from NineStar Press

Connect with NineStar Press

www.ninestarpress.com

www.facebook.com/ninestarpress

www.facebook.com/groups/NineStarNiche

www.twitter.com/ninestarpress

www.ingramcontent.com/pod-product-compliance
Lightning Source LLC
Chambersburg PA
CBHW060232100726
47907CB00003B/600